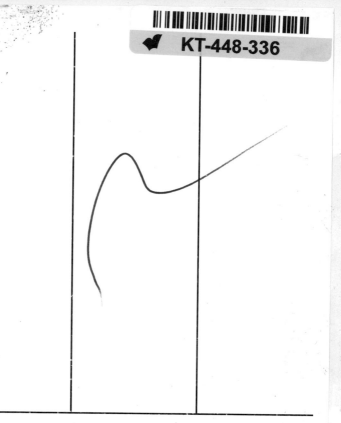

Please return/renew this item by the last date shown. Books may also be renewed by phone or internet.

🖥 www3.rbwm.gov.uk/libraries

☎ 01628 796969 (library hours)

☎ 0303 123 0035 (24 hours)

www.rbwm.gov.uk

Royal Borough of Windsor & Maidenhead

Hayley Webster is a writer and teacher who grew up in Newbury, Berkshire. Her first novel *Jar Baby* was published by Dexter Haven in 2012 and, as Hayley Scott, three books in her Teacup House series for emerging readers were published by Usborne in 2018. She has written for *Grazia* and the *Observer* magazine, did a sold-out event at Edinburgh Festival in 2018, and is a mentor on the 2019 National Writers Centre Escalator scheme. She lives in Norfolk with her daughter.

ONE CHRISTMAS NIGHT

HAYLEY WEBSTER

TRAPEZE

First published in Great Britain in 2019 by Trapeze
an imprint of The Orion Publishing Group Ltd
Carmelite House, 50 Victoria Embankment
London EC4Y 0DZ

An Hachette UK Company

1 3 5 7 9 10 8 6 4 2

A CIP catalogue record for this book is
available from the British Library.

ISBN (Mass Market Paperback) 978 1 4091 8435 5
ISBN (eBook) 978 1 4091 8436 2

Typeset by Born Group
Printed and bound in Great Britain by Clays Ltd, Elcograf S.p.A.

www.orionbooks.co.uk

To Mum
I miss you most at Christmas

3.08 a.m.

Christmas Eve

The Thief

All is quiet on Newbury Street.

The person in the navy beanie hat looks out along the two, grey rows of familiar Victorian terraced houses, taking a deep breath as they watch the Christmas lights shine from the house fronts onto the newly formed puddles. There are flashes of colour as the lights reflect with petrol swirls, reminding them of festive shop windows. It's nearly time.

So many of the neatly spaced archways between each set of ten houses, that lead to the narrow gardens at the back, are gated these days, but people often forget to lock them. Even now. Of all the streets that look like this, stretching out around the centre of Norwich, this one's special. This one's *theirs*.

They let out a slow puff of breath that turns to ice crystals in the dark, waiting for the perfect moment. Timing is everything.

The thief stands far back on the pavement, tucked away in their purpose-bought plain-soled boots. They've chosen to wait, with careful forethought, in the shadows of The Mariner pub at the far end of Newbury street, not quite seen from the CCTV camera outside, nor from the one outside The Stop Shop convenience store over the road, which people had thought would catch wrongdoers so easily when they'd first been installed.

They glance over at Victory House, the four-floored, mostly council-owned block over on the other side of the street, where Brighton Road travels past it. Why the address of Victory House is Newbury Street and not Brighton Road they've never understood, but the three buildings form a sort of safe triangle of dark corners around them as they wait.

They take another deep breath and step forward slightly. They're ready.

The thief has come prepared and wears black clothes, their night-time uniform of tracksuit bottoms, hoodie with button fastenings instead of a zip, and the big rucksack over their shoulder. They have a spare wool sack stuffed inside the rucksack, just in case, and as they lean forward they catch their shadow from the street lamps on the pavement and realise they look a bit like a day-early Father Christmas. They laugh to themselves, because if there's one thing they're not, it's Santa.

Maybe I should wear a fake beard for next year, they think, trying to imagine the incongruousness of all that synthetic hair strapped to their smooth face. *Just for fun.*

The thief has always loved the thick silence that comes at this very specific time in the early hours, when nearly everybody's asleep and everything looks like a child's drawing of night-time. They're often about at this hour. They still love the sneakiness of it, like they're doing something they shouldn't be doing, which, following a pattern that started in childhood, is usually true. They remember they still haven't finished their Christmas shopping, but they've always been one of those high-street-on-Christmas-Eve-afternoon-between-popping-in-and-out-of-the-pub sort of people anyway. There'll be time tomorrow. It's a shame they couldn't give all the things they've taken since this all began, as gifts. People aren't that stupid. Well, not all of them.

The thief pulls back, invisible, while three women in party hats wrapped about with tinsel in badly put on coats wobble across the road, arms linked, probably on their way home from late-night two-for-one Christmas cocktails on the Prince of Wales Road, using Newbury Street as a shortcut. The thief's excursions are usually timed perfectly to fit in the space between the drunks and the NHS workers and shift workers going out or coming back in. Today they're on the lookout for families where someone's insisted they all get up at a ridiculous hour to get to the other side of the country before the traffic. They don't want to be caught out. Not today of all days, so they stay focused, raising themselves up and down from the balls of their feet with excess energy. They can't rely on the usual routines the people of Newbury Street follow as they go about their daily lives, although, by now, they know those particular comings and goings by heart.

The thief checks their watch. It will soon be time for the upmarket milk float to be driven the length of these streets to the loyal customers who keep it going, with this year's promised brandy cream and good cheese to be delivered in the early hours of Christmas Eve. Every morning it hums along the length of Newbury Street like someone has switched on the mains to get the day started.

It's so quiet, and so cold, and the rain is not quite sleet, but it's still got enough freeze to sting on its way down. Once the revellers have moved on, the thief steps out and makes their way along Newbury Street in the dark.

Their quiet boots walk past Number 135, one of the houses split into two flats so the landlord can make a fortune from those who are single and can't afford to rent a house of their own. There are several of these down Newbury Street, usually at the other end, with proportionally high rents when it comes to it, and then the student houses, much further down, split into paid-for rooms that cost almost the same as renting a whole house. They always look ill kept from the outside because the landlords never put any care into them to start with. These houses sit there, not quite knowing what they are, with their overgrown gardens and their neon decorated wheelie bins.

The names Irma Woźniak and Isaac Iwu are biro-scrawled and lit up in their rectangle buzzer slots beside the blue door of Number 127. Flat 1 and Flat 2. A little further along, Number 121 stands out in contrast, with its expensive subtlety, small white and peach star lights around the porch roof and the decorated tree in its green-glazed clay pot, every branch threaded through with glowing white baubles. *John Ellis Housing* says the classic font on the For Sale sign. The house is not for sale, it's just a little well-placed advertising that stays up all year round.

The thief smiles as they cross the road and stop, suddenly, outside Number 118, watching new rain tap into the growing puddles. The sound is comforting. The chill and the lights and that smell in the air, whatever it is, feels like Christmas. Tomorrow, there will be roast dinner and cranberry sauce and Shakin' Stevens impressions. There will be comedy plastic glasses on springs, fortune-telling fish from the crackers and a selection of socks and mugs and keyrings that say Prosecco! or Gin! or Beer! as though these things sum a person up entirely. The thief will nod and join in and be part of it all, while not really being

4

part of it because of their own secrets. They've never liked Christmas, despite putting on a good front, so they're glad of this moment, of everything coming together, of the here and the now. Even though most roads in the city never stop completely, for this moment, everything is still.

Almost everything.

The thief breathes slowly and carefully as they put the key into the Yale lock of Number 118.

They are now an intruder.

It's so easy when you have a key. None of that noisy, time-consuming forced entry. Using a key is so clean, it's almost like being invited, and the last thing any intruder wants is a child staring at them with big eyes from the darkness as though Father Christmas is a day early. Witnesses make things messy, and the thief hates mess. It always ends the same way. With somebody getting hurt. Despite everything, they'd prefer not to have to resort to violence.

Frank Blake and Jen Mullany are the sort of couple who have a special Christmas welcome mat they've brought from John Lewis with subtle mistletoe printed on the bristles. The intruder very quietly tuts. They're not the only one to have noticed the change in Frank Blake since his wife Allie died from cancer and he'd set up home with Jen. Even the way he dresses has changed, all smart-casual, blazer over a pressed band T-shirt and those tan square-ended lace up shoes from Next that look like pasties in Greggs. The thief would feel sorry for Frank, but considering Jen left a loving husband and good father of her kids for the man, their sympathy is severely lacking. *Selfish bastard. Selfish bitch.*

The living room is messy, which surprises the thief. Jen had always been so pristine before. You could eat your food from the floor back then, and she'd never have gone to bed without tidying everything away. But there are toys out and bowls with crisps and dried-out dips on the coffee table. There's the smell of yesterday's baked ham, and the thief turns on the small head torch that has proved so useful in these night-time excursions. *Maybe she lets herself go at Christmas now.* There are games still spread across the floor. Twister, Jenga, and a child-friendly version of Trivial Pursuit. The thief, gently, kicks the loose coloured wedges across the carpet. There's an open box of Roses, with discarded wrappers all about it, shining in the dark and two half-eaten Nutcracker chocolate figures, their foil uniforms peeled down and folded over the broken edges. They hold the torch over the chocolates, pick out a handful and put them in a hoodie pocket for later. It would be rude not to.

Just like in nearly all the other houses the thief has visited so far, the presents are in the cupboard under the stairs. Lots of people on Newbury Street have been keeping them there, even after the first Amazon boxes went missing, even after the hushed voices asking how anybody could be so cruel as to steal people's Christmas presents spread through the terraces in whispered horror. Lots of these cupboards are just covered over with a curtain, so are even easier to get to. People never think it's going to happen to them. This always works in the thief's favour. People rarely change their habits, even after bad things happen that suggest they should. Or they change them for a bit, then go back to exactly the way they did things before. The thief had actually committed some of the smaller burglaries in broad daylight during a chat and a cup of tea.

Because Jen and Frank – well, Jen – have more money than most on the street, there's hope for some expensive tech, and the thief is not disappointed. In the cupboard are an Xbox 360, an iPad, a Kindle Oasis and a child's interactive doll that looks so sad the thief has to withhold the unexpected urge to give it a cuddle. There are wrapped things too, bright in foiled paper, and they're added to the huge sack, along with everything else. The intruder will have fun unwrapping them later.

One large box shakes with Lego with just the slightest movement. 'Shhh,' the thief says, smiling. Lego is expensive these days. Lots of things are. The thief has built up quite the collection.

This whole thing has been easy, one house every five days or so, saving the best till last. All the while, posters being put up saying, 'Be vigilant!' 'Keep each other safe!' People wouldn't know how to be vigilant or keep each other safe if they tried. The thief laughs. Just a little. They try not to be smug, in case it leads to their downfall, but, really, people are ridiculous.

At the other houses it had always been a case of take the gifts and leave. For some reason, tonight, maybe it's because it's the early hours of Christmas Eve and everything in the house still feels so festive, the thief stops to think about how it will make Frank or Jen feel in the morning, and has the urge to do *more*. Money means nothing to them, Jen has enough of the stuff. So, the thief goes into the kitchen and opens the tall duck-egg blue fridge-freezer. It's a spur-of-the-moment thing, and they know the risks of deciding to do something unplanned, but before they can stop themselves, every carefully stacked packet or tub of Christmas food or drink – turkey, pigs in blankets, brandy cream, sprouts, salmon, champagne, the lot – is carefully pulled out and put into the rucksack. There's a bottle of sherry on the side, probably for Santa. 'Ho, ho, ho,' the thief mimes with a grin, sliding it into the sack with everything else.

The intruder starts to grab at the food in an almost frenzy. All they know is that every chocolate, every shiny packet, every little piece of Christmas Frank and Jen have set out neatly in their cupboards and fridge, or laid out to defrost on the kitchen side, must be taken. Nothing must be left behind. They wonder, for a moment, about themselves, about what all this means. But they don't even feel bad as they take the little iced gingerbread people laid out on the wire racks that one of the adults has obviously made with the children, and tip them into the sack, spurred on by the fact all this makes them feel powerful, somehow.

When there's only an old tube of tomato puree, some nearly empty jars of jam and a supermarket packet of parsley stuck to the ice at the back, the thief closes the fridge and turns to leave. It's a good haul. *Joy to the World!* As always, there's that high of just walking in and taking whatever they fancy, a disregard to the laws of hospitality that always gives them a thrill. Sometimes they take the battery out of a wall clock. Or move a bookmark. Or angle a lamp differently. The fact it's people they've looked in the eye, people they've *loved* in their own way, or who have supposedly loved them, just adds to the sense of satisfaction. They know this makes them a terrible person, but that doesn't bother them either. There are worse things than being a terrible person. And lots of people are terrible anyway and just aren't honest about it. *Most people, actually.*

As the thief opens the front door to leave, they find themselves confronted by the stray tabby cat Jen calls Valentino, pressing past to come into the house. 'Shhh. Don't get me in trouble.' The cat looks up and rubs his body against their calves, purring loudly. 'You really do love without expectation, don't you?' they whisper and lean down to stroke him. 'You could teach human beings a thing or two.' They shake their head and give the cat a tickle under his chin. 'See you later,' the thief winks and blows a kiss at the cat. The door closes between them, quietly but firmly, as the quiet boots, and Jen and Frank's first proper Christmas together, disappear along Newbury Street into the navy dark.

9.13 a.m.

Christmas Eve

Joanie Blake

The Patterson House, Earlham Road

Joanie runs her hand along the banister as she steps down the spiral staircase. The wood is polished to perfection and she stops to breathe in the scent of pine, of cinnamon, of the mince pies that were glazed and baked in the oven in the early hours of this morning. Everything about the scene below says Christmas, the sort of Christmas she has imagined since she first walked past Jarrolds front windows with her mum at the start of December as a child. From the dried slices of orange sewn to ivy vines, to the smell of mulled wine slowly warming through with cloves and ginger on the hob, to the birch logs in the grate, crackling, everything is perfect.

Nathan Patterson stands beside the fireplace and looks up at Joanie as she walks down the steps, and they smile at each other. He's warming his fingers around the mug with his name on that one of the children made him at school. He's lit candles. There are tens of them set out like a photo shoot from a glossy magazine, like in church, in clusters on the mantelpiece, and others on top of the bookshelves. He's wearing one of those big grey jumpers you see in expensive catalogues and has pushed his dark hair back so it sits in a kind of off-centre peak. It is ridiculous really, thinks Joanie, that a person should be that well-groomed, that handsome. *That dishy,* as her mum used to say.

'This is for you,' says Nathan, holding a red glittery envelope out in front of him as she walks towards him. 'It looks lovely in here. Thank you.'

'You're welcome. The candles are lovely too,' she says. 'Nice touch.'

As Nathan passes the envelope, she feels the warmth of the fire, smells the birch, and the cloves, and hopes her mum would be proud of her. *Is* proud of her, if there's an afterlife, like her kids keep telling her with great certainty there is.

She takes the envelope and nods.

'A little something extra for Christmas in there too,' he says, his cheeks flushing. 'I'm sorry it isn't more. And I'm sorry about your mum. We miss her. This Christmas must be hard.' He goes quiet.

The money part of this job is always embarrassing, even without the added bit about her mum. Even now, ten months since Allie died, Joanie doesn't know why she's kept on all her mum's cleaning jobs. She hates cleaning, and she could have taken on extra work doing something else. But. There was something about not wanting anyone else to wipe away her mum's fingerprints, her mum's *work*. Something to do with wanting to touch the things she'd touched, to take pride in the work her mum had taken pride in, to keep it going and to prove it wasn't all for nothing. To make her mum *last*.

'Juliette says to have a wonderful Christmas. I'm sure she goes out when you're doing your thing because she'd clean the whole place ready for when you got here! We . . .' Nathan trails off.

Joanie saves them both the agony of opening her wages in front of him. 'You want me here on the 27th, right? Usual time?'

'That's right,' says Nathan. 'We'll probably have a lot of recycling. Bottles and things . . . We'll probably have some toys we'll be getting rid of, if you think either of yours might like them.' He must realise how this sounds because he says quickly, 'Nothing wrong with them, and not that you'd want or need our . . .' But he doesn't finish the sentence.

Joanie slips her arms into her Puffa jacket sleeves, pushing the envelope deep into one of the pockets. 'Thank you. I'll sort through it.' She doesn't mention the toys. 'Don't worry. I'll wash all the tins and bottles out too. After all,' she can't help herself, 'that's what you pay me for. Have a lovely Christmas, Mr Patterson. Enjoy your time off.'

'You too, Joanie,' says Nathan Patterson, brightening. 'I'm still on call for any juicy local stories, and I've got a few ideas of how to push a few bigger stories along. But I've pre-recorded my main slots for the next few days, so my time's my own. Give or take.'

Joanie nods as if in agreement and puts her hand on the big iron door handle just as the mighty red door swings open and in comes Juliette, rosy-cheeked, curls falling loosely from under an oversized, silver beret. She has two of her children on each side of her, bundled up in scarves and big hats, as, together, they heave in a twelve-foot, dark green spruce tree. Joanie tries not to make comparisons with Jen Mullany, although the women are so similar they could be sisters. She'd much rather Jen didn't pop into her head quite so often as she does. She'd liked the woman. Once.

'Might need your help Nath,' says Juliette, laughing. 'We got a bit . . . carried away.' She drops the trunk end of the Christmas tree down on the wooden floor and turns to Joanie. 'Oh! It looks lovely in here. It's practically sparkling. Oh my gosh, your hair!' She looks at Joanie properly now. 'I *love* it.' Juliette reaches her arm towards Joanie, who flinches her head away, but Juliette's fingers are already on her, lightly bouncing. 'Wow! It's set solid. I love the yellow! It looks great on you. I wish I could do my hair like that, but I could never carry it off. My hair's not the right . . . texture.'

Joanie narrows her eyes, wondering what she might say in response about why women like Juliette think they have the right to touch her hair, but, for now, keeps her thoughts to herself.

'Have a lovely Christmas, all of you,' she says in the end. Next time, she'll channel her little sister Tash and say, 'Don't fucking touch my hair.' She bets nobody's ever touched Juliette's hair uninvited. Or Jen's for that matter. *Stop thinking about Jen, for God's sake.* But it's not that easy to stop thinking about the woman your dad moved in with sixth months after your mum died. The woman who used to be your mum's best friend. *Let Dad be happy*, she thinks. Still, it's not always easy.

'We will have a merry Christmas, won't we, darling?' Juliette smiles at Nathan and then frowns, just a little. 'At least he's promised he won't go out on any of those early-hours local interest stories he's so fond of. How many local reporters do you think are off out at three in the morning, chasing stories? None. That's how many. I always say, there's ambition and then there's . . . whatever Nathan's got.' She shakes the tone out of her voice. 'The daft angel.'

'That's quite enough of that!' laughs Nathan, quickly. 'I'm sure Joanie doesn't want to hear all the boring tales about me watching badger setts in Elveden Forest, trying to see how gamekeepers catch poachers or sneaking up on fly tippers off the A47. Say Merry Christmas to Joanie, kids!'

'Merry Christmas, Joanie!' the four Patterson children chirrup together, and then they're all back to it, with Nathan helping them, heaving the big tree fully into the hallway. 'Dad, you won't believe what Mum got to go on top this year. She knows you like that star and it's tradition and all that, but just wait till you see!'

Joanie steps outside and closes the door behind her.

How do they manage to be so . . . perfect? Is it just money, like her dad always said? Money would certainly make things easier, would give her and the kids more choices. She's seen the receipt for the Pattersons' Christmas alcohol delivery – £500. Joanie earns £850 take home a month from her job as a teaching assistant. Cleaning is an extra £32 a week. She tops up her gas and electric on a card and a key. She pays for their water on a card that still has Allie's name on. Different worlds. Her dad's in that world now too. And he's left her and the kids, and Tash, far behind. Even though they still see so much of him, it's different.

She pulls her phone out of her coat pocket.

Dad. 3 Missed Calls. She'll call him later.

As she walks, she thinks of all the years her mum made his pack up for work, wrapping his favourite sandwiches in foil, with him saying proudly to friends, 'Nobody makes sandwiches like my Allie.' She pictures a long road disappearing into the distance, made of all the foil her mum had ever used to wrap them, smoothed out, covered in breadcrumbs, in little fallen pieces of ham and tomato. *What was it all for?*

She turns into Earlham Road. Despite everything she has been forcing herself to look forward to Christmas.

She's tried to keep as many of her mum's traditions as possible. It's important for both her kids, Patti and Dylan, who loved her mum as much as she did. It's important for Tash too, even though she's being closed off and having a go at her for trying to be like their mum. Joanie tries not to think too much about any of it. She reminds herself how lucky she is. Every night before bed she says thank you to the Universe for Patti and Dylan. *Nobody has everything.* Her mum used to say that. And looking back at how this year has progressed, and her mum not even being here at all now, she realises how right she was. *Just keep going.* Some days it's as simple, or as hard, as that.

She walks quickly. The paths are empty, although the road is busy, steamed-up car windscreens and light drizzle, people from outside the city rushing in for last-minute presents. In many ways, she is glad her dad is happy. She will never forget his face when her mum took those last breaths. He'd sat with her as long as he was allowed, his head on the side of the bed and his hand on the pillow. When they got home from the hospital, he got into bed, and didn't get out until the next afternoon, when he had to arrange things, like funerals song sheets and who was going to make the food for the wake and letting people know. Joanie would never let herself forget watching him begin the unthinkable journey of being Frank without Allie and it's why she can't be as angry with him about Jen as Tash, who wasn't there to see any of it. Even though it hurts.

Joanie imagines Tash saying, '*Don't go soft on him. He's betrayed Mum. And us.*' Standing with her hand on her hip, twirling a strand of multicoloured hair between her fingers. They'd already had one argument today, about the turkey of all things. *Mum might have laughed about that.* That's the thing when someone dies. You can only imagine what they'd say or do in all the situations they are no longer here for, but, really, that's the imaginary them you've created. It's not really them. Everybody who loved them is imagining a different person.

She takes a detour, like she always does, past the cemetery and whispers, 'Merry Christmas, Mum' as she goes. She hasn't visited the grave yet. She keeps meaning to but somehow never quite gets past the main entrance.

Just take it one day at a time.

Nobody has everything.

She repeats these phrases to herself as many times as she has to, to stop the wretched feeling sink insider her.

Joanie faces the sky and lets the drizzle fall on her face. It's so cold, but she can't remember the last time it snowed at actual Christmas. Maybe this year there'll be a blanket of white along Newbury Street, a fresh start, the kids making their footprints on all that Christmas perfection. Despite herself, this makes Joanie laugh.

As she turns the corner onto Newbury Street, she allows herself a big breath of damp air, and the comfort of coming home. She loves coming in at the opposite end from where she lives, just to take the whole street in.

The Christmas lights attached to the fronts of so many of the houses flash brightly, even in the daytime, gaudy and joyful like the seaside arcades, and Joanie ups her step. Number 57 has switched-off Christmas lights up all year, they never come down. They are switched on now, row after row of flashing red and green, making the most of the fact that, once again, their time has come. She can't help thinking there's a lesson in there somewhere.

She's relieved to be nearly home. It's always been home here, and Joanie lets herself walk with a Christmas Eve bounce just as she gets to the twenty-metre square 'tiny park' with its slide, its two swings and a duck on a spring for toddlers that rocks back and forth when they sit on it. Its face wore off years ago, but someone has tied a bit of silver tinsel round its neck and put a Santa hat on its head and this makes her smile. Tidings of joy amongst the peeling paint and just-good-enough-to-pass-Health-and-Safety metal.

It's then she sees it. The heap of clothes in a bundle, getting wet on the pavement.

She feels sick, that feeling you get when you know something terrible has happened and there's nothing you can do about it. She runs towards the bundle, knowing it isn't really a bundle, and when she gets to it, she sees it is, in fact, a man. Not just any man either, not a complete stranger, although that would have been bad enough. The man is Mr Finch from Number 133.

It doesn't look like Mr Finch though. The man lying in a bundle, breathing slowly and heavily, with the trickle of blood travelling down his forehead onto the pavement looks like he hasn't eaten a proper meal in weeks. There's a cut on his face, and his body is lying out at all the wrong angles.

Joanie kneels beside him. 'Mr Finch!' she says too loudly. 'Mr Finch, can you hear me? It's Joanie Blake. From the flats. Allie and Frank's daughter.' She flinches at using her mum's name as though she's still alive. 'Mr Finch?'

The man raises his head slightly and nods. His raincoat is almost hanging off him, he's so thin. Joanie's heart sinks. It doesn't look good.

'Somebody bring me some blankets!' she shouts, even though there's nobody else there. She doesn't want to leave him lying in the street, but he needs to be warm. She pulls out her mobile and immediately taps on the green phone icon, keying in 999.

'Ambulance please,' she says, and is connected. A voice at the end of the line starts asking her questions as Mr Finch takes her hand in his. His fingers are cold, and thin, like the cord on the Hoover.

'Check on Wendy,' he says so quietly she can barely hear him, his voice rasping and peculiar. 'She'll not manage by herself.'

'Of course!' she says. 'Of course. And we'll bring her up to the hospital to see you as soon as we can. I'll bring her straight up, don't you worry!' She sounds cheery, overly bright, that voice you put on for children when something awful is happening but you want to hide it from them, want to allow them to believe they are safe when they're anything but. She can feel her smile stapled to her face, like one of the displays on the cork boards at school.

Mr Finch coughs, a deep cough from somewhere far down inside him, and his hand loosens its grip on Joanie's own. She knows then, and reaches towards him, as though there's anything she can do, even though she knew there really isn't. Mr Finch lets out one of those long breaths people do at the end, like her mum did in that hospital bed on the ward, and she feels helpless. She can almost see the life come out of him, can almost see it in the cold and the rain, and she instinctively looks up to the sky to say goodbye.

When she looks back down, she stares at him, gone now, getting wet in the street, and realises she's holding her own breath, tight in her chest. She breathes out. She hadn't even got a chance to ask him what had happened.

The voice at the end of the line is still asking her questions. She tries to put her words together properly. *I miss my mum*, she thinks, but can't let that thought go any further.

'It's Mr Finch,' she says quietly, almost as though someone else is saying it, someone far away. 'He's dead.'

9.40 a.m.

Christmas Eve

Tash Blake

The Stop Shop

Tash hears the sound of the sirens and is dazzled by the glint of the ambulance lights, bright blue through the shop window. Her mind jumps – she'd seen the flash of Joanie's orange coat as it made its way past The Stop Shop only ten minutes before – and she can't stop her first thought from being, *Something's happened. Something's happened to my sister.*

'I need to . . .' She turns to Rocky, her face wild and her eyes wide, the till drawer still sticking out and the receipt barely touching the customer's hand from the last transaction.

Rocky looks at her with a blink, an immediate yes, like he knows what she's thinking because he says, 'Go. I'll take care of here. Just go.'

She mouths a thank you as she slips out from behind the till and through the glass door onto the street. The cold hits her, but she doesn't care. She runs across the road to the ambulance and paramedics without looking for traffic, aware of nothing but the sound of her own heartbeat. She runs and she doesn't stop until her hand is on the white metal of the ambulance.

Tash feels the drop in her stomach that something isn't right and, as she stands ridiculously in the elf costume head office thought would be a good idea for all Stop Shop staff this Christmas, she tries not to let her imagination run away with itself, which isn't easy when there's one of those black plastic body bags like you see after a disaster on the news or in detective dramas on TV.

Not Joanie Not Joanie Not Joanie, thinks Tash and then feels bad, because if it's not Joanie it's still *somebody.* But it *can't* be Joanie. That body under the blanket, lifeless and covered over like some morbid tent . . . and to think the last thing she'd ever said to her sister had been 'Nobody cares about your stupid attempts at a Nigella bin turkey anyway. Stop trying to be mum because you're *not*!' makes her feel sick.

'Joanie!' she calls out. Her stomach feels punched through. She reaches out to touch the blanket covering the body, but a paramedic pushes her hand away, gently, and shakes her head. There's a crowd gathering, and Tash tries not to look at the staring faces, the eyes popping with half shock and half thrill of an emergency on a street under a drizzle of grey blue. 'I think that's my sister!' she splutters, her spine, ice. 'I think that's my *sister*!'

Another paramedic steps forward and asks for her name.

'Natasha Betsy Blake,' says Tash. 'Betsy after my Grami. She died five Christmases ago. And Natasha after Natasha Rostova because *War and Peace* was my mum's favourite book for some unfathomable reason, because, I tell you something, I've tried to read it since she died, but I can't get past the first bit where he goes on and on for all those *pages*. Nobody ever calls me Natasha though. I'm always Tash. Dylan, that's my nephew, calls me Tissue.' She stops talking, aware she hasn't taken a breath since she started.

The body on the stretcher under the blanket is being pulled inside the ambulance. It strikes her it might be the last time she ever sees her sister and she stands with her mouth open.

'The person on the stretcher is an elderly gentleman,' says the paramedic kindly, placing a hand on Joanie's shoulder.

At these words, Tash feels her stomach clench and retract as she leans over to be sick on the pavement.

'Tash!' comes the familiar voice from beside her.

Tash looks up, the taste of sick burning her mouth, dizziness overwhelming her. But there is the familiar orange jacket beside her. The arm that's wrapped itself around her shoulders is familiar too.

The body on the stretcher isn't Joanie's at all. Joanie is beside her, pulling her to her chest and pulling on the tip of her elf hat. Patting her on the back, taking over from the paramedic, running her hands in smooth circles of comfort.

'Joanie!' Tash feels her knees buckle as she sinks into the cold fabric of the coat. The vanilla rose perfume she chose for her sister with her mum last Christmas hits her with love and relief. 'I thought that was . . .' She stops and pushes her face into her sister's shoulder. 'Thank God it's not you. I wanted to tell you I don't think you doing mum's bin-soaking-turkey thing is a stupid idea . . . Not really.'

That morning, Tash had found the massive plucked bird, pink and bobbing in a plastic bin with a weighted down lid, outside the main entrance to their flat. Ever since seeing Nigella cooking Christmas food on TV, their mum had brined the turkey, taking joy at peeking at it soaking with all those cloves and quartered orange segments and surface-floating peppercorns. Tash and Joanie were sent out to find carraway seeds and allspice berries on their

22

way home from school the first year, because it was near the nicer supermarket. This memory makes Tash well up.

Joanie laughs lightly. 'It probably *is* a stupid idea,' she says. 'I found someone trying to get the lid off to put a load of vegetable peelings and God knows what else into it earlier.' She laughs and Tash feels her squeeze her tightly. 'It's not me, and it's not anyone you know well. It's Mr Finch. From Number 133. And he's not made it. I found him . . .' Her face falls. 'I couldn't do anything.' Joanie steps back to look at her sister, and sees she's shaking.

'Oh no.'

'I know.'

'How did it happen?'

'Nobody knows. He seems to have slipped. He was very thin. He was bleeding from his forehead . . .'

'Are you the next of kin?' A police officer is standing beside the two women. 'Oh, hello again. Detective Constable Crane. I was here already, for the burglaries. We met before.'

'Hello, yes I remember,' say Joanie and Tash at the same time. Their flat had been burgled earlier in the month, the only flat in Victory House that had been targeted, although the only thing that had been taken were two polaroid cameras Joanie had bought for Patti and Dylan. DC Crane had been very kind and Tash had liked her. She had commented on the colours in Tash's hair. 'Your hair is brilliant Tash,' she'd said. 'If I was your age, I'd have it sky blue. Maybe when I leave the force . . .' What she has instead is one of those tints that looks black but gleams dark plum under certain lights. Tash wonders if she does it herself.

'I don't know him,' says Tash. 'I mean, I've served him in the shop . . . Not recently, actually. He hasn't been in. Rocky was saving some things Mr and Mrs Finch like for

Christmas, and they're still in the box, out back. He's good like that. He notices things.' Tash goes light-headed at the thought of Rocky.

'The next of kin is his wife,' says Joanie, answering the question. 'Mrs Finch. He called her Wendy to me, just then. And they have no children, that I know of.'

'Thank you,' says DC Crane. 'DC Ado is over there with a doctor now. It looks unlikely that there is anyone to look out for Mrs Finch. Social Services are involved. I just wondered if you knew anything about him. Or her.'

Tash shakes her head as her sister begins to talk.

'They've lived on this street since they were first married,' says Joanie, and Tash looks at her, surprised. How does her sister know these things? DC Crane nods. 'They used to be friends with my Grami, when she first came from Jamaica and then, afterwards, they went to things, I think. Dances and things. Mrs Finch introduced Grami to Grandad . . .' Her face drops. 'I should have looked in on them. Mum used to.'

Tash pats her on the arm. 'You can't look after everyone.'

Joanie pulls away. 'No. But still. She could come to ours for Christmas,' she says suddenly. 'If she'd like to. I don't mind, do you, Tash? We've a houseful, but she can have my room. I can't have her alone for Christmas when her husband has just died. It will be nice to have someone older in the house. Like proper Christmas.'

'That's very kind of you,' says DC Crane. 'We'll need to inform the right people, and it will be up to her, of course. She's being looked over by a doctor herself at the moment.'

'Of course.'

Tash whispers as DC Crane walks away. 'Joanie, do you remember how crowded it was when Mum and Dad lived there too? It's a three-bedroom flat. What about the kids?'

'It'll be fine. They'll be fine. That's what Christmas is about. It's likely the only extra person will be Mrs Finch anyway.'

Tash doesn't say anything. She knows it would be selfish to say she'd love the flat to themselves, to hide away this first Christmas without Mum. If she's being honest, she's afraid of Mrs Finch, in that way very old people frighten her. The way their skeletons stick out of their flesh and their eyes swim. Like mum, at the end, when she wasn't old, but the illness made her look like she was, an image Tash just can't shake, one that presses down over all the other, full-flesh memories, even when Tash tries really hard to retrieve them.

'You get back to work,' says Joanie. 'It's cold and you're not dressed for it. No need for you to be out here. But I do appreciate you running out to check on me. It's good to know deep down you actually care.' She play-punches her on the arm.

Tash shakes one of her feet at her sister and the little brass bell jangles. They both smile at each other, proper smiles, the kind that warm you right through. This is the closest Tash has felt to her sister in months.

'I honestly thought it was you,' Tash shakes her head, the smile disappearing.

'Not my turn yet,' says Joanie solemnly. 'I can't wait to get back to the kids later,' her tone lifts. 'I've got a load of craft stuff out, and we're going to make mince pies. We'll make Mum's Christmas Eve cake too, the treacle and ginger one. Dad said he'd help when I spoke to him yesterday, so the kids will love that.' She pauses as though waiting for a reaction to the word Dad but Tash stays quiet. 'You can have some with custard after work. Or do you want us to wait and make it with you?'

'No, make it without me, but I'll happily stuff my face with it after.' Tash can't face looking at the recipe book full of her mum's neatest writing. 'Come on three o'clock!' she says, laughing. 'Although . . .' She knows she is seventeen and legally old enough to do as she pleases, but she can't get out of the habit of asking her sister for permission. *Joanie is not mum*, she tells herself. But she can't help it. 'I was wondering about going to the Festive Feel Good thing at The Mariner.'

'Of course,' says Joanie. 'I thought about popping in with the kids and Dad, but I'm undecided. We'll see if Mrs Finch decides to stay . . . It depends on Dad too.'

'Yup. Dad is blaming himself, for last night of course. Doing his usual, *this is punishment from the Universe* spiel. If he feels that bad about what he's done, perhaps he should undo it.' Tash rolls her eyes. 'If he was asking for reassurance, he was talking to the wrong person.' She can't forgive him for moving on so quickly, she can't let him be happy, when it should be Mum who's here, Mum who's redecorating. Mum, who used to put her head on his shoulder while they all watched *Love, Actually* and Tash would do her point-by-point deconstruction of all the reasons it's a really bad film until everyone groaned and told her to *just enjoy it*, as had become their yearly tradition.

'Blaming himself for what exactly?' Joanie asks.

'The robbery.'

'The what?' Joanie looks shocked.

'Oh shit, didn't he get through to you? Him and Jen were burgled. Whoever did it took the entire Christmas dinner. The cranberry sauce and the stuffing and *everything*.'

'Jesus Christ,' Joanie shakes her head. 'What. A. Year. Poor Dad. I'll ring him. He should be getting the kids from Irma's in a bit.'

Tash still misses having her dad around in the house. She could have moved in with them. Jen made the, 'Oh you are welcome here too Tash. Think of this as your home,' speech. But Tash wasn't going to move in with Jen and her kids and be the third kid, with her dad all lovey-dovey with someone who was not her mum. Not ever. And soon she'd be old enough to live by herself and it wouldn't matter anyway. She feels weird enough living with Joanie and her kids. Like there's nowhere she belongs, not properly. *I miss you, Mum.* She swallows down the feeling. *What's the point?*

As the ambulance drives away, there is a cluster of onlookers standing on the pavement and as Tash waves her sister goodbye and walks back to The Stop Shop. She can't stop wondering what it would be like to be Mrs Finch, to lose her husband on Christmas Eve. As she walks past Number 127, she looks up at the top flat and jumps to see that young man who usually comes in the shop for cat food and electricity staring out at her from the top window.

She raises her hand to say hello, out of the awkwardness at catching him staring, more than anything. She's always found him a bit odd. But he doesn't wave back, he just stares out on the street, with his hand on the window.

Weirdo, she mumbles under her breath, embarrassed and a bit freaked out. Newbury Street is full of weirdos, when you think of it. Rocky's dad, Larry, had been walking quickly along the street in the early hours, holding one arm out like he was walking a dog, which would be fine, but the Winters don't have a dog.

Weirdos everywhere. Her family included. She could write a list.

Maybe she would and give it to that DC Crane.

10.00 a.m.

Christmas Eve

Wendy Finch

133 Newbury Street

Wendy hears the far-off call of the sirens and the hum of relentless electricity. From the street: a car radio playing Christmas music at full volume, smudges of indecent laughter, a leather football against a wall. She remembers the big Christmas Eve day parties of her childhood. Flags, bells and brass bands in the market. Smart buckles, shoes slick, leathers black. Bunting made from the fabric of old curtains and her mother and father ushering her along in her best clothes. She'd always loved the noise, the colours and the children smiling. She'd always loved the outfits too. She'd still loved going to Thursford, with Len, to see the Christmas show, right up until the past few years, when it wasn't possible for either of them any more.

Dr Allman is very nice. She is gentle and has warm hands and her clothes are well-pressed with the scent of jasmine clothing conditioner, which matters. She has the sort of neat sandy hair that's trimmed very close to her neck, a spray of white at the temples. Wendy Finch is relieved at the gentle manner of the doctor. One drop of goodness in an altogether awful day.

She closes her eyes as she has things done to her, as she must lift parts of herself, is listened to with a metal disc. She breathes in and out, slowly, as instructed. She flinches at the tightness of the band to check her heart rate. She doesn't feel unwell, other than the hunger, and even that she is used to. There were whole decades in the sixties, seventies and eighties where she ate very little too. Back then, it was on purpose and celebrated by those around her as a triumph. All that suddenly feels like a great waste of time, and a very long time ago.

'You're actually in good health aren't you, Mrs Finch?' says Dr Allman, smiling. 'Other than needing to eat more. You're not malnourished, but any longer and it would have been a problem.' She sounds surprised as she says it and Wendy nods proudly at that too. She's had tinned fruit and part of a tin of meat or fish most days. She's had one slice of bread smoothed over with thick gooseberry jam she made several years ago. She only had to scrape the waxy layer of mould from the top and it was as good as the day she'd made it. She had one tin of evaporated milk a week and drank lots of tea. They'd had tins of powdered milk they'd use for the tea. She'd got used to the floating bits. With only one lamp on, she couldn't really see what was in the cup anyway.

It had been different for Len. He'd gone without so she wouldn't. He'd pretended he hadn't, but she could see it, could see him diminishing. It would have hurt his pride for her to try and talk about it. But would that have been worse than this?

The weight of his death presses down on her all of a sudden. It's only half an hour since she was told what had happened and it had felt unreal then. Now it feels like everything's off balance, like the world is moving slightly too fast around her but she is perfectly still, slow. The room is sad in its once fresh pale lemon, cream and brown. Above the fireplace, there are Christmas cards from death-dwindling friends who've never seen how she and Len lived now. They'd hung them up around the painting of Cromer pier that had sat above the fireplace for decades. She'd hoped to have this room hibiscus and gold one day, to match the light on the water. They'd always talked about becoming *sea people*, living in a Norfolk coastal town after retirement, walking along the sand, drinking cold wine by the water in the summer, a dog maybe. It hurts to think of, because this was supposed to be the best time of their lives, the money they'd saved by living frugally throughout their younger years was supposed to bring them comfort and the sort of things they'd gone without.

But that can never happen now.

Dr Allman stands up and begins to pack away her things and the plain clothes detective slips into her space on the sofa. Wendy looks down at her hands, clasping them tightly in her lap.

'You do understand what we're saying, don't you, Mrs Finch?' The male police officer, DC Ado, is talking slowly to her now, as though she's a baby, but he's gentle and she warms to him, even though his face seems almost too young, despite his neat beard, like he should be handing her a Sunday newspaper and pedalling off down Newbury Street on his bike.

She frowns. 'Of course I understand,' she says, proudly, narrowing her eyes as she watches the young man's face as he glances about her living room. It's cold in here, so cold that the ice hangs about his face when he breathes out, like he's smoking. She knows it looks bad. She's done the best she can under the circumstances, but through a stranger's eyes everything must seem much worse. A sudden horror instead of the tiny increments that brought them to now. She tries not to think of all that time trying to hide it, and how people are coming in, uninvited, anyway. The irony of it twists.

'We have a neighbour of yours who's offered to have you stay for Christmas while we work out what to do next, unless . . .' says DC Ado.

Wendy looks up to see Joanie Blake from Victory House, hovering around behind the doctor. She's wearing that big orange jacket, with the shiny rolls of satin fabric, she's always wearing, and has her hands stuffed deep in the pockets. It's her unpolished boots Wendy notices the most. She would never leave the house looking so unkempt. *But then*, she thinks with a sort of embarrassment and wonder, *I haven't left the house for over six weeks now. And Joanie Blake lost her mother less than a year ago.*

Wendy touches the collar of her fake leopard-print coat, and turns it up, so she can sink into it further. She doesn't like having all these strangers in the house. She doesn't like being looked at like an exhibit in a museum of curiosities.

'How well do you two know each other?' the boy officer asks.

'Well enough,' says Joanie Blake. She smiles, apologetically, and nods at Wendy, who doesn't reply immediately. She had known Joanie's mother, Allie, since she was a girl, because she'd been friends with her mother, Grace. A long time ago. Len and Samuel, this girl's grandfather, had allotments alongside each other. For a moment, Wendy is startled by the speed and the cycle of everything.

'I knew your grandparents,' says Wendy, quietly. '*They* always wore polished shoes.' The words come out harshly and she closes her lips to stop more coming out after them.

31

'I'd love to hear about them . . . sometime, if you've ever got time,' says Joanie, and Wendy jolts at the hurt glitch in the younger woman's voice. She's lost people too, but Wendy hasn't got it in her to be careful with the feelings of others right now. Instead, she tries to imagine their house as these strangers see it. Cold, ill-cared for these past weeks, the evidence of their poverty in the damp and the scrunched-up clothes and bedding they'd piled around them to keep themselves warm.

'Yes, I will come to yours for Christmas, Joanie Blake,' she says calmly. She doesn't want to, not at all, but there is no other option. She doesn't want to spend it in a place with other old, ageing people she has only just met, from where she might not be allowed to leave, *for her own good*. But, she feels she would say anything to get these strangers out of her house, to not have their eyes looking over everything her and Len's home had become.

'Oh good!' The younger woman's face lights up. 'I mean, I'm so glad. I'll do my best to make it as comfortable as possible. We're on the ground floor, as you know . . .' She trails off and brings a notebook and pencil out of her bag, opens it on a fresh page and starts to write things down.

Before she goes, the doctor smiles and leans down so that she and Wendy are face to face. 'You make sure you let us know if anything hurts. If you feel worse. You mustn't keep any changes to yourself. Please.'

My heart, she thinks. *It hurts. I feel worse.*

But she doesn't say these things. She would rather lie down in the street herself than say anything like that.

There is some quiet talking that she can't hear, between the police officer, the doctor and Joanie Blake. *How rude*, she thinks. To talk about her and her life without addressing her like a full person. She'd noticed that too, over time. People talking to her like she wasn't there, like she was a baby, or like somebody who had only ever been old. Not the woman she had been – the *girl* she had been – full of life, and dancing, setting her hair with a curl, painting her lips and her lashes with the best make-up she could afford. Laughing with Len. A reel. A jig. How long was it since he'd picked up his violin? Did they even still have it?

I am still all the things I have ever been, or thought I'd be, you just can't see it. Wendy Finch still does her make up every single day and would only stop when it was impossible. Even though she hadn't been out for weeks and hadn't eaten properly in even longer, she still feels it's right to make an effort. Well, she had. When Len was still here. What will become of her now?

She looks up and sees it's only her and Joanie in the room. This happens sometimes. She stares so long at a piece of carpet or bit of light socket, and the time passes. Perhaps she should have mentioned this to the doctor.

'Is there anything you think you might need?' Joanie says slowly. 'Anything I can get from upstairs? I want to make sure you have everything you want while you stay with me. I've texted Dad and he's going to pick anything up, if we put it in the hallway, and let him have the key . . .'

Wendy is still wrapped up in the oversized fake leopard-print coat she's been wearing for days, and she reaches out to pick up the tin of peaches she'd been eating with her one proper silver fork when the police had arrived to tell her the news about her husband.

'Does it look like we're using upstairs?' she says, raising her eyebrow and the fork, waving it about in front of her like a conductor's baton, then taking a mouthful. The tinned fruit has been the biggest luxury of the past months, the sweetness a memory of all that used to be good, but the fork feels very heavy, and her wrist drops.

'Well . . . no,' says Joanie, with warmth. Wendy admires her ability to stay calm and not snap in the face of her rudeness. 'Do you have pyjamas or a nightdress? I have some. Some Christmas ones, you could use, but they . . .' she stops.

'Might fall off me?' Wendy looks down at herself and then at Joanie.

'Yes,' says Joanie, simply. 'The kids have all sorts of onesies and things. Patti is tall for eight so wears 10–11 . . .'

'Eight!' Wendy jolts that she might be so small as to fit into an eight-year-old's night things. 'You heard the doctor,' she says firmly. 'I'm well enough to not have to go into hospital. I'm not quite *malnourished*.' She savours the word, like it's illicit, like it's something to be proud of. She *is* proud, that they have managed, despite all that has happened. Some people would have caved in weeks ago, would have crawled out of the house begging. Wendy and Len Finch would never beg. And here she is, still standing. Almost. 'My nightdress is behind the armchair cushion,' she says matter-of-factly as Joanie reaches behind it and brings out a pale blue, long cotton garment, perfectly folded into a neat square. 'None of this is as bad as it looks,' says Wendy suddenly. 'But if I must get up, I'm afraid you're going to have to help me. I'm not used to asking for help, and I don't really know you well enough for all this to come naturally.' Even saying this takes so much energy, and Wendy feels the heat of shame creep over her.

'I understand,' says Joanie, still smiling. 'I'm not expecting anything of you,' she adds. 'If you want to know the truth, I'm terrified I'll not make Christmas good enough for the others. My sister and the kids especially, but Dad too because he must still miss Mum . . . despite everything. But I'm happy to do anything that makes yours a bit easier, Mrs Finch.'

Wendy gives Joanie a long look. She'd never talk so plainly herself. Her pride is in the secrets she keeps as tight as the girdle she still wore until their fortunes changed. Len and her had talked of the scandal of Frank running off with the best friend only months after the death of his young wife. What had she been? Forty-six? It was folklore of the street, whispered about and pondered over. *They must have been having an affair beforehand*. That's what people said over pints in The Mariner, at the counter in The Stop Shop, and wide-eyed as they walked past Frank and Jen's new set-up. And as for Craig Mullany. What would become of him?

'Do you always spill your thoughts out like that?' says Wendy. 'All over the place and to whoever?'

'Rarely,' replies Joanie, dryly. 'Not at all, in fact.' She narrows her lips. 'Just something about this situation, I guess . . .'

'You should call me Wendy,' says Wendy.

'OK, Mrs Finch – *Wendy* – I'll try. We're going to walk to our flat now. It's not far. You're having my room, no arguments. I've put new sheets on this morning, and everything. They've got little Rudolphs on them. Patti chose them. They're good kids. They'll cause you no bother.'

Wendy doesn't know what to say to that. She is fond of children, but she and Len never wanted any of their own. They were happy. Just the two of them.

She presses her nails into the palm of her hands and looks down at the familiar sage green carpet that's reflected in the condensation on the bay window and for a moment she vibrates with indignation. How had they got into this situation? How had she let it continue, all these months, with Len saying how it was all going to be resolved, how he'd fix it, how things would all work out in the end? What should she have done? Who should she have spoken to? Dealing with money had always been Len's job.

I knew, she thinks, shaking with quiet rage. *I knew when that man sat in our living room and made all those promises. I knew it was all nonsense. But Len knew best and I said nothin*g. She is suddenly angry with him and this feels worse than simply missing him.

'Is there anything I can get to make your Christmas a bit better?' Joanie Blake says brightly. 'I'm not going to pretend you'd have chosen to have Christmas with me if you'd had the choice, but, anything. Food? Drink? Magazines?'

'Babycham,' says Wendy immediately. 'Every year Len would buy me Babycham. If you look in the kitchen, in the top cupboard, there's some special glasses with little deer on. He bought them for me for Christmas 1974. I think there was a promotion. I've never loved a present more. We've used them every year. Every single year.'

'I wonder if they sell it at The Stop Shop . . .' says Joanie, frowning slightly. 'I'll text my sister and ask.'

'They do,' says Wendy. 'Well, they *did*. They've always ordered some in at Christmas. Other years . . .' She trails off. 'There's a chance they might not have this year. I haven't been for a while.' She pauses. 'Nor had Len.'

'I'll go to Asda or something if not.' Joanie is still so calm and friendly, Wendy wonders how she does it.

'It wouldn't be Christmas without it.' Wendy suddenly feels very tired.

'Don't worry. I'll get hold of some.'

Joanie helps her up from the sofa as Wendy wonders what the other woman makes of the sight of her narrow body folded up inside the fake leopard-print coat, her dark plum lipstick and her hair in the neatest bun.

She drops the tarnished fork back into the tin of peaches and catches a sight of some peach slices in the bottom, sliding up against each other like goldfish in a bag from the fair.

'I'm really going to miss him,' she says, so quietly, Joanie doesn't hear her, and, as she takes slow, crumbling steps towards the hallway, Wendy Finch swallows the words back down inside her.

10.14 a.m.

Christmas Eve

DC Crane

Newbury Street

Detective Constable Lucy Crane stands outside The Stop Shop and looks along the length of Newbury Street. She's become used to this street, in so many ways like the one she lives on, the houses set out in their terraces, the same layout, different only in the details. But this one has a poison at the heart of it. One she's determined to find, and feels she should have found much sooner.

She doesn't need to refer to her notes. She knows which houses have been burgled in the past seven weeks. She knows who's missing what, what's turned up in online auction sites, at a Christmas car boot sale off the A47, and what's missing. All of it new and bought especially for Christmas. Whoever is responsible for these robberies, they never take keepsakes, jewellery or valuable old things. It's always whatever has been freshly bought, the receipts still shiny in the buyers' purses or wallets or, like her own filing system when it comes to receipts, at the bottom of soggy bin bags or covered in footprints in the footwell of a car.

It's someone who likes getting one over on other people, she thinks. *It's also someone who likes things shiny and new and uncomplicated.* She thinks over the people she's met during the course of this investigation. Last night's burglary was different, there was a spite to it, as though whoever did it wanted to steal the very spirit of Christmas from under Jen Mullany and Frank Blake's feet. *Craig Mullany. The ex-husband,* she thinks immediately. *Who else would go to all that trouble?* It's not like the man hasn't had the opportunity, working his own hours and having legitimate reason to be on the street carrying all sorts back and forth from a hired van while he's been moving into his new home. How easy would it be to hide things he'd stolen in amongst the boxes of pans and books and crockery? *Very,* thinks DC Crane. *He could be moving the presents around in plain sight.*

She tuts at the thought she still has to get her dad's present, although there's bound to be time later. She could pop into Chapelfield and go to that gadget shop, if there's time. Or get the bog-standard, traditional single-malt whisky and pretend to enjoy a glass of it with him on Christmas Day. He'll be showing her off to her aunts and uncles again, making her job sound far more glamorous than it ever has been, or will be. It's nice, that he's proud of her, but he seems to think she's a cross between Helen Mirren in *Prime Suspect* and Inspector Morse. She stopped trying to tell him about all her Excel spreadsheets and, colour-coded by street/area/crime, pie charts years ago. It's the word *detective* in her job title that does it. She always parks her old Fiesta on the street around the corner so he might still imagine her driving purposefully about the streets of Norfolk in a shiny Jag, listening to opera like John Thaw, rather than shouting wrong answers to Pop Master and replaying her *Best of Queen* or Walker Brothers tapes on loop.

She walks towards Frank Blake and Jen Mullany's house, going over what she already knows. It's somebody who lives in the area, there are too many coincidences, too many exact timings and ease of entries. There are a few known criminals living on the street – petty thieves, domestic violence, benefit fraud, a sex offender, the usual – but it seems unlikely to be any of them. They are being kept an eye on anyway, vaguely and without clear purpose, from a distance, on neat colour-coded databases, because of other crimes, but none of the offenders seem to fit with the Christmas present thefts. Not really. Which is why she keeps coming back to Craig Mullany. But if it's him, where is he keeping the stuff?

The papers keep asking why don't they just have police on the street twenty-four hours a day. But it doesn't work like that. And the thief – or thieves – are clever. They've always left it just long enough between burglaries for the dust to have settled, slightly.

DC Crane rings the doorbell and looks sideways at DC Ado, who's fallen into step beside her. This is the first time they've been sent out on this case together, although they've been in each other's work orbits for a good half a year. They're getting used to each other. She likes him and thinks the feeling is mutual. He has a careful way of watching people that she appreciates. He's neither an optimist nor a cynic, and if he painted portraits, they'd just look exactly like the person who sat for him, just like a photo, with none of this interpretation of character or soul in the brushstrokes. *I'm not here to be Freud*, he's said more than once. It makes her laugh, because his fashionable little beard isn't unlike Freud's own.

'Hello.' Frank Blake stands at the door with a mug of something hot in one hand and the other leaning on the doorframe. 'It's good to see you. Come in. Excuse the mess.'

DC Crane notes that the only people who ever apologise about the mess are people whose houses are unusually tidy, and this is the case here too. She resists saying, 'You should see the state of mine,' because one of the many good things about living alone with dogs is that nobody *does* have to see the state of hers.

The scene of crime team had done a good job going over the place with a fine-tooth comb earlier, and there were no longer other people in the house other than the family themselves. Jen Mullany is sitting on the floor, playing with her two boys and a big box of Lego. She has her long ash-blonde hair in a ponytail down her back, and the younger of the children has the end of it between his fingers, twisting it over and shoving it into his mouth, sucking it, then spitting it out again. His mum doesn't seem to mind.

'Would you like a cup of tea? I've just made a pot,' says Frank. 'Shall we make the officers a cup of tea, boys?' He talks to his partner's children in a way DC Crane hears so many adults talk to children after being victims of crime, like they're made of precious stuff that might break. She feels the same about her dogs.

'No thank you,' she says.

'Yes please,' says DC Ado.

The oldest boy jumps up and goes with Frank to the kitchen, while the youngest stays on the rug with his Lego and his mum, one hand on her leg protectively and the other rolling an ill-made car back and forth on the wooden floor. Jen Mullany turns on the television and he's soon stretched out watching something with dinosaurs and people fighting in it while feeding a very content-looking tabby cat from a packet of pink Dreamies.

'Don't give him too many,' says Jen softly. 'I think Valentino gets his Dreamies all over Newbury Street.'

The boy sets out a row of the little biscuits across the wooden floor and onto the thick mustard rug, so they look like something left by Hansel and Gretel, and the cat works his way enthusiastically through them.

'I just wanted to ask you about your ex-husband,' says DC Crane, surprising herself, as she hadn't meant to ask about Craig Mullany outright. DC Crane thinks of the face the man had pulled the first time she'd met him and they'd somehow come onto the topic of his ex-wife's new family set-up. Like he wished he could make them vanish.

'When I came down this morning and saw the kitchen, I must say I thought it *might* be *Craig*,' Jen mouths his name and DC Crane presumes this is to avoid speaking ill of the child's father in front of him. She immediately likes that about the woman. It's rare. Jen fiddles with her long ponytail herself and continues, 'He's not exactly had a good year.' She says it as though it's something that happened to him by accident rather than because of a choice made by her and his best friend.

Stop judging, you know nothing about it. Be more Ado.

'You think this is the sort of thing he'd do?'

Frank hands DC Ado his mug of tea. He's doing nothing to hide his incredulity. 'I doubt *C-R-A-I-G* has the energy to carry things in bags around, let alone plan and engage in strategic theft along Newbury Street.' The man's face darkens.

DC Crane doesn't disagree with him, but stranger things have happened, and how many times has she seen people turn their whole personalities around after experiencing trauma? After feeling betrayed?

'I *can* spell, you know,' says the oldest child with a frown and Jen shoots Frank a frustrated look.

42

'Sorry,' says Frank. 'You know I love your dad.'

The boy shrugs and joins his brother on the rug in front of the TV.

'I do feel bad for him,' says Jen softly. 'I wouldn't like not to be with these two every morning. But I've tried to adapt. He takes them to school two mornings and has them at least two nights every week. It'll be more or less structured now he's found a permanent base. I've not asked for any money from him, and I won't do either. I know we hurt him.'

'A permanent base from where he can practically see into our bedroom window . . .' tuts Frank. 'Life is short,' he says quietly. 'There's no time to let the years go by just not to hurt his feelings.'

DC Crane has no wish to hear a justification or explanation. People talk to her like that sometimes, like she's a priest, a conduit straight to God, and she never encourages it. She'd rather say nothing and change the subject.

'Well, do call if you think of anything,' she says, handing them her card.

'Nanna and Grandad are taking us food shopping later!' says the oldest boy. 'They said we can choose anything we like, anything at all!'

'That will be exciting,' says DC Crane.

'I'm going to choose chocolate,' he says. 'And three jars of marmite. And bananas.'

'Ice cream!' calls out his little brother. 'Chocolate ice cream.'

'Marmite to go on the ice cream,' says the older brother and the other boy pulls a face.

DC Crane is impressed with how the two adults have kept the children so happy and calm after the burglary. Maybe it's just their age though, both still under six, blissfully unaware of the darkness in the world.

Or maybe not. Not all children are kept safe or innocent. Sometimes keeping children innocent in ways adults think they need to be causes more problems too. She swallows down memories of the worst cases she's been involved with since doing this job. Children see lots of things they shouldn't.

Frank Blake shows them to the door and DC Ado hands him back an almost full mug of tea.

'Thank you for everything,' Frank says.

'Have a lovely Christmas, all of you,' says DC Crane. 'We'll let you know when we know anything. We will do everything we can.'

Frank nods and closes the door calmly behind them.

When the two officers step out onto the street, DC Ado turns towards her.

'Strange, isn't it? All these people trying to make new families out of old families, painting houses, booking holidays, updating their relationship status on Facebook, as though it's ever as easy as that?'

'Ain't *that* the truth.' DC Crane ponders the history of her own personal life, which reads like a series of discarded openings to romance novels nobody ever bothered writing. She'd never had the energy to pursue relationships to the happy-ever-after stage. She isn't sure there is anyone out there who wants the sort of relationship she'd like, which would include not living together, spending lots of time by herself with her dogs and never having children. From what she's seen, she often thinks people are not designed to keep starting again without pause. Or, if they are, others are not designed to watch it.

'Problem is when we start thinking we own people,' DC Ado continues. 'We don't. Marriage tricks people into thinking that they do.'

44

'God,' DC Crane shakes her head. 'All this is rather morose for Christmas Eve, isn't it?'

'Not really,' DC Ado smiles. 'I'm a happily married man, and that's because both me and my wife think like this. I don't want to own her. I like choosing to be with her, and her me. It's good.'

'I'd *love* to meet your wife.'

'You should come over. We're having an open house on Boxing Day.' He must see the look on her face because he adds, 'The invitation is dogs included, obviously.'

'We might,' she says and smiles. 'Now, the thing that gets me most about this particular burglary is whoever did it waited exactly until we weren't surveying the street anymore. Almost to the half-hour.'

'Yes.'

'I'm willing to consider Craig Mullany. Shall we go and visit him?'

'Yes,' agrees DC Ado. 'Let's do that. There's something about him that's off. He's like a man who's got a secret in his mouth and each time he speaks he nearly spits it out.'

'Interesting observation.'

'Watch him and see what I mean,' says DC Ado. 'It's something about the jaw.'

DC Crane walks with purpose along the long street and wonders about the ways people unintentionally, or intentionally, reveal their own and others' secrets. The rumours people had shared with her during the length of the investigation so far were myriad and had already led to other investigations. Some people are just waiting to share all the things they think they know about their neighbours to a police officer. Others don't mean to, but end up doing so anyway. She admires DC Ado's ability to take it all in without showing one inch of judgement or surprise. She wonders if inside he's like her but just does a particularly good job of keeping a passive facial expression.

When they get to Number 113, DC Crane notices two things. One, the front door is already open, and two, there are cardboard boxes of all shapes and sizes squashed flat and getting damp all over the front lawn.

'Shit!' a voice comes from inside the house, and then Craig Mullany steps out of the door with more flattened boxes and a roll of old velvet curtain. He looks up, red-eyed like he's been crying, and shakes his face, as though he's shaking off water. It reminds DC Crane of one of her dogs, Freddie, after a long walk on the beach at Holkham. *When he's got something in his mouth he shouldn't have.*

'Good morning, Mr Mullany,' says DC Ado.

'Good morning, Mr Mullany,' says DC Crane.

'Hey,' says Craig Mullany. 'Sorry about the swearing. For some reason that I can't seem to remember now, I thought it would be a good idea to kit my new house out with roomfuls of new flat-pack furniture on Christmas Eve.'

'This is a lot of boxes,' DC Crane acknowledges. She leans forward to try and get a glimpse of what he's got hidden amongst the cardboard mountain.

'I'm renting, but it came unfurnished. Other than a sofa that smells of cat biscuits that nobody will let me donate to them that I might leave out here to piss off the Ellises as a special Christmas present.' He smirks as he says this, and DC Crane makes a mental note to look into his history with them.

'If you have a moment,' says DC Ado. 'We'd like to talk to you about . . .'

'Jen's burglary,' he finishes for him. 'I have a moment,' he laughs, slightly. 'I have lots of moments these days. Do come in, and please excuse the mess.'

The house is indeed, disproving DC Crane's theory, a mess. Piles of clothes, shoes and magazines, dirty cups and plates and a few pizza boxes are strewn on the carpet. The start of a plastic Christmas tree is being assembled, there are boxes of new baubles and unstrung lights, plugged in and flashing in a multicoloured pattern across the floor like neon snakes. A half-built TV stand and a coffee table upside down, and a new sofa, grey marl covered with mustard cushions, still wrapped in cellophane and pushed against the far wall. Split logs are stacked around the fireplace, with an axe leaning against the tiles, and along the mantelpiece are photograph after photograph of the two boys DC Crane and DC Ado have just seen playing with Lego on the carpet at Number 118.

'Can you tell us where you were this morning between 2.30 a.m. and 4 a.m.?'

'I can, pathetically,' Craig says, picking up a full glass of Baileys and ice from the side, then taking a seat on the sofa. 'I was here. Asleep on the sofa. I fell asleep crying while watching *Love, Actually*. They'll show it tonight on one of the main channels because it's Christmas Eve, won't they? I'll watch it again, probably. I say fell asleep, I passed out. I'm not a drinker, you see.' He looks sheepishly to the glass of Baileys. 'Not usually. It's just . . .'

'No need to explain yourself to us, Mr Mullany,' DC Crane says in her most neutral voice. But Craig Mullany continues nonetheless.

'I'd been scrolling through Instagram before that, looking at everyone's Lovely Christmas Drinks and Lovely Christmas Families and Lovely Christmas Engagement Rings . . .'

'Social media can be especially difficult at this time of year,' says DC Ado, and Craig Mullany nods in return.

47

'I pretended to everybody I'm doing something exciting for Christmas,' he says, standing up and walking towards the kettle. 'But I'm not. I'm just going to be here, waiting until I have the kids on Boxing Day. Trying not to pester anyone.'

DC Crane thinks pester is an interesting choice of word. 'Like who?'

'Oh, you know. Anyone.'

Craig Mullany has sandy hair that's swept to the side and back and shaved close to the scalp at the back, like it was once those thick curtain undercuts everyone had in the 90s and he hasn't quite worked out what to do with it since he got older. *He's good-looking*, thinks DC Crane, not that that has anything to do with anything. He has the body of a keen cyclist. Very different from Frank Blake, who's handsome but twice the width and height, with thick dark hair. Craig Mullany is hairy too, sandy bursts of it at the collar of his T-shirt and down his bare arms. *It's probably all over his body*, thinks DC Crane, immediately jolted at the uninvited thought. *Best not think about people involved in this case's body hair at this particular moment, Lucy,* she admonishes herself for her quiet appreciation of hairy men that, looking at the evidence, it seems she shares with Jen Mullany.

The difference between the two men isn't just in looks, though, she thinks, getting her thoughts back to where they should be. Craig is a self-employed systems analyst, working from home most days, or brought in when companies need his expertise. Frank is a groundsperson at the high school and the local milk delivery person. There is the obvious class difference. The difference in education. Craig seems apologetic about his new life, but DC Ado is right, there's something about the way he holds his jaw that says, 'Don't underestimate me.'

48

'Have you thought about moving elsewhere?' asks DC Crane. 'I mean, it's none of my business. But it might be harder. Living on the same street. Right over the road, more or less.'

'Undoubtedly,' says Craig. 'But I want to walk the boys to school. I want . . .' he pauses for a bit. 'I want to be nearby if they need me.'

DC Crane understands what he's saying, could lean towards sympathy and admiration for the man, but she's seen situations like this before when the motive isn't as wholesome as Craig Mullany makes it sound. Not letting a partner move on, being there, in the foreground, can be a sign of something else. Something darker.

'You could probably see what time I liked some posts on Instagram,' he says suddenly. 'If that's any help.'

'It might be,' says DC Crane, deciding there's nothing more for them to ask the man right now, and making to leave. 'I hope you have a lovely Christmas.'

'I will,' says Craig. 'I'm going to have dinner at The Mariner. And everyone knows Sue does the best Christmas dinner this side of Costessey. I tried to convince Jen for years to go, but she's not a pub-at-Christmas person. I can do what I want now. Small mercies, hey. And I can go out for a drink on Christmas Eve too,' he adds. 'I'm going to the charity shindig Sue and Larry have put on, to lift the mood and get some present money to the people who've been burgled.' He looks at DC Crane. 'You should go . . . you know. See if you can spot anyone being dodgy.'

'We will very likely be there,' says DC Crane, realising it sounds like she's agreeing to see him there. 'Well, I hope you have a lovely Christmas,' she adds, ignoring Craig Mullany's vaguely flirtatious tone and the long look being given her by DC Ado. It's interesting to her that only a moment ago the man had said he wasn't really a drinker. He could be lying, or he might just not want to be home alone. She'd reserve judgement until she knew more.

'Call me Craig,' he says, and smiles warmly. 'Ah look! It's Rosemary Woodhouse. Hello, young lady!' Craig bends down, and the two officers turn to see the tabby cat they'd seen not long ago walking about the living room of Number 118 being called Valentino and being fed Dreamies from the younger Mullany boy's little hand.

'We'll leave you to it, Mr Mullany,' says DC Crane, ignoring his request to be called Craig, and the man nods, not looking up from the cat he's, almost aggressively, stroking.

Outside, the two officers look at each other.

'Rosemary Woodhouse is an interesting name for a cat,' says DC Ado.

'It's a creepy name for a cat is what it is. You ever seen *Rosemary's Baby*?' asks DC Crane, who'd named her dogs Freddie and Walker after two of her own long-lasting musical loves.

In the front garden, she looks over the cardboard boxes, and is unsurprised to see several with the familiar Amazon labels.

'What do you think?' she says, as they walk together towards the other end of Newbury Street.

'I think there's nothing more dangerous than a rejected, angry man,' replies DC Ado.

'Would we say he seems angry?' DC Crane thinks back to the way Craig Mullany was making a new home from scratch, from the inside out. 'I think he seems quite . . . accepting of his fate.'

'Maybe,' says DC Ado. 'What about the boxes?'

'I'm not sure. Yet.' She shrugs.

'It's possible that he's behind all of the burglaries. To get some power back. He's had a bad year. Whoever it is really wanted to ruin Jen Mullany and Frank Blake's Christmas.'

'But his children's too . . .?' DC Crane doesn't want to jump to any conclusions.

'People do awful things to their children when they've lost control. You know that. What about the Lessing case?'

DC Crane shivers.

DC Ado is right. They can make no assumptions about any of them. Whether it has anything to do with the burglaries is another matter.

'Do you feel Christmassy?' she says as they pass one of the heavily decorated houses. She doesn't herself, isn't quite sure what the difference between a Christmas Day and an ordinary day should be. She'd put up a little tree in her living room, so Freddie and Walker would get to destroy it enthusiastically off and on throughout December, as was their right, and stocked the fridge with food she liked. But she did that the rest of the year too, so the difference was negligible.

'Yes,' replies DC Ado. 'Very much because of the kids, and my wife, and time together. But then again, deep down, I don't really believe in Christmas.'

'Neither do I,' says DC Crane lightly, shrugging. 'I just pretend to on behalf of everyone else.'

10.20 a.m.

Christmas Eve

Sue Winters

The Mariner Pub

Sue puts the plate of bacon sandwiches and pastries down on the bar and lets out a deep breath. Christmas Eve is always the busiest day of the year, and the pub will be full of people who only come on this one day, as well as the regulars she knows better than she knows some of her own family.

This year is even more important. She'd had the idea to do a charity Christmas Eve party with all proceeds going to the people who'd been burgled since November, other than themselves and the Ellises, who, in her opinion, are both well off and not in need of charity donations. Christmas presents, and money, came thick and fast once the news was out and now they have so many gifts, they decided they'd give the extras to local children's care homes ready for opening on Christmas Day. Thank goodness Tim and Rocky had been there to help with the wrapping.

She's cooked sausage rolls, and mince pies, and made expensive-looking Christmas-themed table decorations with holly and foil and gold candles she bought cheaply from a market stall in the city centre. The ceiling is covered in fairy lights and glass red and gold baubles, and it looks quite magical, considering it's a no-frills pub for the rest of the year. She knows they're good landlords. They've dedicated their entire married life to it. The perfect hosting team.

So where was he, last night, when I woke up in the early hours to find the space in the bed beside me empty?

She pushes the thought away because there is no definite answer. Larry has always been a light sleeper. He was probably having a cigarette and a sneaky port out in their private courtyard. She'd ask him about it later. Larry was too dedicated to their life together to be getting up to no good, she knew that. But he's an attractive man, robust, white hair, a strength in his forearms after years of changing barrels. They both see John Ellis get up to all sorts with various women in the pub all the time. *Is he ever jealous of him?* she thinks. *Is he ever tempted to be* like *him?*

She shakes her head. *You can't start doubting your husband on Christmas Eve, come on, Sue.* She stops herself from overthinking. There's too much to do, for a start.

'I can't believe old Len Finch died in the street,' Larry says, gently, placing a hand on her shoulder. 'Of all days. His poor wife.'

'It's just horrible,' says Tim from his spot polishing the bar, one last time before opening time. He's already dressed in his running gear and once again Sue's impressed with his tenacity when it comes to his fitness. He wouldn't dream of taking a day off, not even for Christmas.

One of the best things about Christmas for Sue is having the whole family sleeping over in the pub together again. Larry had tried to sway both his children to join the family business, but one, Rocky, goes to art college and is a supervisor in The Stop Shop the rest of the time, and the other, Tim, would rather work for 'that prat John Ellis'. It was Sue who convinced Larry to let it go when his blood boiled with betrayal and he was almost ready to cut Tim out of his life entirely. *You'll only lose him otherwise,* she'd said. She was right, of course, and now he and Tim are back to how they used to be, with him leaving his own DIY project house to come back to the family pub for Christmas.

Larry had always been terrible at letting things go, a grudge holder, who without her intervention, could easily swing towards revenge, even over the smallest of slights. She'd always loved the passion in him. It was just a question of helping him keep the right side of the line.

'No kids, no family,' continues Larry, 'Nobody to have the wife for Christmas. Imagine that. Imagine being old and all alone on Christmas Day . . . Fancy some of this?' Larry nods to the plates of bacon sandwiches and pastries.

'Bacon sandwich maybe,' says Tim. 'And, don't worry, I'll look after you and Mum when you're old. Some whisky in the coffee?' He laughs and holds his mug out to his dad. 'It's Christmas after all. I'm surprised you haven't asked her to stay here . . .'

Sue smiles as she watches Larry get a bottle down from behind the optics display.

'Thank you. That's very reassuring. And no need. Joanie Blake's having her. She just said so on the charity WhatsApp group. Otherwise I'd have let her have one of the guest rooms,' he says and pours them both a large shot into the mugs. 'Do you remember the first time you tried one of these? You were twelve. You were sick on the carpet.'

Tim laughs. 'Ha! Yes. You didn't let me forget that in a hurry.' Tim takes the mug from him and Sue feels happy at the warmth between them.

'All harmless fun,' says Larry, smiling and nodding to the wall of photos of them over the years behind the bar. 'People like feeling like they know us, that they're part of the family. It's why we do so well. They feel safe here.'

Tim takes a big sip of his coffee. 'That's true. No room for secrets round here either, that's for sure.'

Sue thinks about this. She has several secrets of her own, but a much bigger collection of secrets belonging to other people. They can't help but spill them with their pints and shots, like they're just waiting for the truth to come out. She's heard the sort of sordid stuff that would make some people's eyes pop out. Seen it with her own eyes, too. But she'd never use it to her advantage. Not unless she had good reason.

'I was thinking,' she says slowly, wondering if Larry will go for it, 'of us offering a reward for information. On the burglaries. What do you think?'

The two men stare at her, and she wishes Rocky wasn't at work as he's usually on her side in any family debate. She's wearing her new Christmas dress, black wool with a sequin design in the middle that brushes one way to make a Christmas tree and the other to make a snowman. Her earlobes glint with the diamond earrings Larry bought her last Christmas. She stands her ground. Larry will come round in the end. He always does.

'I'm not sure,' says Larry. 'A reward. With our own money . . .?'

'Just think of the look on John Ellis's face,' she says, appealing to a soft spot she knows Larry can't resist. 'When you're named in the papers for helping catch the burglar.'

Larry pulls her to him and kisses her on the lips, a wet kiss she returns eagerly. 'I'm liking the sound of this,' he says. 'You know I like to do good, first and foremost.'

Sue smiles. He does, of course. And it's pure coincidence that every time he does a good thing, people come through the door to tell him what a good man he is, the takings go up and they mention him in the news. A win-win.

'I knew you'd like it,' she says, then she laughs, the same laugh he says made him turn around and ask who she was while waiting for his pint of Guinness to be pulled in The Ten Bells in the city centre all those years ago. Or so the story goes – one she loves to hear again and again because it reminds her they were young once, and that he'd wanted her long before she ever made his life easier.

'I'm ready,' says Larry. 'Christmas in a pub always feels exciting. No matter how many times we do it . . . A reward for what, *exactly* by the way?'

'Information that leads to finding who's behind these burglaries,' says Sue. 'A nice juicy amount too. We can afford it. Someone should *do* something.'

'You know what,' says Larry, holding out his mug for more whisky. 'I like that idea.'

'Nothing to lose hey, sweetheart,' says Sue, wondering what a good amount would be.

'I'd rather you gave it to me, obviously,' laughs Tim, putting his coffee down on a beer mat on the bar. 'What do you think of my handiwork, Mum?' He stacks the cleaning things away in the store cupboard, then gestures to the area he's just spent the last half an hour cleaning.

'It's perfect, darling. Like a Mr Sheen advert.'

'You know I only do the cleaning so I don't have to help with the sandwiches,' laughs Tim. 'Poor Rocky, always with the short straw. I wouldn't be surprised if, after last year, he has nightmares about tubs of Flora.'

'You've done a good job here today,' says Larry happily. 'Fancy a cleaning job on top of flogging houses and getting people perfect bodies?'

'Thanks, but no thanks. If it's all right with you,' says Tim, 'I'm going for a run in a bit. But I'll have my bacon sandwich first.'

Sue looks at their son. It still amazes her that she and Larry have made a person so into his health and fitness. Tim is all tight biceps and thigh muscles and he's been doing pull-ups on a bar he's attached in the door frame to the pub cellar despite only being home for a couple of nights. It just goes to show you can never tell how your children will turn out.

'We can add Mrs Finch to the reason we're having the Festive Feel Good – get a few things to her as well as those who've been burgled,' says Sue. 'It's going to be hard for her.'

There's a bang on the door then, a little too early to be a punter, and Larry unbolts the latch to see a wet-haired Frank Blake standing the other side of it.

'I'm really sorry about what's happened,' says Larry, ushering in his friend, who brushes the water from his shoulders onto the welcome mat.

'It's OK,' says Frank. 'I'm just popping in before I pick up Patti and Dylan to say I'm not sure we'll all be coming to the Festive Feel Good. I know Jen was going to help out a bit, and all the rest, but . . .'

'Don't be silly,' says Sue, going over to him and putting her arm around him. 'We don't expect anything of you at all. Just tell Jen we love her and she's welcome at any time and we'll think nothing bad of her if she stays away.'

'Will do,' he says, smiling. 'She will still come and pick up all the gifts for the care homes. I know she'll want to do that. Ray and Barnie are spending some time with her mum and dad while she sorts out some new presents. You know what she's like – determined to do it herself.' He smiles and Sue can see this is something he loves about her. 'Who the hell does a thing like that though? You know they took the Christmas dinner with them? The turkey, the home-made cranberry sauce . . . even the gingerbread men the boys made.' Frank shakes his head.

'A bitter and miserable arsehole is who,' says Tim, passing Frank a whisky, which he downs in one. 'The thing I don't get is why the police haven't found whoever it is. It's been going on for too long.'

'They *should* have found who's behind it by now,' Sue feels angry at the thought of it. The first burglary was in early November. Seven properties had been hit all in all: John and Cynthia Ellis at Number 121 first, then The Mariner, a few houses further on, and now Frank and Jen. She remembers how Larry had laughed a bit when he'd heard about John Ellis. *Never laugh at another's misfortune, as next time it will be you.* That's what Sue always said. And, of course, they *were* next. She managed not to say I told you so. She was too upset at the thought of a stranger riffling through their things.

'It makes you wonder what the point is,' says Frank sadly, the whisky hitting his positivity immediately. 'All that effort we put in, to make Christmas just right, to make it feel like we've made a proper family.'

Tim comes round from behind the bar. 'You *have* made a proper family. Family doesn't come down to presents and a trussed-up cooked dinner.' He puts his arm on his friend's shoulder.

'No, I suppose you're right.' Frank doesn't look convinced but pats his own hand over Tim's. 'I just wanted to make it nice for her, you know. I wanted to show her I *could*. I wanted to have a fresh start.'

'I'm going to offer a £5000 reward for information that leads to a conviction,' says Larry, decidedly. 'I'll announce it at the Feel Good.'

'You are?' Frank looks surprised by this, but is smiling. Sue smiles too. She's always loved her husband's generosity.

'Yes. We have to look after each other. Take things into our own hands.'

Sue does a little cough to make her presence known.

'It was Sue's idea,' Larry says quickly, and she nods in agreement.

'You mean we get people to be vigilantes?' Tim pulls a face Sue can't work out.

'Not vigilantes. Like people who won't take this shit anymore,' Larry explains. 'It's not OK to steal a family's Christmas dinner.'

'I can't help but feel,' says Frank, his smile fading, 'that we're cursed. Me and Jen.'

'Humbug!' says Sue, brightly. 'Of course you're not. Take loads of photographs tomorrow,' she continues. 'There'll be lovely memories with Jen and the boys. And it's never about what you give them, or even the bloody turkey. It's about how you show them how to deal with things when they haven't got everything.'

'You should write cracker messages, Mum,' laughs Tim.

'She's got a point,' says Frank, finishing his whisky. 'I just hate not being able to keep them all safe. And I want to prove to Craig his boys are OK with me.'

'Of course they're OK with you!' Sue believes, strongly, that it's about time Craig Mullany accepts Jen and Frank's relationship. She's one of the only people who doesn't think they were having an affair before Allie died, and as one of

Allie's closest friends, she knows a few things other people don't, but it's really not her business to share, despite sometimes wanting to. 'You've known those boys since they were born. You can't help that you fell in love with their mother. Allie would have understood, I'm sure of it.'

'Urgh,' Frank's shoulders slump again.

'Fancy a run?' Tim takes a mouthful of bacon sandwich, then leans down to change into his trainers. 'Take your mind off it?'

'Today? Do you never take a day off?' Frank asks.

'I'm eating a bacon sandwich and drinking whisky with my coffee. That's having a day off. I like running. It's relaxing!'

'I'll leave it thanks,' says Frank. 'I've got to pop in and get the kids from Irma's. Maybe on Boxing Day.'

'I'll take that maybe as a yes,' says Tim.

Frank shrugs, and smiles again. 'Right I'd better be off. Thank you, Sue. Thanks, Larry. That's amazing about the reward money. I hope it pushes someone to come forward. Enjoy your run, Tim . . .' The two friends smile at each other as Frank leaves the pub through the side entrance.

Tim finishes his sandwich and immediately leans down to tie his neon laces carefully while Sue arranges the Christmas table decorations. Sue takes a deep breath, relieved at the simplicity of her family life. She doesn't envy Frank and his complications. Maybe it's time to say something. What would Allie have wanted her to do?

Why did you have to go and die on us, hey? She shakes her head. Some things in life make no sense, and there's no point trying to make sense of them either.

'What we need,' says Sue, suddenly, 'is music!'

'Time for a bit of "Blue Christmas"?' This is Larry's favourite Christmas song and when it comes to karaoke he fancies himself as a bit of an Elvis.

'Give it a rest, love,' says Sue. 'People don't want that at half ten in the morning!' She taps numbers into the jukebox and on comes the jingle bells that introduce Mariah Carey's 'All I Want for Christmas Is You'. *The* festive classic, in Sue's opinion.

'I doubt they want this either,' laughs Tim. 'Shall I let everyone in on the way out, or go out the back?' Tim turns to his Dad as he puts his headphones on.

'Let everyone in. We're late opening as it is! Gotta let the hungry, thirsty hordes in,' says Larry, smoothing down his shirt and then his hair. 'Christmas Eve is supposed to be the best day of the year.' *Not for poor Frank and Jen, or Mrs Finch either*, thinks Sue.

Tim leaves as the first of the regulars enter the door. There are eight waiting and Euan Barratt from further up the street at Number 88 is straight in at the bar ordering his first pint of what will be many. Larry knows he'll have to keep an eye on him.

'Merry Christmas everybody!' says Larry.

Sue sings along in time to the music. 'All I want for Christmas is youuuuu!' and points at the people coming in. 'Who's for a bacon sandwich?' she says.

There's a showing of hands from the regulars.

'Do you know anything about what happened to the man from Number 133?' says somebody else and Sue looks up to see Nathan Patterson, local newsman and long-time friend of Larry's, standing in the doorway with his camera and a smile. 'I thought I'd come early. Spend a couple of hours here before it all gets going later, if it's all right with you?'

'Of course it is, come in. Sue's done bacon sandwiches. On the house,' Larry offers.

'Perfect,' says Nathan, smiling, with his perfect TV teeth, and leaning his tripod against the bar. 'I'll just blend in. You'll barely know I'm here.'

Somehow Sue thinks that seems unlikely, but at least Nathan so often gives the pub good publicity.

'You might be able to help me as it happens, Nathan,' Larry says, leaning conspiratorially towards the TV newsman. 'I want to offer a reward to catch whoever did these burglaries. Ten thousand pounds. What do you think?' Sue laughs to herself at how easily Larry has doubled the amount to something more ostentatious as soon as he's with Nathan.

'Do tell me more,' says Nathan Patterson, helping himself to one of the bacon sandwiches and taking a big bite.

'I also wanted to talk to you about last night.' Larry leans forward and grins and Sue wonders what her husband wants to discuss about last night. There's not much time for worrying though, because Christmas Eve at The Mariner is in full swing.

11.03 a.m.

Christmas Eve

Irma Woźniak

127 Newbury Street

'I'm so sorry to hear about the burglary, Frank,' says Irma kindly as her girlfriend's dad picks up his grandchildren. She's had them since Joanie dropped them off on her way to work and they've started Christmas Eve laughing and cutting shapes into their toast with plastic scissors. She feels it already might be the best Christmas she's ever had.

'It's OK, Irma,' he says, taking the children's hands and grinning at them enthusiastically. 'We've got far too much to be getting on with to worry about a little burglary. Haven't we, kids?'

'We have!' says Dylan, the younger of the pair, who's dressed warmly in a big coat, gloves, bobble hat and striped scarf.

'We have!' says Patti, older but just as excited. She's wearing the deerstalker hat she'd bought with her birthday money last month, and a silver Puffa jacket, a smaller version of her mum's.

'But are you OK?' Irma mouths to him.

'I'm *always* OK,' smiles Frank, pulling them to him as

they step out into the hallway and he opens the main door to Number 127. 'Have a lovely day, Irma. See you later on. Or tomorrow.'

'One of the two,' says Irma. 'I hope you all have a lovely day too.'

'Love you Irma,' says Dylan, out of the blue, stopping to call the words out over his shoulder as the door shuts behind him.

'Love you too,' says Irma quietly, the small boy's words grabbing at her unexpectedly so she has to lean onto the doorframe on her way back into her flat. This is definitely the best Christmas Eve yet.

With the children gone, happy with their grandfather, Irma puts the plates with the remnants of their Christmas Eve breakfast of mincemeat swirls and strawberries into the sink and begins her yearly Christmas Eve ritual.

She lights a rosehip candle, draws the curtains tight and puts a record on her old record player that she roots out from the bottom half of her wardrobe. She will only play one piece, Puccini's 'Signore, Ascolta' aria, before packing the player away until next year. She's played it every Christmas Eve morning, since Christmas 2006.

She was fifteen then, had dreamed of being an opera singer since she was a small girl. She's twenty-eight now and doesn't sing anymore, nor listen to opera either. It seems such a ridiculous and old-fashioned dream. Like it was an ancestor of hers who'd been that girl. Her record of Puccini's *Turandot* is the same one she's had since she was a child, but she only ever listens to it on Christmas Eve. That's all she allows herself. The rest of the time, she has the radio on, or playlists Joanie makes her, and the record player is put away at the bottom of her wardrobe.

As the music floods the flat, Irma places her palms flat on her dressing table and closes her eyes. It all floods back, the heat of her skin, the sweat at her forehead, the scents of disinfectant, of blood, of flesh.

'*Ma se il tuo destino, doman, sarà deciso, noi morrem sulla strada dell'esilio . . .*'

She remembers the warm head in her lap and the baby's soft, surprisingly thick, hair against her skin like autumn marsh grass. The love, all the love, in the tips of her fingers at the base of her hairline, gently foraging for flaked scalp; seeking out evidence of whatever it was she lacked. She didn't want to let her go with a head full of neglect, clustered at the nape of her neck, or all across the top, like fallen petals; a string of rotting beads.

She's learning to put the memories in pockets, has begun to enjoy things more, to know she is allowed to, but it has taken so much time, and she still isn't truly used to it. Joanie has helped with that, always reminding her that sometimes an outcome is about the luck you have, the people you have around you, a tick of the right clock. This year has been the best she's had since it happened. She is, as much as she can be, happy.

But, still, in hidden corners of herself, it consumes her. Like now.

The memory of Klara is like a war drum inside her, as though all her innards – lungs, heart, entrails – beat with the loss of that face – that face which was half hers, the blue eyes, forget-me-nots, the lashes, moth wings.

She closes her eyes and smells the candle, sees her daughter's face, so clear it's as though she's right there with her. She remembers her fingers around her own. The thumbnails, neatly trimmed, the suck, suck as she slept, her soft limbs spooled around her like a new cat, furless yet warm.

Then she was taken away. Given away. By people who were supposed to love her.

The hot rosehip wax smells of bright, blue-skied, sunny days, not of frost. Christmas comes with its own rituals, and later Irma will be at work in the pub, whipping up festive cheer, listening to people talk about their own prides and losses as they sit at the bar and have one too many, or five too many. Seeing the youngsters, not much younger than her really, back from university, meeting up with their old school friends now they're grown-ups, laughing, putting 'Last Christmas' on the jukebox, snogging, being sick, pretending they haven't been, ordering one last drink for the road.

The past year has been better, she's made real friends, has fallen in love, which she'd truly believed was impossible, and some days she forgets to remember. Or remembers that it isn't everything. Thirteen years is a long time to feel wretched. What did Joanie say when she'd told her? 'I hope you know none of that means anything bad about you.'

'But you *kept* your child,' Irma had replied. 'I mean, you had the courage to keep yours. You *fought* to keep yours.'

'I didn't fight, I had my mum,' Joanie had said quietly. 'I couldn't have done it without her. It was never a question of fighting. She literally asked me what I wanted to do, that was it. She asked. I answered. We all got on with it. You didn't have anyone.'

But Christmas Eve is always hard, wondering what Klara is doing, what her name is now, what she dreams of on Christmas Eve. She is thirteen. Out there, somewhere. That's if she's still alive, which, Dear God, she must be, surely. Irma finds it unbelievable there's a person who grew inside her, who was so wanted, and people around her somehow thought it would be better for her to grow up elsewhere. *Is* actually growing up elsewhere.

The candle flickers. Irma tries to remember, without disappearing into sorrow. It's Christmas Eve after all. Patti and Dylan had laughed with her for the past two hours while Joanie had been cleaning. They are always a tonic, and she'd not begrudge them a joyful Christmas.

Irma has promised herself she will try and enjoy Christmas in her own way. The flashing lights earlier, the sight of Mr Finch, covered and taken away in an ambulance, it shook her and it reminded her too. She mustn't waste her life in blankets of regret.

'Ei perderà suo figlio, io l'ombra d'un sorriso . . .'

Who knows, she thinks, blowing out the candle. Maybe, if what she's got planned later works out, motherhood will come to her a different way. Stranger things have happened.

She's never allowed herself to imagine another child. Never that. She'd cut Joanie off every time she'd asked her about it. But then she spotted someone carrying books out of the library part of the Forum and something lit in her. *Maybe Klara will come back to me after all.*

The music stops and Irma puts the record away in its sleeve. Such beauty. She'd love to sing again, but she can't. It would be like slicing herself in two and letting everything fall out of her. She'd be worried she wouldn't be able to put herself back together again.

Once the candle is blown out, the record player and record put away in the depths of her wardrobe, Irma does the last few bits to get ready for work, where she will get everyone in the festive mood, then listen to their stories. Betrayal. Buffoonery. Sex. She'll swing the pump, down, up, down, up, and the beer foams high in the glass, in

67

which she will see the reflection of her face; the cut of her cheekbones and the decorative arch of her eyebrow. She is good at make-up. Her brows are like calligraphy, a lover's pen, a curve and a flick. The punters tell her she's beautiful. The words flap about her like sparrows. A rise, then falling to fragments. Flattery sustains nothing. All Irma wants is to work out how to live with hope, to stop dreaming about the day they took Klara away. When she hears her daughter cry in her sleep, she is always a baby, and she's always just out of reach.

Irma prepares herself for the inevitable chat-up lines that will come her way, made even worse by the fact there's this underlying idea that people should get together at Christmas. Knocking people back is tiring. *You look like a woman in a black and white movie. A Greta or a Gloria, a Gina or a Gene. Dark hair, abundant handfuls, like a princess in an old story. Your skin is like marble. Your lips are like wine.* That's the older ones. The younger ones. Well.

She stands at the sink and sorts out the recycling. Nobody dares overstuff the wheelie bins in the shared houses. They've been warned about it before. People with clipboards and earnest, grey identity photos laminated on yellow lanyards, knocking at doors. Another thing that can be added to their Database of Inadequacy, like the children playing too loudly in the so-called park, or the rusting electrical appliances and the noisy barbeques in summer, when the beer cans fall out into certain parts of the street like broken mosaics and the tin gleams.

Upstairs, her neighbour, Isaac, is dragging something across his living room. She can't remember the last time they spoke to each other, meeting only once in the hallway downstairs in the past half-year. Irma has lived on Newbury Street for six years, in this same flat, with the shared entrance hall, and always somebody living above her upstairs. Isaac has been here for just under a year. She'd been surprised to see him, a familiar face from her later teenage years, but he just shook his head when she mentioned it and they'd continued as though those years had never happened. As though they'd never met.

And then she'd spotted someone else, a while ago. Someone she hadn't expected to see again. It was like the universe was egging her on to *do* something. It was only the past few days she had any idea what that could be.

The handle of her front door turns.

For a moment, she sees Klara as she might be now, the half of her that's hers and hasn't gone. She's popping over for a cup of tea, a mince pie, a ticket to *The Nutcracker* at the Theatre Royal. They're close, she hugs her and brings her a pot of holly, armfuls of poinsettia, of amaryllis, rustling, damp in wax paper.

It's a thought too far, and Irma hurts with longing.

When she allows herself to look up, it's Joanie in her living room, not an imaginary Klara, and she's holding two cups of coffee from The Stop Shop coffee machine and a bunch of gig fliers, crooked under her arm.

'Happy Christmas Eve!' exclaims Irma, rushing forwards and throwing her arms around her. They kiss. Joanie tastes of coffee and blackcurrant, always some kind of trace of fruit on her lips, from her brightly coloured collection of lip balms.

'Your make-up looks *so good!*' says Joanie, passing Irma the coffee and putting the fliers down on the dressing table, kissing her on her neck. 'Happy Christmas Eve to you too. I mean, not happy. But . . . you know. I thought we should go to a gig on Boxing Day. When the children are with their dad. What do you think?'

'I think that sounds good. And thanks. I'm going for Christmas Bette.' Irma bats her eyelashes and pulls the most elegantly disinterested face she is capable of. They both laugh.

Since she was a child, Irma has collected photographs of movie stars from the thirties, forties and fifties and has practised doing her make-up to look just like them. For today she's taken a look from *The Man Who Came to Dinner*. She's pinned her hair up too, just like her heroine, and put on some simple (fake) drop pearl earrings that catch the light as she tilts her head. She wonders what she'd do if she didn't put this thought and effort into her appearance. People misunderstand. They think her vain. But if she didn't do this, if she didn't use herself as a canvas, she might have never left the house at all. And it's not their business anyway.

Irma keeps most of her make-up in the fridge, like *Just Seventeen* told her to all those years ago, her mother newly married to an English man, who, at first, was generous to them both. It's the secret of her oft-admired eyebrows – a fridge-cold pencil and cold foundation rolls out smoothly across her face like the finest marzipan over a Christmas cake, and it stays there. Cold liquid eyeliner shines like new printer ink. These things are satisfying in their moments. They make Irma feel calm. Even though it rarely lasts.

'I've only got fifteen minutes,' says Joanie. 'Did the kids get off OK? I've somehow invited Mrs Finch for Christmas. I can't quite believe what happened. God. I've got so much to do.' Irma sees her girlfriend's face flicker with overthinking. Joanie's generosity and the way she takes care of others is something Irma loves about her, but since Allie died it sometimes seems she's forgotten that she has to look after herself too.

'I saw the ambulance. I wish I'd spotted him sooner. This time of year is shit for so many people . . . Thank you for this,' Irma sips the coffee. 'The kids got off fine. And that's so lovely of you. About Mrs Finch.'

'She must feel awful. Imagine losing someone at Christmas.' Joanie slaps her hand up to her forehead. 'Oh God. I . . .'

'Don't worry. I know what you mean. And yes, it must be awful. Unless Mr Finch was awful, in which case, his wife will be celebrating in her heart.'

'You say the funniest things.' Joanie puts her hand on Irma's cheek while Irma sips the coffee and leaves a faint print of her lipstick on the cup.

Irma looks at Joanie. Her girlfriend's hair, often different colours, often different lengths, is, today, cornfield bubbles around her head, yellow and beautiful, black at the roots. She's startling to look at, all stripes and limbs and earrings, and she wears the sort of dark lipstick that makes Irma think of vampires, fruit and wine.

'What about you do my cards?' Joanie nods enthusiastically. 'If you want to, that is.'

Whenever she's with Joanie, Irma feels like she's getting it right. Like this is life and all the things, the endless things – the disappointment, mistakes, destruction, guilt – are just a tiny part of something bigger, and not everything. And they laugh so much together, so easy. So right.

'Good idea. A quick past, present, future.'

Irma keeps her tarot cards in an old Weetabix mug. She gets them out, in their green cloth bag she made when she was going through her sewing-will-make-me-a-real-mother phase, when she was expecting Klara, before she knew what her stepdad was planning. She puts them carefully on the table. They used to belong to her German grandmother,

her mother's mother. They are soft through time and use. First by her maternal grandmother, then by her mother, until she put them away when she no longer wanted to be the sort of person who did tarot, and then by Irma, who inherited her grandmother's talent to read them, and more besides.

Irma can see people's auras. She's been able to since she was very young. Everybody has colours and stripes and sparks around them. Some people walk through clouds of candyfloss, others in dark sheets of rain. Some trickle through a spectrum of both. She sees Joanie's heart beating, a pink and yellow haze about her head and shoulders. *She is kind*, she thinks. *I am so in love with her*, she thinks too, and the fact that her heart can feel anything like this at all, after all the times she'd tried to cut it off, or close it down, feels like it's her own sort of Christmas miracle. She doesn't want anything in return. Just to feel it, and be around her, is more than Irma had hoped for. She has felt so happy these past months and is giddy with it. She'd always lived like joy was something to be metered out, measured by the spoonful, in case being greedy brought a sort of punishment that she'd always thought she deserved. But now she is beginning to think that maybe she deserves a little of that joy, though nothing more than that . . . Irma knows how to be thankful, and makes sure she finds way to show it every day.

Breathe. Breathe. Breathe. You're allowed to feel happy. She remembers Klara in her cot, curled around that bunny she bought her from Woolworths. It had a cloth cap and a lemon-yellow bib. It had plastic, orange eyes and satin ears, stitch-scattered with purple moons and stars. She rubbed the ears into her cheeks and chin, and when she woke up, they were soggy with night spit. Klara always seemed to breathe so deeply. Irma sat up all night just to hear her breathe. She couldn't believe the Universe had let her be that happy.

Irma sets out three cards: *past, present, future.* The illustrations are in black and white ink with silver edging.

'Oh, look. *The World.*' Irma looks at the picture of the naked woman holding two staffs, surrounded by a wreath of green.

'I like the sound of that,' says Joanie. 'Does it mean we're going to go on a trip or something?' Joanie reaches out and holds Irma's hand. 'Patti and Dylan would *love* that.'

'Not quite,' says Irma. 'It's more like a pause before a change . . . a sort of shift between something past and something future. I feel like . . .' She stops. The card is reversed. *Stagnation. Unable to finish something. Failed plans.* She doesn't want to say what that might mean, and wonders if her own fears are affecting the reading. 'I'll be late for work,' she says. 'We'd better go. We can do cards later.'

'Maybe it means you're going to stay the night tonight!' She gives Irma one of those grins. 'Don't worry. No rush. We don't have to, you know that. But, you could. I'd love it. The kids would too.' Joanie gives Irma one of those big smiles that makes Irma, despite her best efforts not to, go weak at the knees.

She doesn't tell Joanie her actual plans for later.

Those plans are secret, for now. Irma knows that sometimes you can't talk to the people you love about the things you need to do, just in case it means it will make them stop loving you. Just in case you lose courage.

11.25 a.m.

Christmas Eve

DC Crane

Newbury Street

'You can tell a lot about a person by the way they treat another person's cat,' says DC Crane. 'I mean, I'm no cat person myself. It's always been dogs for me. That's what people do, don't they? Decent people? Make a fuss of other people's cats?'

She watches the cat she's heard referred to by two different names already today walk off along Newbury Street, and thinks of the look on Craig Mullany's face as he greeted it earlier.

'I don't much like them, *as you know*,' she adds and looks at DC Ado, who's smiling and shaking his head. 'What is it?'

'Well, there is a difference between being nice to someone's cat and making a fuss of it.'

'Right . . .'

She watches Frank Blake let go of the hands of his two grandchildren as he stops to bend down and pull his own hands along the length of the cat's spine. As the cat pushes into his palms, purring heavily and looping its tail round and about his calves, the children join in too. It's a happy scene. *Isn't it?*

'Just because someone's nice to someone else's cat, doesn't mean they're a nice person.'

'I wasn't saying that,' says DC Crane, walking along Newbury Street to Victory House with DC Ado beside her. 'It's just . . .' She isn't sure what she's trying to say. There's something about the way Frank Blake is stroking the cat now that makes her forget what she was going to say about both Jen and Craig Mullany having the cat in their houses, calling it by a different name. 'I think you're reading too much into this.'

'And well you might,' says DC Ado. 'But if someone was cuddling up to my cat like that,' he nods in the direction of Frank Blake, 'I'd feel a bit like they weren't respecting the fact that it was *my* cat.'

'Animals can't belong to anybody, Michael,' she says, with a half-smile 'We are only custodians of their spirits.' That's what she thought when she watched Frank Blake stroking the cat. He acts like he owns everything. A sort of confidence in the space he inhabits. *Too confident?* She's not sure.

'Now I *know* you're taking the piss. If someone tried to offer Christmas Dinner to Freddie, you'd have their guts.'

'I'd politely ask them to sod off,' laughs DC Crane. 'But dogs are different. Dogs need humans in a way cats just don't. Who even *owns* that cat, anyway?'

At this moment, Isaac Iwu from Number 127 appears from the far end of Newbury Street and the cat pads away from Frank towards him.

'Fickle git,' says Frank, laughing loudly as he leads his two grandchildren further up the road towards Victory House. They are laughing and skipping, and the shorter one, the boy, is carrying a cuddly snowman and the girl is dressed like a robotic Sherlock Holmes. The other man pats the cat and Frank Blake shakes his head, giving one last kissing sound to see if the cat will come back to him. It doesn't. Isaac Iwu looks between the big bag he's carrying and the cat, then back at Frank and the children with a look that can only be described as disgust.

Frank shrugs, pulls Patti and Dylan to him, and starts to whistle as he walks. Isaac nods at the cat, a small smile forming on his lips and an almost puff out of his chest.

Crane and Ado watch the man, and the cat, enter Number 127 together and the door shut firmly behind them.

'No love lost there,' says DC Crane.

'Indeed,' says DC Ado. 'As I said. People don't want other people making a fuss of their cats. It's territorial.'

'What about their cars?' The two detectives stop by John Ellis's out-of-place BMW M4, which is parked on the street outside his and Cynthia Ellis's home. It gleams in the pale light, a very competitive green. As far as DC Crane could work out, John Ellis and Larry Winters, the landlord of The Mariner and self-styled *local charity organiser extraordinaire*, are always in competition with each other, and while it might have been expected that John would park away from here, at one of his other houses, or in a lock-up, like Larry does with his Jag, it was obviously here on Newbury Street as a reminder to anyone who might have thought otherwise that John Ellis is on top.

'Cars are a different thing altogether,' says DC Ado, who is about to say more when Cynthia Ellis steps out of the front door, dressed in expensive clothes that seem, in DC Crane's opinion, far too big for her, collecting the post from the little box that's attached to the wall next to their glazed house number.

76

'Good morning, Mrs Ellis,' says DC Crane, remembering the older woman's nervous shaking the night of the burglary at their house. 'How are you doing? All ready for Christmas?'

Cynthia Ellis nods. 'Oh yes, absolutely. John wouldn't have it any other way. I've made some things for the Feel Good at The Mariner later. Quiches. Doilies too. Have you ever made lace? With bobbins? I could do it for hours.'

Both detectives shake their heads.

'I'm going to stay for the whole thing. I haven't been to a party for ages.' She's vibrating with a sort of childlike excitement that seems utterly genuine.

'Since the burglary?' asks DC Crane.

'Since before then,' says Cynthia Ellis. 'As John says, I'm not really a party person.' She takes the letters from the box. 'I'm quite a nervous person, I suppose. I always have been. John's so gregarious. I'm lucky someone like him married someone like me. I'm good at charity things though. And organising. So I'm not completely useless!' She laughs then, a loud sort of seal-like laugh that comes from high up in her chest. The laugh doesn't reach her eyes.

'I'm sure he's lucky too,' says DC Ado, and this makes DC Crane warm to her partner even more.

'Ha, oh yes, of course. My daughter says that quite often. Shame she lives in Australia. Will I see you at the Feel Good?'

'It's highly likely, DC Ado nods, politely.

'Good, good,' says Cynthia Ellis, doing an almost-curtsy as she turns around and goes back into her house.

DC Crane can't put her finger on it, but there's something off about Cynthia Ellis. It's not that she comes across as duplicitous or anything like that, more that she always seems to be on high alert, her eyes flicking back and forth, her body in an about-to-run position, even when she's standing talking at her front door.

'Have you noticed that every time we've seen Cynthia Ellis, she's wearing clothes that are several sizes too big for her?' says DC Ado, as the woman disappears back inside her house.

'I have,' says DC Crane. 'I was thinking it just now. She wears top notch stuff. Worth a fair bit, but they fit awfully. What do you think it means?'

'She might have lost a lot of weight.'

'She might not want to attract attention.'

'She might not have as much money as you'd think.'

'It's a mystery,' DC Ado concludes.

'Oh good, another one,' says DC Crane, shaking her head. 'Shall we pop in The Stop Shop and have a look?'

'Good idea. Let's.'

The two detectives enter the main entrance of The Stop Shop and look about them. It's already beginning to be Christmas Eve busy. Alcohol and expensive mince pies and emergency instant bread sauce packets. Booze. Chocolate. Booze. The Stop Shop has everything a person might need if they don't want to go to one of the big supermarkets, or into the city. All slightly overpriced. Never quite exactly what you want.

DC Crane picks up a packet of rhubarb and custard boiled sweets to keep in the glove compartment of her grey Fiesta.

'Do you think they sell single-malt whisky?' asks DC Crane.

Rocky Winters, one of the supervisors, despite also studying full-time at City College, and the youngest of the Winters brothers, comes over. 'Hello again,' he says smiling. 'You're becoming quite the regulars.'

'Hello again, Rocky. Absolutely top-notch elf outfit,' says DC Crane warmly. 'Do you sell single malt? I'm looking for a gift for my dad. Left it a bit late, really.

'Sadly not. But we've got miniatures . . .' He nods his head so the bell on the end of his hat jangles in the direction of behind the till, where a selection of more expensive alcohol is set out neatly next to paracetamol, antihistamines and an assortment of cigarette lighters.

'Your outfit is splendid,' smiles DC Ado.

'I know right! Oh, but you should see Tash!' He nods towards the till, where Tash Blake is serving customers in an elf outfit of her own. 'Nobody's laughed at *her*,' he says, smiling. 'But for some reason *I'm* the height of hilarity.' There's no bitterness to him. He seems easy-going about it and DC Crane can't help but admire his attitude. 'Who's going to be cross when they're dressed up like an elf?' He adds, grinning. 'I kind of like it. I'm not bothered by what other people think anyway.'

As the three of them head over to the counter, Tim Winters half jogs in through the main entrance, sweat-wet in his running gear. He slips his headphones from his ears to around his neck and calls out to his brother, 'Rocky! What are the chances of me doing my Christmas shopping in here? Did you get anything for Mum and Dad? Can we go in together?'

'Not you too.' Rocky laughs a little. 'The detective constable here is doing hers. And we had Craig Mullany doing some of his. And Frank, in fact. But that's understandable, considering what happened.' He nods at his brother. 'And no, I haven't. I kept meaning to. I thought I'd make them home-made cleaning or dinner-out vouchers, or something?'

'I've done Mum's,' Tim says, drawing an invisible halo above his head. 'I just need something for Dad. Good morning, detectives.' He nods politely at DC Crane and DC Ado.

'Good morning, Tim,' says DC Crane. 'You and me both re our dads. I'm thinking single-malt whisky.'

'Good one,' says Tim. 'But what does a loving son buy a father who lives in a pub?'

'Alka-Seltzer?' DC Ado nods a hello into the conversation. 'A year's subscription to something?'

'Maybe,' says Tim. 'Maybe I'll buy him an *experience*. Like a supercar day at a race track or something.'

'I can't see Dad doing that,' says Rocky, frowning.

'*I* wouldn't mind doing that,' responds DC Crane.

'Neither would I,' smiles Rocky. 'Not dressed like this though.' He nods down at his elf tights and shoes and jangles the bells on one of his feet. 'Are you going to be around all day? It would be nice if you are. People are unsettled. I've already had some in here thinking Mr Finch's death is something to do with the burglaries.'

'We're going to be around on and off, most of today,' says DC Crane. 'And uniform.'

'I've got a box of things for Mr and Mrs Finch actually. He was going to pick it up. I don't know what to do with it.'

'We can take that,' offers DC Ado. 'We need to pop into Victory House as it is.'

'I'll check with Tash.' He nods towards Tash Blake, who's still standing behind the till serving customers. DC Crane knows the look of love when she sees it and she turns to DC Ado to see if he's noticed too, but he's looking at Tim's trainers.

'You training for a marathon?' he asks.

'Yes!' says Tim Winters. 'London next year. I'm running for a cancer charity. Did the Manchester this year.'

'Brilliant,' DC Ado smiles. 'I want a pair like that myself.' He nods at the trainers. 'You'd recommend them?'

'Absolutely,' Tim nods. 'Best ones I've had. Other than the blue Dunlops I had in Year 8.'

The two men laugh and DC Crane wonders what it might be like to start running. She walks with Freddie and Walker. A lot. Long afternoons over the dunes and salt marshes. For hours every weekend. Early in the mornings, late at night. How would they respond to running, their shaggy legs and soggy faces? *How would I respond to running? Why am I even thinking about this?*

Just then there's a disturbance at the till.

'The card has been declined, I'm really sorry.' Tash Blake's voice is wavering. 'Is there something else you could pay with?'

The man DC Crane remembers as Euan Barratt has his hands on the counter. 'It's a present for my girlfriend,' he says angrily. 'And no there's not. There's probably some dust on it or something.'

'I'm really sorry, Euan,' says Tash quietly. 'Your card has been declined. I tried wiping it. I tried tapping it. I tried waving it in front of me. None of it worked. Look . . .' She shows him something on the screen that he obviously disagrees with because this is the moment before the eruption.

'For fuck's sake!' He bangs his fist on the counter. 'I need to buy these now.'

Rocky is at the till before DC Crane and DC Ado.

'Euan mate,' he says, 'we don't want any trouble at Christmas, do we?'

'Who's this *we*?' Euan turns on Rocky and puffs out his chest.

'Any of us. You included.' Rocky stands tall, shoulders back, fists clenched at his sides, the elf costume having no effect on how he stands his ground.

81

'Does there seem to be a problem here?' DC Crane keeps her voice calm and steps nearer to the angry man. She can feel the rage, and alcohol, in him, but it won't deter her. She may not have the uniform to show her authority, but she's met plenty of men like him before. And she knows the way she stands is intimidating when she wants it to be.

'I'm not sure,' says Rocky. 'Euan?'

Euan Barratt looks at DC Crane and then at DC Ado and back again. There's something in the way he looks at DC Ado that sets off DC Crane's warning bells. Even from here, the man's breath smells of sour beer and cigarettes. She looks up at the analogue clock on the wall behind the till that someone's decorated with red tinsel. It's only just gone twenty past eleven.

'No,' says Euan, calm now. 'There's no problem. I just wanted to buy these for my missus.' He nods at the flowers that are lying flat on the till – carnations with pinecones and a red sparkly Christmas-stocking skewer down through the middle.

DC Crane stares him out, but he doesn't look away. There's something about the man she doesn't trust, even though he's not on any list, has no previous, is, for all intents and purposes, an innocent man. She knows, too, that this time of year is horrendous for people on low incomes. The expectation of what they're supposed to give and be, versus what they can. The sparkly shoes and cocktails and *boy done good* on Instagram and the reality of having your card turned down for some four-quid flowers in the corner shop. She softens towards him, very slightly.

'Right. I'll be back later,' Euan promises.

'Go and have a cup of tea, Euan,' instructs Rocky. 'Or coffee.'

Euan nods and turns to Tash. 'I'm sorry,' he says. 'For all that.'

'No worries,' says Tash unconvincingly.

DC Crane notices the girl is shaking, slightly, the reverberations going all the way to the bell at the end of her elf hat.

Euan pushes his way out of the door, pulling a packet of tobacco out of his jeans pocket, rolling himself a cigarette as he walks.

'Today is weird,' says Tash, to the others standing at the till after Euan has left. 'I'm quite looking forward to the end of my shift.'

DC Crane sees Rocky slump a bit. 'Can I make you a hot chocolate?' he asks gently. 'You're having quite the day.'

'Yes please,' says Tash, and she smiles at him in such a way that DC Crane knows Rocky's feelings are requited. She wonders if each of them knows. She should probably not interfere.

'Maybe I should buy Dad some vape stuff?' says Tim, stepping towards the till, continuing the conversation as though the altercation with Euan and the others had never happened. 'He's always saying he wants to be healthy, then he smokes several pouches of pipe tobacco every week. I could get him a flavour he likes. He can smell like lemon drops or whatever it is. What sort have you got?'

'We only have a few here,' says Tash. 'You'd need VAPE IT on St. Stephen's for a big choice.'

'Dad isn't going to vape,' tuts Rocky, turning to go through to the kitchen.

'I can't be bothered to go into the city,' says Tim when his brother has gone. He's smiling at Tash, twinkling. DS Crane notices this and the edge between the brothers. Not quite the happy family. 'So I think I'll get one in here. Even if there's only a cigarette-smelling one, or whatever.'

'OK, so we have . . .' Tash starts to explain the different e-cigarettes they have behind the counter.

'Cheerio all,' says DC Crane, popping the bag of rhubarb and custards back on the shelf. 'I'll be back for these later. Hopefully we have no other reason to see you today. But have a good day either way.'

'Bye, and thank you,' says Tash. She's showing Tim various vape equipment and he's leaning in closely to her, but she doesn't seem to notice.

'If you ever fancy a run around here just shout,' says Tim, looking up from the selection on the counter, and from Tash, to DC Ado, who holds up his hand to say goodbye.

'Thanks,' says DC Ado, and the two detectives leave the shop.

Outside on Newbury Street, it's so cold that DC Crane pulls up the collar on her coat. She still doesn't have a present for her dad. Her mum's had been easy. She'd bought her a signed book by a local author she likes, someone who writes Victorian mysteries about a cook in a grand house who solves crimes from the kitchens. If only her dad had such obvious interests.

It starts to snow, ever so slightly. Watery flakes fall, far apart from each other, transparent and barely visible, but definitely there.

'Do you see that?!' DC Crane says, excitedly.

'Snow!' says DC Ado and, as soon as he says it, it stops and turns to a thick sort of rain instead. 'Great,' he adds. 'What was the point of that? Was that the shortest snow flurry of all time?'

'I wouldn't mind if it held off until today was over,' she says. 'But I hope it happens. There's something about snow at Christmas, isn't there?'

'I'm not sure I remember ever seeing any,' ponders DC Ado, and she remembers he's at least ten years younger than her.

'I like the idea of it snowing once I get home tonight and then me and the dogs being stuck at home for all of Christmas Day. Maybe until new year. I've got a full freezer. And cheese always lasts.'

'I can see the appeal of that,' replies Ado, shivering slightly.

DC Crane turns to look the other way along Newbury Street and sees Euan Barratt spit a couple of mouthfuls of saliva onto the pavement as he walks back in the direction of his home. He's looking about him, side to side, smoking the roll-up he was working on when he left the shop. At the last minute, he has a change of heart, double backs on himself and crosses the road in the direction of The Mariner, flicks his cigarette against the pub wall and pushes the big door to go inside.

'Instinct tells me he's not a nice piece of work,' says DC Crane, looking at DC Ado, her early softening towards the man, hardening again. It doesn't matter how miserable you are, you don't have to take it out on other people. She doesn't have many rules, but she does try not to pass on her misery or anger to everyone else. If she can help it.

'Evidence too,' points out DC Ado. 'Considering the way he behaved in there. It didn't seem out of character to me. Shall we go in there later, for the fundraising thing?'

'My thinking entirely,' says DC Crane, as they cross the road to the other side, like Euan Barratt, and walk past The Mariner to take another long walk along the length of Newbury Street. As they pass Craig Mullany's house, they see his garden has gathered more flattened boxes.

'Interesting,' says DC Ado.

'Very interesting indeed,' replies DC Crane, as they keep on walking.

Midday

Christmas Eve

Joanie Blake

Flat 5, Victory House

Joanie looks at the bloated turkey on the kitchen side, pokes it with a skewer and mumbles, 'This can't be right. Should I have left it longer . . . Why the hell is that leg swollen like that?' then steps away and turns towards the others.

The children are weighing out the ingredients for their grandmother's famous Christmas Eve Treacle Cake with Frank. He's smiling, with his shirtsleeves rolled up, while Patti spoons treacle into a Pyrex bowl, and Dylan, who's six years old and full of misplaced confidence, holds the bag of self-raising flour carefully in his little hands, his arms wobbling with the weight of the thing, as he sticks his tongue out of the corner of his mouth and says, 'Nearly there, nearly there, nearly there,' while watching the arrow on the scales go up, until he tips it all too far and a big heap of flour falls out in one go and puffs up into his face. 'Come on!' he says, pushing out his cheeks but laughing easily. 'I nearly had it that time Grandad!' The boy is smiling. Frank is smiling too as he tilts the silver weighing pan on its side and scoops all the flour back into the squished-up bag.

Joanie thinks of her mum. Sometimes the pain of her not being here is too much. Everybody moves around in the spaces she used to live her life and it makes her seem more visible than ever.

If only you were still here, thinks Joanie, dabbing her eyes. *You could tell me what to do with the bloody turkey for starters.*

'You *could* put some into a smaller bowl,' says Mrs Finch, from her seat at the kitchen table, interfering with the baking in a way that presses Joanie's buttons, which she immediately feels bad about because of what happened to Mr Finch. 'So it's easier for the boy to lift it.'

'I could,' replies Frank slowly. 'But where would the fun be in that?'

It's all too much, the whole lot of it.

'I'll get that Babycham now,' Joanie says suddenly. 'If you guys are all right with the baking?'

'Of course we are,' says Patti, licking treacle from the spoon.

'Just look at us!' says Dylan, whose hair is sprinkled liberally with flour dust.

'What could possibly go wrong?' says Frank, and Mrs Finch does a little grunt that can only be interpreted as derision.

'Love you all,' says Joanie, at the door and in her coat already. She just has to get out of there before she suffocates on things nobody else can even see.

Outside, Joanie takes a deep breath of cold air and leans against the wall, breathing slowly. She can't wait to see Irma, everything is all right with Irma. Having Dad in the flat being Dad is hard enough, and just as she thought Mrs Finch might be enjoying being there with them, the woman went cold.

People's feelings are harder to handle than the turkey. Which, if she's being honest, looks a mess. How did Mum used to do all of it?

Merry Christmas Joanie, she says to herself, and walks towards the shop, pinching her fingers tight around the handle of her two tote Bags for Life, which, of course, she'd remembered to grab on her way out. Sometimes she wishes she was the sort of person who'd forget to take her own bag, recklessly spending 10p on a new one, or even *20p on two*. But it's just not her. She seems to spend so much of her life being responsible.

When the children go with their dad, Jamie, she'll let her hair down a bit. Maybe she can convince Tash to stay at Dad's, *just for one night*. She feels bad then, because she can hear Tash say, 'You see, everyone wants rid of me!' and knows she could never ask her.

She enters the shop and sees her little sister behind the till, scanning chocolate and wine through and smiling at the couple buying last-minute Christmas Eve treats.

Joanie steps aside as a tall, young man in a black hoodie and grey tracksuit bottoms walks past her with a basket full of cat food. She recognises him as the man who lives above Irma. What did Irma say about him? *I knew him. Before. At The Lodge.* Irma doesn't say much about her time in care, and she didn't say if he'd been someone nice or someone not and Joanie hadn't pushed it. Irma's past was her own, and if she wants to share it, that's fine. But if she doesn't, that's fine too.

When she gets to the alcohol aisle, Joanie finds, much to her surprise and relief, they do sell Babycham in cardboard packs of four 20cl bottles. She wonders how much Mrs Finch will want and decides to put the whole lot into her basket. There are six boxes stacked on the shelf, so she puts as many that will fit into her basket like a badly set out game of Jenga, then puts the others under her arms and ends up pushing one more along the floor with her foot. There must be an easier way to do this, and she knows she could put them down and get a bigger, wheelie basket, but she reasons that, her luck being what it is, she'd probably end up with some other person coming in and getting them all when she'd left them. It's safer to hobble and slide down the centre aisle of The Stop Shop with her vast amounts of Babycham than to leave Mrs Finch's supply to the cruelty of the gods.

Rocky Winters is putting reduced family bags of posh crisps into one of the end of aisle baskets as she squeezes past them. He smiles at her.

'Thirsty, Joanie?'

Joanie laughs. 'Um. Yes. Not sure I'll be drinking this though . . .'

'Babycham!' Rocky laughs. 'Reminds me of my mum when I was a kid. She always had the blue bottles out at Christmas.'

'I'd never heard of it until today,' says Joanie. 'Mrs Finch. It's her one request for Christmas. Thank God you had some. I might have wept if I'd had to drive out to Asda on Christmas Eve.' She is reminded of how easy it is to talk to Rocky. He's so nice. She can see why Tash likes him, not that Tash would ever tell her that. Tash would never tell anyone about her actual feelings about anything.

'Ah, that reminds me. I've got a box Mr Finch ordered out back. I'd put some things aside. Babycham included. DC Crane and DC Ado said they would take it earlier, but they forgot before they left.'

'Ah . . .' Joanie looks at her basket as the queue gets longer. 'I'm not sure I'll even manage this. My Bag for Life is looking inadequate as it is.'

'Don't worry,' says Rocky kindly. 'I'll bring it all over later. If that helps?'

'That's really kind,' says Joanie, relieved. The last thing she wants to do, she now realises, is come back out again once she's gone back into Flat 5 after this. She wants to stay in, be with the children, get cosy. She won't be going to the Feel Good either, despite Irma being there. Irma will be working and they won't really get to spend any time together anyway, the kids will be overexcited and want to tear about, and there's no proper pub garden. Sometimes, when there are more people, the space where her mum should be seems even bigger. She's hit with the urge to hide away. For as long as possible.

'I'd better nip behind the till,' says Rocky. 'But I'll see you later. In fact, if you want to leave some of that behind after you've paid . . . I'll bring that later too. Saves you getting all Stretch Armstronged on the way home.'

Joanie smiles, 'Thank you. I think I'll be OK. But thank you.' Sometimes a moment of kindness can be the sort that makes you cry. A shop supervisor she's known since he was little, dressed as one of Santa's elves, offering to carry her shopping is one of them.

'Any time, honestly,' says Rocky, as he jogs over to let himself behind the counter and onto the till beside Tash. They both look too adorable, next to each other in their elf outfits, although Joanie will keep this opinion to herself as she joins the queue behind the man who lives above Irma, who's shifting his weight between one foot and the other, with so much nervous energy that it makes her wonder if he's actually unwell. She must find out his name. She's sure Irma must have said at some point, but with everything else she needs to remember, this useful piece of information has deserted her.

'Oi. Oi you. Where were *you* last night?' someone in the queue calls out, aggressively. When Joanie turns around, she sees it's Euan Barratt from Number 88, who seems to think he can interrogate members of the public, in public, loudly and embarrassingly just because he feels like it. 'Yes I'm talking to you,' he says loudly and Joanie realises he's talking to the man who lives above Irma. 'You're always walking about with that great big bag, up and down the street. Where were you last night when that Jen and Frank were broken into, hey?'

The man in front of Joanie looks down at his basket and fiddles with something in his pocket. He pretends the other man isn't talking to him and has the stance of someone who's experienced this before. He pulls out one of those sticks people use to top up their electricity from his pocket and keeps looking forward, saying nothing.

'You ignoring me, are you? Don't you speak English?'

The man still says nothing. He counts the packets of cat food in his basket with his fingers, rearranging them in some kind of order impossible to work out to any onlooker. They are an expensive brand, the sort they used to advertise with a woman putting it in a silver dish with a sprig of parsley on top, sniffing at it as though she'd eat it herself, before setting it down on an oak polished floor. When Joanie feeds Spock, the stray tabby she's become rather attached to since her mum died, she always gives him the same brand. She knows she's thinking about this so she won't have to think about what's happening in the queue. Hopefully Euan will stop and everyone can pretend it never happened.

Nobody says anything. Euan Barratt is snarling at the man now, no longer in the queue, but beside him, hopping about in his personal space, his breath full of beer fumes and the smell of cigarettes. Joanie looks at Tash and then at Rocky. Everybody else is looking down at their feet, at the contents of their baskets, at anything else but what's happening between the two men.

Joanie can't keep quiet. 'Everything all right?' she says, not to Euan.

The man looks at her and nods his head imperceptibly, a tiny movement that matters.

'Joanie . . .' Euan looks momentarily sheepish and she can't work out why. 'This isn't a relative of yours, is it?'

She stares at him. 'A what?'

'Well . . .' Euan Barratt looks between her and the man several times.

Something snaps in Joanie. It's usually Tash who gets into rows in public, who calls people out, who is a great defender. Joanie is the subtle one, the patient one, the one who listens then acts. But not this time.

'Well, you're being a racist prick, because do you really think I'm related to every person with a different skin colour than you?' She stares him out. 'You're being a dick. I could just as likely say it's *you* who's been stealing the presents as you can this man.' Joanie's voice is calm, although her heart is thumping in her chest.

'What the . . .' Euan seems taken aback at this.

'You hang about on the street at all hours. Everybody's seen *you*.'

'I fix cars.'

'Yes. Yes you do. For *business* purposes on a *private* street.'

'Wait there . . .'

Joanie doesn't let him finish. He's had his turn and she wants to make her point without his excuses. 'You're not the only one who can throw accusations around, you know. So, I'd keep it shut.' Joanie is shaking with rage. How dare this angry man, in his Budweiser T-shirt, leather jacket and Timberland boots call out a stranger in this way. How dare everyone stay silent while he does it? She doesn't know who she's more angry with, and she realises that somewhere, deep inside her, she's been angry with lots of people, for a very long time. She still has the four packs of Babycham under her arms, the basket in her hand, and one foot against the bottles she'd been pushing along the floor. This makes her laugh. She starts laughing and thinks she might not stop.

Behind the till, Tash is clapping, loudly.

Rocky comes out from behind the counter and stands next to Euan, who's shaking his head and holding his arms out in front of him, with his hands up like he's in a film, trying to say, 'Surrender!'

'I'm not having any of this in here, mate,' Rocky says, addressing Euan Barratt and not Joanie, nor the man with the cat food, who's standing very still, and holding on tightly to the handles of his basket.

But Euan has turned to Joanie. 'Who's going to listen to *you*? We all know what your girlfriend gets up to late at night, huh?' Euan squares up to Rocky then, bouncing back and forth on the balls of his feet, which doesn't do him any favours. 'She has to get a bit of what you can't give her, Joanie?' He sneers at her and Joanie knows if she didn't have the bottles under her arms, she'd have struck him.

'I suggest you leave,' says Rocky calmly. He may be wearing his elf costume, but he has a calm energy that seeps out around him. Irma would say something about him having a green or pale blue aura. The calm in a storm. 'I would hate to have to call the police. Especially with everything else that's going on round here. You wouldn't want to be on their radar for Christmas, not any more than you are already after they saw your performance in here earlier shouting at Tash. Pissed at 11.30 a.m. . . .'

'I'm not a fucking racist,' says Euan Barratt back at Joanie as Rocky marches him over to the door. 'That bloke's a serious weirdo. Creeping about. Just you see. I knew you lot'd stick together.'

'I only came out to get Mrs Finch's Babycham,' says Joanie loudly, thinking she might be in shock. She's still laughing. It's always been the same, even when she was at school, the moment she's afraid or thinks she's in trouble, she laughs. It's rarely made things better. She knows Euan only said what he said about Irma to upset her, and, despite knowing better, it makes her worry.

'I suggest you have a coffee or seven and sober up,' says Rocky. 'You can't barge about in here saying stuff like that. It's bad enough you think it. I thought we were mates.'

Euan doesn't reply to this, he's pointing to the door.

Behind the till, Tash is talking loudly. 'Oh, Euan. Euan, Euan, Euan, Euan.' She's tutting and shaking her head. Joanie isn't sure this is a good idea.

Irma's neighbour is still standing looking into his basket. It's like he's been frozen in place. Joanie can see him trembling. She looks in his basket and smiles kindly.

'Is that your Christmas dinner?'

'Not the cat food,' he says eventually and laughs. 'Although, she eats better than me, most days.' He looks away, sheepishly, as though he's said the wrong thing. 'She only likes the expensive stuff. I've tried her on everything.'

'Cats are like that,' says Joanie. 'They want what they want. I know one like that. I'm really sorry, I can't remember your name. I'm Joanie.

94

'Isaac,' the man answers.

'That's right. I knew it was something biblical.'

'You turning your back on me?' Euan Barratt is louder now. He comes quickly away from the shop door where Rocky had been chaperoning him out and he'd been faking like he was about to leave, into the space where the man and Joanie are standing and jabs at the man's chest with his hand. He smells of too much aftershave. Joanie's thoughts go to Magda, Euan's long-term girlfriend, quiet, sweet, quite the opposite of him. She dreads to think what Magda's Christmas Eve will be like when Euan gets home and Joanie feels immediately guilty for maybe making it worse.

You're not responsible for his behaviour, she tells herself. But she can't help thinking somebody should be.

'I'm listening,' says the man with the cat food, answering Euan for the first time, 'but I don't have anything to say.'

'It's time to go now, Euan,' says Rocky, moving towards him. 'I'll use force if I have to, and as soon as I have to, the police will be called.' He reminds Joanie of his dad then, calm, forceful, the strength and authority of a pub landlord, even though he's only nineteen.

Euan begins stepping towards the door once more. People in the queue shuffle and look down. Joanie wants to scream at them all then, the cowards. So this is how it is? All these others in the queue, and it came to her to step in. What would they have done? Let Euan Barratt hassle the other man out of the shop and pretend it never happened?

'I didn't want any trouble,' says Euan. 'I just think it's sick. Whoever's been nicking these presents. Sick.' He's looking between the man with the cat food, Rocky and Joanie.

'We all do. Now out!' says Rocky. He's already got his hands on Euan's arm, to lead him to the door, and it seems like it's sorted.

Then, on the way out, Euan turns around to face the man with the cat food, his face pure rage.

'I see you creeping about at night. *I see you*. The police should tear your place apart. Or someone should. Probably find all the presents tucked under your bed or something. But I suppose they're not allowed to . . .'

'That's enough,' says Rocky.

The young man in the hoodie is shaking. He seems so young, and vulnerable, all of a sudden, and the cat food in his basket looks so ridiculous in there, like the least threatening thing a person could ever buy. That, and the cheapest block of cheese, and the white slices of value-range bread.

'You're barred,' Rocky tells Euan. 'Until I tell you otherwise.'

Euan stumbles out onto the street and the door closes behind him and Rocky lets out a long sigh. He's obviously disappointed. The two men had been on The Mariner darts team together since he was a kid.

'You can't bar me!' shouts Euan Barratt as he starts off down the road, not to his house, but back to The Mariner. Joanie thinks of Irma having to deal with him in there, for anyone having to deal with him, including Magda at home, and really how nobody should ever have to. How dare he say what he said about Irma. How dare he even look at her, let alone judge her. Joanie is shaking with rage, and something else she can't articulate.

When Euan has finally gone, Rocky comes to see if they're OK. 'Nice work, you two,' he says to Joanie and the cat food man.

Some people in the queue start to clap. Joanie feels her rage increase. What good is the applause if they weren't actively with them when they were in danger? She smiles though, and so does the man in the hoodie.

'You live upstairs from my girlfriend, don't you?' says Joanie.

He nods, still looking down at his basket, and shaking.

'What are you doing for Christmas?' she asks.

'This and that,' he whispers. 'You know.' He's holding tightly to his basket. He looks up at her and smiles, a bit.

'Well, Isaac,' Joanie speaks softly, trying not to make a big thing of it, while at the same time trying to make sure that he knows she means it, 'you are most welcome to mine. I'm in Flat 5 Victory House – we have a bit of a houseful, I mean, a real houseful. But that's how I like it. You'd be welcome. For Christmas dinner. And for the rest of the day and evening. Whatever you fancy. If you don't mind eating your dinner off your lap, and little kids everywhere, and . . .'

'Mandatory cracker hats at ours,' calls out Tash, as the man moves towards her till.

He laughs.

'Don't worry,' grins Tash. 'My head's massive and they always break. And by break, I mean I rip them moments after putting them on so I don't have to wear them. But it's the thought that counts. You should come!'

'They're not mandatory,' promises Joanie. 'But you'd be welcome. We usually eat early, so we can have party food later. Just after midday for round one.'

'Thank you,' he says. 'I'm busy. But thank you,' he says. 'That's very kind.'

'Well, you can change your mind at any time. Just so you know. Even halfway through dinner. Even *after* dinner. Number 5 remember.'

Isaac smiles, a small smile, but it's there nonetheless. 'I'll bear that in mind.' Isaac looks at her, and for a moment it seems like he might say something else, but then he's at the front of the queue and Joanie watches him pay for the things in his basket, handing over the stick for his electricity. Tash smiles kindly at him and gives her sister a thumbs up.

'I didn't know you had it in you,' she says, proudly.

'There's a lot in me you don't know about,' Joanie says mysteriously and smiles at her sister. The adrenaline coursing through her belies her outward serenity. She just hopes Irma won't be cross with her.

What *had* Irma said about the man, from when she knew him before? It's at moments like this Joanie wishes she had a better memory. She decides to pop into The Mariner on the way home to warn her either way.

She pushes Euan's words out of her mind. What does a nasty little drunk know about Irma anyway? He was only saying it to wind her up. But there is a little seed planted. Maybe he'd seen her doing something she shouldn't be? How well can you really ever know someone? *Stop it. Irma loves you. The end.*

Joanie will ask Irma later rather than spend days worrying about it. There's only one person doing things they shouldn't be at night, and that's the thief. Irma would never steal from anybody. Would she?

12.28 p.m.

Christmas Eve

Sue Winters

The Mariner Pub

The official Festive Feel Good doesn't start until around four o'clock, and Sue doesn't want it to blend into the rest of the day. There needs to be an official opening, which she's roped Nathan Patterson into leading, then witnessed a heated conversation between him and his wife on his mobile phone when he was out the back having a cigarette. She doesn't feel bad about it. They need today to be a success.

She's set herself the task of keeping the pub as clean as possible, making sure it doesn't get into a state before the official opening and the auction and raffle. She hasn't said anything to Larry, but she's started to feel suspicious about so many of the regulars. The burglaries were too close to home, and she hasn't forgotten the feeling of waking up to find all her carefully chosen gifts gone.

She moves carefully over to Nathan Patterson in his favourite booth, the one he uses on quiet afternoons to interview people for local profiles but is now surrounded by a family group of people drinking snowballs and pints of cider and, for some reason she couldn't work out, pina coladas.

'Raffle tickets, Nathan,' she says, holding out a few books of the tickets. 'Just a tenner a book? Shall I put you down for, say, three?'

Nathan looks amused. 'Make it five. And if I win, give the prize to the care homes with the others. What's the prize again?'

'Champagne. Computer stuff. Xbox. Cuddly toys. Workout sessions with my eldest,' she says the last bit proudly. 'He's a professional, you know.'

'Impressive,' says Nathan. He's sitting with a few of the people from the early numbers of the street. The Smiths from number 6 – Rob and Janice, and their grown-up daughters, Lily and Sara, both back from university. *The first in the family, either side, to go,'* as Rob likes to tell people as often as possible. Sue can't begrudge him that though. She's proud of her boys too, even if neither of them have followed the path she thought, or hoped, they would.

'I'll buy one. Does he always look that good?' Lily nods in the direction of Tim, who's behind the bar, making Jägerbombs for the back-from-University crowd.

'He always looks that good,' laughs Sue proudly. Women of all ages were always asking her to pass on their regards to her son. Sometimes she passes them on, others she doesn't. This time she might. Lily is pretty, the acceptable side of quirky, and is drinking a white wine spritzer, slowly. The last thing Tim needs is another drinker. His last girlfriend was a disaster.

She hands over the tickets.

'So what do you think is going on with these burglaries?' she hears Nathan Patterson say to Janice.

'I think it's got to be someone on the street,' she says, loudly because she's on her third pina colada. 'Someone who *doesn't really belong here.'*

Just as Janice finishes her sentence, the door swings open and in comes Joanie Blake, carrying two tote bags full of bottles of something. She looks worn out, hurried, and her hair is wet.

'Joanie!' Sue dips in and out of the customers without knocking anybody, or their drinks, in a way that makes it look much easier than it is. She's been doing this long enough to know all the tricks of the trade when it comes to swift and elegant crowd navigation.

'Sue!' The two women give each other a hug.

Sue can't help thinking that Joanie looks so old, suddenly. Here she is, twenty-four years old, young still, looking like she has the weight of the world on her shoulders and Sue supposes that's how it must feel for Joanie most days since her mum died. Sue's own mum and dad will be here tomorrow, for Christmas Day like always. They infuriate her from time to time, of course they do. But she can't imagine life without them. They've always been there in the background. Joanie and Allie had been so close. Two peas in a pod. She feels tears in her eyes. She misses Allie too.

'We did good,' Sue smiles, nodding not wanting to get maudlin or add to Joanie's woes. 'Just look!' She opens her money holder and nods to all the gifts and prizes stacked up beyond the boundary under the huge, sparkly tree as it sags ever so slightly under the weight of her enthusiastic decoration.

'Wonderful,' says Joanie. 'Mum would have loved this.'

Sue agrees. She and Joanie's mum Allie were friends for so long it was hard to remember how their friendship started. Sometime at the school gates when Rocky and Tash started infant school, laughing at missing a costume day, their two the only ones all neat in their school uniforms, both furious. The two women's friendship continued, all the way through their children's schooling, so much water under the bridge. All the children were so close at one point, she'd even wondered, with a flash of horror, if Joanie's firstborn, Patti, was Tim's for a while, back when she was in Year 11 and he was nineteen, in his final year of his personal trainer qualifications. It had turned out to be a false alarm – the father was a boy in Joanie's class – and she'd felt bad for thinking the worst of her eldest son. But, of course, it wasn't a false alarm for Joanie. She saw Allie's strength then, as other parents, and many of the teachers, whispered in hushed horrors at something Allie didn't seem to take as a problem at all. 'It's never a bad time to be a mother, if you want to be. I'd feel different if she'd been coerced, but the two of them thought they were in love. Soppy sods. Where's the point in me having a go at them? It won't change anything.' Allie had been so relaxed about it that Sue had been shocked. She kept thinking, *You're supposed to be angry and upset. You're supposed to be sobbing on my shoulder saying,* 'My little girl.' But it wasn't like that at all. When Patti was born, Allie and Frank bought all the locals a round and said, without any hint of remorse, it was the best day of their lives. And Allie had been right, it was just a shame she wasn't here now.

'What you drinking? I think some of the old lot you went to school with are about over there.' Sue nods to the table where a bunch of Joanie and Tim's schoolmates from their respective year groups, grown-ups now, sit drinking and reliving the old days.

'I don't want to peak too soon. But I will go and say hello. I've only popped in to see Irma,' Joanie says. She looks at Sue seriously then, 'And to warn you and Larry about Euan Barratt. He was just in the shop, causing a stink. Pissed. Threatening customers. I thought you should know.'

Sue rolls her eyes. 'Of course he was. Thank you for the warning. He's been on a weird bender all day. Let's get you to the bar.'

Sue expertly leads Joanie through huddles of people to the bar, where Irma is pouring several pints of the Christmas guest ale, Jolly Holly, a dark beer from a local brewery with *notes of mince pie and cranberry*, so it says on the pump label. Sue had tried some. It tasted like the same sour froth that beer always tasted like to her. She saved that opinion from the punters, of course, and was known to really love her beer. Sometimes it's best for everyone if you lie, is Sue's thinking.

'Irma!' Joanie's face lights up.

'Darling!' Irma's face lights up too. This amazes Sue, as Irma is singularly the most serious-faced person who's ever worked for her. The fact that she's ridiculously beautiful, good at listening, and gives clear, non-fussy advice means people don't seem to mind, and she's probably Sue and Larry's most popular member of staff.

'I've left Dad and the kids in charge of taking out the treacle cake,' says Joanie. 'I had to get Mrs Finch Babycham.'

'Babycham? I think that's the first thing I ever got drunk on . . .' Irma nods as she pulls the pump down.

'It's her favourite, apparently. She's got special glasses from the seventies. I also wanted to warn you, and Sue, about Euan Barratt. I just saw him in The Stop Shop. He's totally drunk and was having a go at Tash, making up shit about you, being a racist drunk and general disgrace. Rocky was a hero, of course. And I may have accidentally invited your upstairs neighbour for Christmas dinner.'

'What?' Irma raises her voice slightly.

'He won't come, he said as much. Euan was starting on him, being really awful. He seemed . . . really lonely.' Sue is impressed at Joanie's kindness, even now with so much on her plate, thinking of others.

Irma doesn't say anything for a while. 'I doubt he'll come,' she offers eventually. 'He's always liked his own company. So, what did Euan say?'

Joanie lowers her voice, but Sue can still hear. 'Just some crap about you getting up to stuff at night, or something . . .'

Irma looks startled. 'I . . .'

'Oh don't worry,' says Joanie. 'I know he was just trying to cause trouble.'

Sue's memory leaps to something Tim said about Irma. *'Everyone thinks these burglaries are done by a man, but how much do you actually know about Ms Irma Woźniak, hey?'* At the time, she'd told him to stop being silly, but two people saying the same thing means there could be something in it. Irma does wear a lot of new clothes, is always buying new make-up and vintage accessories. Her job as a supervisor doesn't pay that much. Is it possible the younger woman is topping up her income by stealing Christmas presents?

Sue takes a side glance at Irma. She really hopes she's got nothing to do with it. You can't trust anyone is the eternal problem.

'I'll tell Larry about Euan. I don't want anyone ruining today. Least of all him. And thank goodness for my Sylvester.' Very occasionally Sue will use Rocky's given name. She'd never quite got over the fact he'd rejected it and always gone by his nickname instead. The fact she'd named him after Sylvester McCoy and not Stallone only made it more of a rejection.

'Come round whatever time you like later,' says Joanie to Irma. 'And if you want to wait till the morning, that's fine too.'

'I can't wait to try your turkey . . .' says Irma, laughing, 'having heard so much about it.'

'Yes, well, the less said about that at the moment the better,' Joanie laughs back. The two women smile at each other, and both nod reassuringly. 'I'll see you later. Thanks Sue. For being brilliant,' says Joanie, and Sue smiles at her friend's daughter. How she's coping after everything that's happened, she doesn't know.

For a moment, as the young woman turns from Irma and walks across the bar, she looks like the twenty-four-year-old she is, smiling carefree in a pub, on Christmas Eve. But she'll never know what that feels like again.

Allie, why did you have to die? thinks Sue, a tightness in her chest. *There's something I really need to talk to you about. I need to ask you if it's OK to tell them about what you told me, just before you got ill. It could change a lot of things for a lot of people, but I don't want to betray you.*

'I didn't know you could smile, Irma,' says Tim, popping more shot glasses into the next round of Jägerbombs for the youngsters playing darts, when Joanie is out of earshot.

'Well, I can. When it's someone I *actually want to smile at*,' says Irma, without looking at him, finishing off pouring the last of the round of beers she's been working on. Sue jolts at the unexpected and outright animosity between her son and her best member of staff. What on earth is that all about?

'Play nicely you two,' she says lightly.

'We always do, don't we, Irma?' says Tim, smiling at his mother, as she pushes away the thought that there's more to this than meets the eye. Does Tim really think Irma is responsible for the burglaries? Does he know more than he's letting on? She just hopes they can be polite to each other when the Feel Good starts. And when Christmas is over Tim will go back to renovating his new house up the road, and his work with John Ellis and his personal training, and whatever it was will all be forgotten. She'll always be on Tim's side. But Irma is too good a member of staff to lose at the busiest time of year.

'You not going to say hello to your old schoolmates?' asks Sue, smiling at her son.

'Them?' says Tim dismissively in the direction of the laughing table. 'The day I left that place was the best day of my life.'

Sue leaves the bar area, there's no point talking to Tim when he's in that sort of mood. She makes sure she's got her raffle tickets and secure money pouch with her. 'Larry!' Her husband is standing with a group of regulars and their families who are only really allowed in the sacred space of The Mariner on this one day over Christmas. 'Larry, can I borrow you for a bit?' she says, still smiling her best landlady's smile.

'Of course!' He turns to his assembled group, who seem to be hanging on his every word. 'And then it only turned out to be a pigeon!' he says, and they all start laughing.

Larry moves away from the customers and raises his hand. When they're out of earshot Sue whispers, 'Joanie said Euan Barratt caused some problems in the shop. I think we should be looking to bar him if he comes back in here.'

'I'm starting to wish that man wouldn't come in here to drink at all,' sighs Larry. 'He's a walking disaster.'

'Too late,' says Sue, because before Larry has even finished his sentence, Tim is jumping over the bar to hold

Euan Barratt in some kind of headlock because he's pushed Joanie Blake over on her way out of the pub, and she, and six four-packs of Babycham, are strewn like skittles across The Mariner's burgundy carpet. This isn't how the Feel Good is supposed to start at all.

12.40 p.m.

Christmas Eve

Craig Mullany

Newbury Street

Craig makes his way towards the pub, and sighs.

How could he be forty-six with so many regrets? Wasn't he supposed to have those when he was eighty, ninety, *dead*? Forty-six is young. Forty-six is the new thirty. Forty-six is . . .

Who's he kidding? He doesn't quite fit in anywhere any more. The friendship group he'd relied on all those years, he and Jen, Allie and Frank, had disintegrated in such a drastic and final way that it seemed incongruous that the four of them had ever hung around together at all.

In the absence of his friends and wife he's trying more to do what he wants and be damned with the conse-quences. Who knows where he'd be now if he'd started thinking like that earlier? He used to be more of a think-about-it-for-ages-and-let-it-fester-until-it's-too-late kind of person. *And where did that get you, hey?* He knows, despite the new house, and the new furniture, and the body he's created by upping his cycling, he isn't in a good place. He's still making too many bad decisions.

Terrible decisions. And he doesn't even feel bad about any of them. Not yet.

As he heads towards The Mariner the air is cold and wet. It's almost as though it wants to snow, and he wills it onwards. The kids would love it if they could make snowmen, or have a snowball fight, and as he's got them for the second half of Christmas Day and all of Boxing Day, what a wonderful thing that would be. The thought of little Ray in his snowsuit, and Barnie in his Pokémon hat and glove set that feature so regularly in the photos he's set out on his new mantelpiece fills his heart. He can imagine the photos he'd take in the snow, and how often he'll look at them when his sons are not with him. Bittersweet. Love.

Sometimes it feels like all the old memories had been cut up and shredded and that everything is new. How do you start everything again? Craig's life has changed so much, you'd never recognise him as the same man from a few years ago. From last year, even.

Craig's memories of Allie's last Christmas, before anyone knew she was ill, are still so clear in his mind that when he closes his eyes, he can see her as she was back then perfectly. There she is, coming out of the entrance door of Victory House, not knowing she was being watched at first, holding a dress on a hanger, covered in cellophane, and a big trifle in a crystal dish.

'Are you watching me?' she'd said, raising an eyebrow and laughing. Shaking her head, that way he'd seen her do so often when she'd make a joke of something.

He'd nodded, just a little shift of his head, nothing so obvious as saying that he had been, and she'd given him this look he couldn't make out. Derision? Anger? Neither of those. It was a look he'd never seen her pull before. That was the last time he'd seen her before everything that had followed.

How could he have known what would happen with Frank and Jen? Craig shakes his head. It's too much to think about. And there's nobody to talk to. Sometimes he thinks about calling them up and having it out with them. Saying, 'I know you think I'm angry with you both, and I am, but it's not always for the reason you think . . .' But it's too far gone to have that conversation now. At that moment, standing in a fall of almost-snow at the far end of Newbury Street, Craig has never felt so alone. It's a dangerous feeling.

He shakes his head again. The sky is white, like someone has rubbed out all the colour, and it's so cold that when he lets out a breath, it hangs about him, like a soul leaving the body. *Melodramatic bastard.*

He tries to laugh at himself, knowing it will help, but it doesn't work, so he takes a deep breath and attempts to use the technique from his mindfulness app the doctor told him to download to help him. As always, all it does is make his heart flutter in his chest. He finds the man's voice smug, annoying. *You must be doing it wrong*, thinks Craig. Anyone would find all this hard, maybe he should just accept that and look forward to next year. He's never been the type to wallow. He isn't the type to say, 'Christmas is ruined for me because of what's happened.' But that doesn't mean that Christmas isn't ruined for him because of what's happened.

He puts his hand upon the door handle to The Mariner. His intention is to stay all afternoon. To eat. To drink. To take part in the charity bits and pieces. *To relax.* The thought of such a thing makes him laugh out loud. He might be able to relax for a few hours in the pub but how is he supposed to relax in a house full of unmade furniture when his sons, who don't even live with him, are coming for the second half of Christmas Day?

Just as he's trying to enter The Mariner, Euan Barratt comes hurtling out of the door, with Tim Winters' hands firmly on his shoulders. Craig steps backwards, and leans on the outside wall of the pub, watching, not sure if he's supposed to take part or not. He knows Tim is fit. He's been paying him to train him into his new future self. Working from the outside in, which he knows won't work, but at least it will *look* like it's working.

'Stay out, for the rest of the day, OK, Euan? It's only going to get worse. You've just struck a customer. A female customer at that. The police will be involved.'

Euan says something else, but whatever it is, it's lost in translation, so he takes a swing for Tim, misses and falls over.

'Is this what you hoped your life would be?' says Tim, shaking his head, with his foot on the fallen man's back, reminding Craig of one of those statues of people who've claimed a piece of land for themselves, or for a country. 'I won't have you in there, scaring my mum and pissing people off who're trying to have a good Christmas.'

'Fuck off,' says Euan. This bit Craig understands.

'You want some help?' Craig hears his own voice say as he walks towards the pair.

Euan is back on his feet, somehow, and the two men are now spinning each other in staggering circles, with their hands holding each other's shoulders. Neither one willing to let go.

'Could do,' says Tim from somewhere behind Euan's forearm. The music from inside the pub surrounds them. *Have a holly jolly Christmas.* 'We just need to calm you down, don't we, Euan? Sober you up.'

Craig knows what he's going to do with the bucket of liquid next to the bench before he does it. He has no idea what it is inside. It could be water, or disinfectant or poison, even. But he picks it up anyway, angles it exactly and with care, then, whooooosh, throws the entire contents straight over Euan Barratt's head. The man splutters as it goes over him, his whole jacket and T-shirt soaked, his hair wet through. Tim escapes unscathed.

'I . . .' Euan lets go of Tim, hunches over, shivering and shaking himself off like an animal.

'You think you might go home and sober yourself up?' suggests Craig. 'How is any of this going to get any better, the state you're in now?'

'It's not,' says Euan, still shaking out the water and putting his hand down the back of his coat collar, pointlessly trying to feel himself dry with his wet fingers.

'Dad's said you're barred for the rest of Christmas Eve. He might let you back in tomorrow as you and Magda are booked in for lunch with your in-laws, is that right? But not if you carry on like this.'

Euan doesn't say anything. He wavers, slightly, as he tries to stand straight. He's a big man, and tall, a good five inches taller than Craig.

Craig puffs out his chest, for a moment, feeling like he's achieved something of worth today, buzzing from the adrenaline and the success of his aim, and from last night.

Euan gives him a look, a threatening one that runs all the way from his eyes to his knuckles, and Craig steps back, some of the bravado fading. But the other man turns and starts to walk away, crookedly, along the length of Newbury Street.

'Tell your dad I'm sorry all right,' he says over his shoulder. 'I'll be in for Christmas dinner as planned. And I'll pay my tab off.' Craig thinks the younger man doesn't sound sorry. He thinks he looks like he's angrier than ever, and the chances of him going home for a cup of tea are slim, but Euan doesn't stop, and they wait for him to disappear into the distance.

'Good,' says Tim, grinning at Craig, then calling after Euan. 'Make sure you do!'

The two men are left standing in the afterglow of an almost satisfactory interaction where they had emerged the victors.

'Glad you came along when you did, Craig, mate,' Tim says, shaking his head. 'I don't know. You volunteer for a day's shift at your parents' pub and the next thing you know you're putting people in headlocks. Mum'll be mortified. She's put so much into making today a family day.'

'People know what he's like,' says Craig, still bristling with pride at his intervention. 'I wonder what was in that bucket anyway.'

'Best not think about it.' Tim pulls a face and they both laugh. 'Let's go in. Mum's bringing out more sausage rolls in a minute.'

Craig feels good entering the pub with Tim. Inside, it couldn't be more Christmassy. There are huge silver stars hanging from the light fittings, rows of fairy lights hooked about the walls and ceiling, around mirrors, around the paintings and photos of the pub and Newbury Street over the past one hundred years. There's a silhouetted light show, row after row of red and white reindeers leaping over imaginary hills and projected onto the wallpaper. Larry and Sue have really gone all out, and he's suddenly glad he came.

The pub has an oddly familiar and comforting smell of beer, sausage rolls, perfume and sweat. It's warm with everybody's breath, and Craig's glasses steam up immediately. He pulls them off and pops them in his jacket pocket. He looks about for people he knows, but Tim is beckoning him over to the bar, making space for the both of them to stand together.

'Thank you, love,' says Sue Winters, rushing over and squeezing her eldest son tightly. 'Thank goodness you were here. Do you think he'll be back?'

'Not sure. He certainly went off in the right direction. Couldn't have done it without Mr Mullany here,' he pats Craig on the back, and Craig feels himself expand with the praise.

'Ah, Craig, thank you so much,' gushes Sue. 'Today's really important to me. Drinks on the house. Do you like sausage rolls?'

'Told you,' says Tim, grinning.

'I certainly do, thank you,' says Craig as Sue rushes off into the kitchen to get them.

'What'll it be?' asks Tim.

'A pint of that Christmas ale, I think,' Craig replies. 'To start.'

Tim clicks his fingers at Irma, who's come from the back with a full ice bucket. She gives both men a look of utmost disdain and Craig flinches.

'Click at me again and you'll wear it,' she says, walking past them both, straight over to Joanie, who is smoothing out her clothes, and packing Babycham into two Bags for Life. The women kiss each other goodbye and Joanie leaves by the main entrance and Irma slides back in behind the bar.

'You do know this is my mum and dad's pub, don't you?' says Tim, not retracting his demands. 'So, in a way, you work for me.'

'Yes, you're right. In a way I do. *In your head.*' She rolls her eyes.

'There's no rush,' says Craig. 'I'm not in a rush.'

Irma smiles at him. 'No, no, I'll get you your drink. I'd certainly think about the company you keep though.' She flicks her eyes at Tim, but when Craig looks at him, he's grinning, as though he's enjoying this, and he wonders if there's a history to the two of them he doesn't know about. He's never seen Tim so dismissive, he's usually so polite and gentlemanly. This is his point. Most people do terrible things, but they just hide it. Craig lifts his pint, takes a long swig and looks around.

All about him are familiar faces, laughing, talking, excited for Christmas, pleased to have time off work. He remembers when the four of them used to have drinks together on Christmas Eve. Where did things go so wrong?

Allie, why did you have to die? There was so much I wanted to talk to you about.

He thinks of Jen and Frank playing happy families safe in the beautifully decorated warmth of Number 118, the place he'd called home for ten years. He drains the rest of his dark ale quickly and without ceremony.

'Is it too early to have a round of shots?' he says to Tim, who is only a quarter into his pint and looks amused at this suggestion.

'I don't see why not,' the younger man replies. 'It's not like you're Euan Barratt, is it?'

Tim clicks his fingers in the direction of Irma, who gives him a look of pure ice.

'Tequila shots, with salt and lemon,' he says. '*Please.*'

Irma rolls her eyes but pulls out two clean shot glasses and holds one of them to the tequila bottle.

Craig doesn't want to think about anything anymore. Nothing he's doing to forget about everything is working. Tequila seems as good an idea as any.

1.20 p.m.

Christmas Eve

Cynthia Ellis

121 Newbury Street

The two police detectives are sitting on the guest sofa. One is drinking tea from a Melba teacup so fine that the rim is the width of a playing card and the handle barely fits one finger. Cynthia wants to laugh at the incongruity of the thing in his big hand, although it feels nice to be able to make proper tea in a proper cup, at least pretend that this sort of thing is still her life, instead of John *socialising for work* and her waiting patiently at home like she always, for years, has agreed to.

She gave up complaining about not being invited to the majority of John's work dinners long ago. Knowing when to give more, knowing when to take. Knowing when to speak up, and when to turn a blind eye. That's what makes a happy marriage. And theirs *is* a happy marriage. Cynthia knows it is. People tell her often enough. Also, how lucky she is.

Yes, she thinks as she watches the detective lift the cup to his mouth. *How lucky I am.*

The cup in the detective's hand has the crocus pattern on it and is from their wedding set, bought for them by

116

John's parents. Her cheeks feel hot at the memory of his mother's compliment, *'A very fine girl indeed. Very fine.'* Like bone china: neat, decorative, perfect for bringing out on special occasions. She was made for entertaining. She'd been led to believe that was what her life would be. She'd felt special for being chosen.

She watches the officer try to purse his lips around the delicate edge of the cup, the flowers bright at his palm. They look almost as good as they did on the day they were given. She knows how to look after bone china. No soap, drain, then dry with brown paper.

'We're just asking all the neighbours, again, if they saw or heard anything suspicious, anything different, last night,' says the male officer. 'We could have asked to pop in when we saw you earlier, but we had a few leads to follow.' He wears a signet ring on his little finger. Was it his initial, or that of a loved one as is now the thing? Cynthia had a signet ring, bought for her by her mother on confirmation day who'd made her a little felt hat with a white net veil and satin gloves, moon smooth. Cynthia had felt so special when she wore them. They were a perfect fit.

'I haven't really been looking,' she says, which is true and not true. 'I realise Jen Mullany and Frank Blake live only across the way. I was fast asleep by ten o'clock. I took one of my tablets and went straight to sleep.' She suddenly feels horror that they might think she's one of those women who is addicted to sleeping pills, so adds, 'Herbal tablets. Recommended by Lois Rowntree. You might know her? Her husband does a lot of charity work with the rotary club.'

Both detectives shake their heads and Cynthia feels herself shrink. Why is she explaining herself? She's done nothing wrong.

'I'm very sorry for the things that were stolen earlier in the month,' the male detective says, putting the cup, too carefully, so it teeters back and forth, back into its saucer.

'It's more the fact that they came into the house,' says Cynthia quietly. 'I keep hearing things that aren't things. I'm on edge. John tells me not to be silly. He's bought an upmarket alarm. But . . .' she thinks carefully before saying this, 'he's often not here during the evening, and you do worry. Being on your own. And now Len Finch . . . If somebody *did* something to him, it means none of us are safe.' She shivers. It's frightening.

'I can imagine and I'm sorry,' says the female detective. 'You're doing really well. Even the slightest thing you might have noticed might have significance. Just so you know, we'd never think you'd be wasting our time if there is something. And we think Len Finch was an accident of sorts, not related to the burglaries at all. So please let that put your mind at rest in this instance. We just want to know if you've noticed anything unusual, anything at all?'

The detective is tall and broad-shouldered, and wears an impressive pair of shiny black laced boots. Funny, if it was anybody else, Cynthia would have asked them to remove them, but she'd never dream of asking a member of the police force to remove their shoes to spare her carpet. She wonders if they're even allowed to take off their shoes in front of members of the public. This is the sort of thing she worries about and John tells her means her brain doesn't work like other people's. *If you were at school now, Cynthia, they'd have you marked down as someone special*. He says it cruelly, but she knows he means it kindly. She'd never have half the life she has now if she hadn't been so lucky to have him choose her as his wife. He told her just that morning.

Cynthia feels slightly thick-headed, the tablets from the night before have not quite worn off properly, but she wants to describe Newbury Street and how it's changed over the years in case it helps. She remembers so many of the families who've been and gone. She remembers how neat and tidy they once were, children safe on the street (or were they just afraid to tell grown-ups the sort of things that went on? She has wondered about that, since), and the houses were the same but different, always changing, always echoing with things it's easier not to think about. Things are unusual all the time. Cynthia has lived here for thirty years – although people often say she looks too young for that – and still human beings surprise her.

'Not anything that isn't unusual already,' she says. 'This end of the street is . . .' She stops. She doesn't want to appear a snob. She doesn't think she is one, not really. It's apparent to anyone who walks along Newbury Street that it's a street of two halves, give or take the odd interloper, or landlord who rented a nice house out in segments. 'Fairly quiet.'

'Yes,' says the male officer, who seems to have abandoned his tea. He seems short, even sitting down, although maybe that's in contrast to the woman. Cynthia thought police officers had to be a certain height. Height gives a sense of authority. She's not sure this man would be any good in a life-or-death scenario, although she's sure he's pleasant enough.

'Just make sure you lock up carefully, use the bolt locks, don't leave it on the Yale. And don't leave any windows open, make sure you all look out for each other,' says the woman.

'Yes, well,' says Cynthia. She bites into a pink wafer biscuit. She really does dislike them. They powder up in the back of her throat and make her want to sneeze, but they look best on the side plates. And John likes them. They remind him of his childhood. 'I haven't really been speaking to people the way I used to. We are very involved with the wider local community. Lots of charity work, and such.'

The woman officer, who Cynthia thinks is called after a bird that she can't remember, stands up. 'Well, that's good, Mrs Ellis. Do let us know if you think of anything. Same to your husband. Do you know when he'll be back?'

'Yes, of course,' says Cynthia and she ushers them towards the door. 'And no, I don't know when he'll be back. He's working today too, even through Christmas. He's a terrific worker, is John. He never takes his money for granted. Built everything up from scratch.' She feels the usual pride, as she always has done towards her husband's career. 'I'll see him later at the Feel Good. We're both really looking forward to it.'

'It must be lovely,' says the other detective. 'To have the other homes to visit, and the boat on the broads. Really lovely.'

'Yes,' says Cynthia slowly. It must be lovely. It *would* be lovely. If John ever took her to those places, but he doesn't. He says they are for *entertaining clients*, and for *the future*, when her *nerves aren't so problematic. What would we do, Cynthia, if you had one of your little panics on the water?* She doesn't say this to the detectives, however, for fear of seeming gauche. Or like the embarrassment she sometimes fears she is.

On their way out, the female officer gives Cynthia her card. DC Crane, it says in a lovely dark blue font. Ah yes, that was it. A bird. Just as Cynthia had thought. She tucks it away in the pocket of her skirt, and knows it's unlikely she'll ever need it. There's nothing for her to tell them, not really.

When they've gone, she tidies away the tea things. She takes through one cup at a time to the kitchen and deals with the china immediately. She's never left washing-up undone in her life. Not once. She rarely uses the dishwasher John bought, which he teases her about. She likes to take pride in how she cares for things. Some things are important and will always be important, no matter how much money you have.

She puts the uneaten biscuits back in the biscuit tin. She's not sure why she does this. She'd usually throw them away, as she doesn't trust other people's personal hygiene.

Then she rearranges the foliage she's put in a vase at the windowsill and looks down the garden. She had cut it from the back garden herself and arranged it in one of the vases she'd bought from the ornament pitch on the market last time she was in town. It's made of rose glass and it makes the stems look thicker than they are, distorted and bubble-furred. Ceramic vases are better, but she couldn't find any of hers. She wonders where the spotty one James had bought her a few Christmases ago has gone. Somewhere in a cupboard, still in its box probably. People she loved always presumed she wanted things for the home as presents. She tries not to think about what this might mean.

There is a miaow coming from the back door, and Cynthia opens it to see the cat she sometimes lets in the house to feed standing there, looking up at her expectantly.

'Come in, Sir Tom,' she says as he pads through the crack in the doorway. He follows her into the kitchen, where she pours him some food from her secret stash of Felix that she hides in the cupboard under the sink – a place John never goes – but he doesn't seem hungry.

She walks through to the front room, where the Christmas decorations glow with a bright happiness she can't quite feel. She sits down in John's chair and picks up the *Radio Times* and television remote. She'll watch some of the Christmas repeats of shows she used to love when she was younger while she waits for John to come home.

Sir Tom is soon on her lap, where she holds him to her, breathing in the smell of his fur and feeling the tightening and relaxing of his muscles. She has the thought that if she could just sit here with him like this, every evening, just sit, and never have to see anyone, she might be happy. She could get her food delivered. And do everything else online. She wouldn't have to interact, or think, or even speak again. She could learn to speak cat. She realises John doesn't feature in this strange and solitary imagining of her future.

'Now I'm being ridiculous,' she says aloud. 'But I'm glad *you're* here.'

The cat buries his head deeper into her shoulder. It's the closest she's had to real touch in years. She feels his breath there. At that moment, the phone rings and she's glad the handset isn't attached at the wall so she doesn't have to disturb the cat. She pushes her fingers into the fur under his neck and he purrs deeply. She presses the button to take the call and is pleased to hear her daughter's voice, clear as if she was in the next room, all the way from Australia.

'Sarah!' she says. 'Merry Christmas Eve!'

'Merry Christmas Eve, Mum!' Sarah replies, enthusiastically. 'I looked online and saw they're playing *White Christmas* on Channel 4. I wanted to check you were watching.'

'Oh! I hadn't realised. How thoughtful of you,' Cynthia feels her heart swell. Sarah has always been thoughtful, even as a little girl. She hadn't realised how much she'd miss her until she was gone, far away, and it was too late to make contingency plans.

'Would you like to talk to Albie?' Cynthia's heart swells even more at the thought of talking to her only grandchild.

'Yes! Yes please! I bet he's all excited about Christmas. What time is it there? Is it past his bedtime? We might have snow here. Wish you were all here to see it.'

'It's 8.30. I've told him he has to be in bed by nine. He's so excited and I haven't got it in me to quash it. Here's a thought. Maybe next year you could fly out to have Christmas with us? Paul would love that. And his family. I think you'd like it here, though of course there'd be no snow.'

Cynthia laughs. 'Maybe,' she says slowly. She can't imagine John going for it. When she'd mentioned it before, he'd pointed out her anxiety, and her fear of flying, and how she rarely even left Norfolk, let alone travelled across the world. *'I'd like to,'* she'd said quietly, but he'd laughed it off. *'You're like the mouse who thinks he can climb Mount Everest,'* he'd said, still laughing. Later that day she'd turned on the computer to see if any rodents lived on Mount Everest. She'd been delighted to discover that deer mice, *Peromyscus*, live at high altitudes and flourish there, are accomplished runners and jumpers. But she hadn't said this to John, of course. It kept her quietly happy nonetheless.

'You should get something to do video calls with, Mum,' says Sarah. 'Skype, or something. You can do it from the computer. You don't need a mobile.' It is an ongoing source of confusion for her daughter that Cynthia doesn't have her own mobile when John has several. John is right though. She'd get into a muddle with it, and probably rack up loads of debt in calls, or fall for scams, or send people accidental viruses. She doesn't say that now, although she knows seeing Albie in his Christmas onesie in real life would fill her heart enough to make her float. 'Right, Albie's here now, Mum,' says Sarah. 'Merry Christmas Eve. Love you lots. I'll call tomorrow.'

'Love you too, precious one,' says Cynthia. She refrains from telling her how much she misses her. There aren't really the words to explain that and she's worried if she says it then she won't be able to piece herself back together again. That she'd fall like the Lego bricks she's sent to Albie for Christmas, with the card with *love from Gran and Grandad* in her neatest pen, onto the carpet, never to be reassembled again.

'Hello, Gran!' says Albie, his lovely Australian accent even more obvious now his words are clearer.

'Hello, gorgeous one,' replies Cynthia, stroking the length of the cat on her lap and closing her eyes. 'Are you looking forward to Christmas?'

'Yes,' says four-year-old Albie slowly. There is a sort of whispering in the background, and then he says, 'Thank you very much for my present, Gran.'

'You are most welcome.'

There are more unidentifiable whispers. 'Come and see us very soon,' he adds.

'Oh I will. Don't you worry. I will come as soon as I can.' She feels her heart ache at how much she wishes this were true. It seems unfathomable that she's yet to even hold her grandchild.

'Love you byeee.'

'Love you too, Albie,' says Cynthia, but he's already hung up. She holds the phone in her free hand, gently, as though Sarah might call back and the two of them might hatch a plan for her to be there in time for New Year. But that's another life, another her, so she puts the phone on the side of the chair and flicks the channels until she's found *White Christmas*, just like Sarah said. They used to watch it together when she was a little girl. The cat in her lap reminds her of what it's like to feel that sort of closeness to another living being. To be bonded to the breathing in them.

The phone rings again, and she grabs it, enthusiastically.

'Sarah!' she says, excited.

'Sorry. Wrong Ellis,' comes John's familiar voice over the phone. 'It's only me.'

'She's an Eastwood now,' says Cynthia, not sure why she feels the need to point this out.

'She'll always be an Ellis to me.'

There's noise in the background, people and music, and Cynthia narrows her eyes and stares at the familiar scenes on the television.

'I'm at The Mariner,' John says cheerfully. 'The Festive Feel Good will start around four, but there's a lot of greeting and encouraging before then. I was thinking I'd do my duty as early as possible. Hand out a few prizes, then come straight home. No need for you to come out in this weather. Stay warm at home.'

'I was looking forward to it,' says Cynthia quietly. 'I've dressed especially.' She looks down at her woollen skirt and shiny shoes. At her new tights, with a slight leaf pattern in the knit.

'Honestly,' says John firmly, 'you'd hate it. It's rammed tight in here. Lots of drunks. Stinks of sweat and cheap perfume. Don't do it to yourself. I know you. You'd hate it. I won't be long. We can have a nice Christmas Eve in.'

Cynthia tries to find an answer to this, something including how they'd not had a nice Christmas Eve in since Sarah and James had grown up and left home, or how the likelihood of John being home 'soon' was low, incredibly low in fact, because the usual pattern when he says something like this is he'll come home long after she's taken her tablet and fallen fast asleep. But Cynthia leaves these words inside her head and doesn't share them with him. She doesn't have it in her to fight for her place beside him. She's also, she realises, quite happy, in the armchair with Sir Tom and the bright glow of her favourite Christmas movie. A different life. *A better one?*

'Have a lovely time then,' she says. 'I'll see you soon.'

'Yes. Yes. Good idea. I didn't think you'd want to come. See you soon. Don't forget to take your sleeping tablet. You don't want to be awake when Santa comes . . .'

She pretends to laugh, although the mention of the sleeping tablet when it's so early in the day makes her wonder what time he's really intending on being home. Then she says, 'Goodbye John.'

When the phone has gone dead, she sits holding it, and the cat, for what seems like a very long time.

2.30 p.m.

Christmas Eve

Irma Woźniak

Newbury Street

There are a few things Irma has noticed about Jen Mullany: she wears lots of rings and her hands are almost robotic with silver. She doesn't repaint her nails, just waits for the polish to flake off, so she has flashes of dark berry gloss at their middles and the tips are torn and slightly ragged, which doesn't suit the rest of her overall look. She likes foxes (necklace, phone cover, on the socks you see a flash of when she reaches to arrange the laces of her burgundy brogues). When she empties her handbag onto the coffee table, she sets out her Kindle, a Samsung Galaxy, a packet of fruit Mentos, a packet of Sainsbury's own-brand tissues and a tube of cocoa butter lip balm, neatly, in some kind of secret order. In public places, she pretends to do the *EDP* crossword but really just fills it in with names of bands and TV programmes she loved when she was a teenager. Her usual outfit is a version of jeans, a Breton top and a well-cut navy pin-striped blazer.

Now, as she sits on her sofa, in full view of anyone who happens to be looking into her living room through the big windows they've had fitted, she picks up and puts down her phone every few minutes, presses, scrolls, sighs and puts it back down again. She's never still for more than a few moments, folding and unfolding her legs, smoothing out her long, blonde ponytail and brushing imaginary specks from various parts of her body. She always looks busy, even when she's not doing anything at all.

Irma is on her half-hour break and this counts as the fifth time she's followed or watched Jen Mullany, always waiting for the right time to put her plan into action. She knows following her's not right, but, also, she hasn't been able to stop doing it. Every time Irma thinks of her, a thousand words fill her head and she wants to say them, but they get muddled up. That's how she ended up following her, because she wants to talk to her, but Irma never plucks up the courage. Somehow it's turned into something she never meant it to be. She knows it must stop. How would Joanie feel if she knew? Five times is still five times too many. People deserve their privacy, and their safety and to not be watched when they don't know they're being watched.

Yet, here she is. Badly disguised in a huge duffle coat and hat, looking into someone's living room through the window.

Irma sucks on her cigarette and stares into the house and watches Jen plump the cushions on her sofa. She has one of those living rooms that's set up perfectly for a family. Corner sofas, beanbags, big plastic boxes of toys that once had lids but are now rammed with all the bits that no longer belong to anything but are too expensive to ever get rid of. There are purple canvas tube lamps, some wall art of buildings in New York, family photos in crafty frames and stacks of books, although not very many DVDs. There are expensive-looking glass reindeer decorations stuck up across the ceiling, and a Christmas tree that has those lights that change colour every few seconds.

Why do so many people have photos of New York on their walls? wonders Irma. She always hoped she'd get to go to New York, although she knows that Jen has probably already been.

She isn't sneering at her. She wouldn't do that. It's just she can't imagine living in a house like hers. A family home. But she wants to. She wants to believe in that for her future, her and Joanie's own version of it.

Even the front of Jen's house looks lovely. She has one of those ceramic mosaic tiles with the house number on, and sometimes, Irma knows, she jet-washes her wheelie bin. She has a Vote Green diamond sticker in the front window from the last election that she's not taken down, and big blue-glazed pots of herbs and flowers placed around a floor of black and white tiles. Everything looks like it's from a storybook. Or an advert for an expensive shop on TV.

Jen's boyfriend and her children are out. Irma's timed this perfectly. The older woman is by herself, which gives Irma more opportunity to do what she needs to do.

Jen hasn't changed much at all from when Irma knew her. She has different, shorter, hair, but that's pretty much it. Irma can see her in her head as clearly as she was at The Lodge. She was the best of them. Irma couldn't believe it that day she'd first seen Jen at The Stop Shop, all these years later, buying oats, to make biscuits, she said to Rocky Winters behind the counter. Irma had dropped her basket and stared at her. She'd been too afraid to go and say hello, just as she'd been too afraid to say hello to her every day since then.

She's surprised Jen hasn't noticed her outside her house because she's not exactly hiding. She has her hoodie on and the big coat with the grey toggles pulled tight through the loops that is nothing like her usual style, and her hands in the deep pockets.

When Irma was fifteen, Jen was the most important adult in her life. Some of the things she did she still remembers as if it were only yesterday: taking her to an American diner for burgers and ice cream on her birthday and paying for it with her own money, buying her her first Stephen King book, teaching her how to wash and fold her laundry.

Foster homes had been hit-and-miss for Irma. Her problem was that she never knew who to tell about the worst places. She'd moved back and forth between care and home with her mum and her boyfriends at various points in her childhood. Sometimes everyone in her life was paid to be there, and she knew it. She also knew she couldn't trust anybody.

She is thrown back, as she plucks up the courage to do the next part of her plan, to the woman who'd fostered her when she was seven, Mrs Ellwood. Irma had had such high hopes for her, and she wasn't even one of the worst people who'd crossed her path in childhood.

On her first day, they'd had such a good one. The best of days. Mrs Ellwood had held Irma's hand in the supermarket and bought her a Wispa bar and a comic. She'd taken her for a haircut. She'd bought Irma a balloon from the man at the market; a hopeful silver blob of helium that bobbed about above her as she drifted it home, the feeling that this was what life was about, this was happiness and maybe everything would be different now.

That night, Mrs Ellwood had put her face right against hers. Irma had felt so happy. She didn't dare believe it, but it had been a whole day with not one drop of anger, not one thing that confused or upset her. Mrs Ellwood had

130

smiled at her. She'd held her hand. Maybe things would be OK. She had said she'd sing Irma a song, so she sang her a song, *Row row row your boat, gently down the stream*, and stroked her hair. Her voice was like having your face stroked and all the smiles in the world in front of you. She felt happy. She felt like the world was safe, and she'd started to cry. *I'm so happy. I'm so happy.*

And then she wet the bed.

The heat of it spread around her, but still Mrs Ellwood sang and Irma didn't think to check what she said before she spoke. She forgot to remember and, instead of keeping it secret, she said, 'I've had an accident.'

'What?' Mrs Ellwood had stopped singing.

'I've weed myself.'

The woman had looked up at the ceiling and then towards the window. She said nothing. Irma reached up to her for a cuddle. She wanted a cuddle. For a beautiful moment, she thought that was going to happen because Mrs Ellwood leant over the bed and put her face very close to Irma's again, this time so that they were almost rubbing noses. Irma reached up and put her arms around Mrs Ellwood's neck. She wanted to pull her face to her, to feel the warmth of her cheek.

'Why,' said Mrs Ellwood very slowly and very quietly, 'do you kids have to ruin absolutely *everything*?'

Irma felt herself get smaller.

'What's wrong with you? You got something missing in your head or something? You defective?' Mrs Ellwood's voice had changed. It was fierce and her features had rearranged themselves to resemble an angry dog.

Irma lied in the wet in terror.

'You can fucking sleep in it too.'

'I don't want to,' she says quietly.

'You don't want to?'

'No. No I don't.'

What happened next was so fast that, afterwards, Irma lay in the wet, with her pyjama bottoms sticking to her legs and the taste in her mouth and the feel of the cotton. The wretched stink of it all. Mrs Ellwood had ripped the wettest part from the under sheet, tore it into shredded scraps and pushed several of them into Irma's mouth. The smell and the taste were vile and she'd gagged, but the woman had just pushed them in further.

'Don't speak to me,' she said as she left. 'Don't ever speak to me.'

The next day, Irma was taken away by a different social worker, one she'd never met before, after Mrs Ellwood had told her about things Irma hadn't done, talking about her as though she was an animal, and then she found herself in The Lodge for the first time.

She'd been back and forth between there and home four times between seven and sixteen. It was at The Lodge she'd met Jen. Miss Bray, she was then. She sat with Irma when she crawled under the table in the common room, and she read her *James and the Giant Peach* until she came out long after it was dark. And she kept reading then too. Irma loved *James and the Giant Peach* because it showed that adults can be cruel through no fault of a child. She had spent most of her life around people who pretended that wasn't true.

Now, nearly thirty, Irma watches Jen curl up on her sofa through her expensive windows. It amazes her that people sit there like that with their curtains or blinds open, unaware that anyone could be looking in at the secret fragments of their life. She knows she should look away, but she can't help herself. She wants and needs her privacy so much that she would have all the velvet curtains, and all the iron bars and all the locks and chains. And then she'd sit in the corner and wish she could see the sky and someone smiling.

Irma is determined to make changes this year, to make things different.

Step by step.

Starting with now.

Irma takes a deep breath, folds her coat collar down, as neatly as she can, and runs her hands over her hair. She practises her opening line, over and over, trying to get it right so that she doesn't bumble or splurge, or mess up her words as she walks up the path to Number 118, which looks so different in daylight, and knocks at Jen's door.

When Jen opens it, they stare at each other for what feels like much longer than the few seconds it takes for her to open her mouth. Irma sees fear flash across the other woman's face, and her push the door slightly towards being closed, so the gap Irma's looking at her through is narrower. She doesn't look comfortable, almost like she's been caught in the line of a zoom lens camera and is searching for a way to hide her face.

Irma looks down to see the mistletoe-print door mat over the threshold and a cascade of smartly snipped paper snowflakes stuck to the stained-glass window in the green door. There are fairy lights around the hallway mirror, all green and gold, flashing intermittently. There's a *Santa Stop Here* sign to the right of the doorstep, with a striped candy-cane post and a plastic hand pointing to the entrance. She realises she's just standing there, silently, watching the woman as she slowly closes her front door in front of her.

But she isn't going to give up that easily. Not today. She's come this far.

'My name is Irma Woźniak,' she says calmly, putting one of her feet inside the doorway. 'And I don't know if you remember me, but I've got only fifteen minutes of my break left. I need to talk to you, and I need it to be now.'

3.17 p.m.

Christmas Eve

Wendy Finch

Victory House

Wendy leans over the sink and washes her face in gentle circles with the tips of fingers. The soap is one of those scented pastel bars with a logo pressed into the surface. Joanie presented it to her still in the box, in a little basket of toiletries, alongside a stack of pale blue towels. Wendy is touched and enjoys lathering up the bubbles in the sink full of warm water and the feel of it on her skin. They'd not had hot water at all, unless they boiled it, in the past month. The steam in Joanie's bathroom feels like the ultimate luxury.

The Babycham sits hot in Wendy's stomach, fireworks and bursts of thunder. She thinks she might take up Joanie's suggestion of a nap.

'Would you like a hot-water bottle, Mrs Finch?' The little girl Patti is outside the bathroom and calling through the door. 'Mum wants to know.'

Do I want a hot-water bottle? Wendy stands up fully and looks at her soapy face in the mirror. So strange to see all the lines in such close focus. To be standing in somebody else's bathroom on Christmas Eve as though the past sixty years of marriage had never happened.

'Yes please,' she says. *What harm could it do?*

She's thinking of last Christmas. *'It won't always be like this,'* Len had said, apologising for the lack of Christmas presents and the lack of heating after he hadn't been able to afford the bill. He'd been right too, because here she is. Alone. Washing her face in someone else's basin. And it's nothing like last Christmas *at all*.

She hears the voice before she sees him, booming, confident from the other side of the bathroom door. His voice makes her freeze. She hadn't got as far as thinking about what she'd say to him when she sees him again. She hadn't got as far as thinking about him at all, other than the seething anger that this man had tricked Len into giving up all their life savings. To give up their *house*. She doesn't care if it is legal or not. What that man did was unforgivable.

She's wearing her nightdress, early in the day for her, with a dressing gown loaned to her by Joanie, so big on her small frame that she can almost wrap it around herself twice. *I'm going to stay in here until he's gone*, she thinks. *I'm going to stay in here until he's gone and then I'm going to carry on as though nothing's happened.*

'That's OK, Joanie,' comes the voice. 'I'll wait until she's ready. I wouldn't feel right if I didn't get to wish her a Merry Christmas. And give my condolences. I thought very highly of Len Finch.'

Wendy grips the side of the bath. *He's going to wait*, she thinks. He's going to wait and then . . . what? What's the worst he can do? The house is full of Joanie and the kids. She's not going to give him the pleasure of seeing her frail in her nightdress. If he wants to wait, then he can wait.

She reaches for the clothes she was wearing before her shower. The dress, tights and the purple cardigan with the butterfly brooch Len had bought her on their wedding day still pinned to the left-hand side, just beside one of the big buttons. She pulls on the clothes, folding the nightdress and dressing gown neatly and putting them on top of the little unit Joanie had said was just for her while she stayed.

She will not rush for him, so she stands at the bathroom mirror and applies her make-up from what Joanie has given her. Really, she'd shown such kindness. She chooses a lipstick, different from her usual colour, pinker, with a bit of a shine instead of the usual matte, and applies it in her usual way, blotting her lips on a piece of folded toilet paper and smacking her lips together. She fills her eyebrows in with brown pencil and flicks mascara along her lashes. Joanie didn't have any face powder or foundations suitable for Wendy, so she taps out some talc into her hand and uses a brush to pat it lightly over her cheeks, nose and forehead.

When she looks in the mirror she reminds herself of Miss Havisham.

The man is still out there. Part of her had hoped that if she took her time, he'd lose patience and leave, but his voice is doing that sing-song public voice that she knows is fake, fake, *fake*. *To lull people into a false sense of security.* Like he had with Len, but not her, never her.

When Wendy is finally ready to leave the bathroom, she reaches into the pocket of her leopard-print coat that she's hung on the back of the door. The neat parcel wrapped up in patterned foil paper is still there. The present Len had put on the mantelpiece before he left the house that morning and never came home, the present with the little label written as neatly as he could manage, *To my wonderful wife at Christmas. One Day. Your Len x.* Tomorrow morning she will open it, so slowly and carefully, and remember the man she's loved for over fifty years.

How can you be gone? Her throat feels sore and rasping.

She knows she has to leave the bathroom, and so puts her fingers around the door handle, turning it as slowly as possible.

'Wendy!' comes the familiar voice when she enters the kitchen. The man puts his arms out towards her and pulls her to him, and she stiffens. She doesn't want him anywhere near her, let alone next to her like this. He smells of expensive aftershave. *And money.* For the moment there's only one thing she can do. She must pretend she doesn't know what happened to the house, and to the money, nor to any of the things Len had organised with this man. She must pretend she's ignorant of the game, of the scam, of *all of it.* She must act like she's happy to see this man, and even though the thought of it sickens her right through, she smiles and puts her hands out to meet his. Everybody round here knows this man, *admires* this man even. She has to think before she acts.

'Hello!' she says, brightly, although her hands are shaking and her feet lose power beneath her as she takes a seat at the kitchen table. 'How kind it is of you to come and find me.'

The man flashes her one of his most winning smiles. 'I couldn't not come. I wanted you to know if there was anything I could do, please ask. And to bring you this.' He holds out a cheque signed by himself for £3000. 'It's what I was going to put towards today's Festive Feel Good. I'd rather you had it directly. And I'll give a separate amount to the pot.'

'That's very kind of you,' she says, calmly, taking the cheque and watching it droop between her fingers. *So, it's as easy as that. To give money that would pay bills and buy food. As easy as that.* 'You really didn't have to do that. This is too much. Really.'

'Three thousand pounds? Woah,' says Dylan, leaning in to take a look at the writing. 'That's a lot. How many Pokémon cards is that, Patti?'

Patti gets a whiteboard and wipeable pen stuck next to it with White Tack. 'Right,' she says. 'If we did it in booster packs, they're, say, eighteen pounds . . .' She starts drawing lines on the whiteboard and counting out dots into each column.

'Maths has changed a lot since my day,' says the man, smiling at Wendy, leaning back onto the kitchen side, and he runs his hands through his thick hair. 'There's no rush to decide what you'll be doing next, but this will help when you do.'

Joanie brings him the mug of tea.

'That's really kind of you,' she says, smiling. 'It's really unexpected to see you here, I must say.'

'Not kind enough. Yes, I'm not sure why I've not been here sooner, really.' He turns to Wendy. 'I'm so sorry about Len . . . Did they say what happened? Why he died?'

Wendy watches him. He looks so confident, like he hasn't got a care in the world. But there's something about how he's wringing his hands over, how his leg is at an odd angle, how he leans in towards her like he wants to shake her and demand she tell him everything she knows. He's worried, she thinks. And this gives her a new sort of courage.

'I'm sure it was old age,' says Wendy. 'Although they did say they might do a post-mortem . . .' She can't remember if they said that, but it wouldn't hurt to put the idea in the man's head. 'It comes to us all in the end,' she says. 'Whether we're rich, or poor. Whether we're famous and everybody knows us, or we're all alone and nobody notices we're gone.'

He doesn't say anything to that. He just stands there in Joanie's kitchen, out of place, acting like it's the most natural thing in the world.

Wendy's still holding the drooping cheque. Three thousand pounds. What is she to do with three thousand pounds now it's too late? Three thousand pounds would have bought food and heating and *dignity*. What is she to do now? Invest in a time machine and go back to the first time she sat like this, with him, in her own kitchen, waiting for Len to come back from the building society, putting out the best milk jug and teapot, delighted Len was doing something that would give them a good future. At first.

Was it that first conversation where she became suspicious? Maybe. Or maybe later, when Len was so regularly going out to the building society while this man with the familiar face had turned up, for a reason nobody had ever explained to her, waited on the sofa with her at home, making small talk, not letting her get on with her day. What had she said to Len? *'It feels like he's waiting here with a gun to my head until you return. Like he's making* sure *you return. With the money.'* Len had laughed it off. *'Of course not, love. He waits with you to keep you company.'* She'd asked Len that one time, how it all works, and when would they see the returns they'd been promised.

'Oh, I leave all that to him,' Len had said.

'Maybe we should change our minds,' she'd said. 'It's never too late to change our minds.'

Len had visibly shuddered, she'd seen it, and he'd gripped the side of the armchair, pushing his fingers into the flowered material. 'Oh, it's too late for all that!' he'd said cheerily. 'He owns fifty per cent of our house now. That's what equity release is.'

'So the money we've released is in our building society account?'

Len had pulled a face as if to say, *Oh, you don't understand all this, this is men's stuff*, and she'd wanted to say more, wanted to say *lots* more. But he'd shook his head vigorously. 'No, no, no. We still pay him because he's investing the equity in high-return stock. It means we're not only releasing equity, we're doubling it, *tripling* it even. He's so well known, Wendy. He would lose too much to be doing something like this wrong. He's a philanthropist at heart. He likes helping people. You've seen him when he's on local TV. Always helping people.'

'Len . . .' She'd reached out and put her hand on his. 'I don't think that sounds right.' It was the only time she'd outwardly doubted his decision. Len had kept them safe financially all these years, and she'd never once questioned him before. It worked for them, just like it worked that the kitchen was her domain, as was the decor and the meal planning. They'd always worked. Always. This was something new.

'Hush, Wendy love,' he'd said quietly. 'I know what I'm doing.'

She'd let it go. She'd let it go and his visits to the building society had continued, until one day he announced, 'Well, that's it. He owns our house. But soon we'll be able to buy a bigger and better one.'

This grand announcement was followed by their first week of not being able to afford their groceries. She remembers Len's face, confused, as he came home empty-handed from the shops. 'It must be a mistake,' he'd said unconvincingly. 'I'm sure it will be sorted quickly. These things happen now everything's done on computers.'

But it hadn't been sorted quickly. And they'd started living on their pension alone. The day Len admitted they were now paying the man rent and that was why their pension didn't cover everything was the day Wendy knew they'd truly lost everything. *'There must be something we can do, Len,'* she'd asked. She was worried about how they would survive, but mostly worried about Len, who'd been looking more and more lost by the day. *'Stop talking about it. I'll fix it.'*

Now here she is.

'Look, Wendy . . .' the man says gently, turning his full attention towards her as he reaches out his hand, which is holding his business card, 'I want you to know you can call and ask for anything at any time. Please. Come to me if you want any advice, or anything at all. Don't go to strangers. Stick with your own. We'll see you right.'

She nods, wondering if her acting is as good as his, or at least he thinks it is as the card burns its shape into the palm of her hand while its owner sits across the table from her and she pretends she's really that stupid as to not know what he's done. *Or what he's threatening to do if you say anything about any of this to anyone.*

'Listen to this!' Patti turns up the radio, stopping the conversation immediately. The station had been playing David Bowie and Bing Crosby's version of 'Little Drummer Boy' that Wendy has always loved.

'We just had this tweeted to our show page,' says the over-friendly DJ who sounds to Wendy like he probably paints his teeth white. 'Local Norwich Landlord and

142

all-round nice guy, Larry Winters of The Mariner Pub, who's running a Christmas Feel Good event at his pub this Christmas Eve afternoon, has just informed us he's putting up a £10,000 reward for any information that leads to prosecution as regards the Christmas burglaries on Newbury Street. I'm reliably informed that this amount has been matched by John Ellis of John Ellis Homes, making the entire amount £20,000. So it's worth thinking about. Maybe you, or someone you know knows something . . . And now for an old favourite!' The familiar opening to 'I Wish It Could Be Christmas Every Day' blares out too loud in the kitchen and Patti quickly turns down the radio again.

'*Twenty thousand pounds*,' she says, her eyes wide open as she draws dots onto her neatly drawn bar model. 'Imagine how many packets of Pokémon cards you could get with *that*, Dylan. If you could get four booster packs per hundred, and there's ten one hundreds in one thousand, and there's three of those . . . That's—'

'Twenty thousand pounds,' repeats her brother. 'Maybe it's time we became detectives,' he says. 'You're good at finding stuff out, Patti.'

'Twenty thousand pounds is a lot of money,' says Joanie, 'What generous men.' She prods at the gingerbread pieces she's just pulled out of the oven. 'Kids, I know you said we had to make a gingerbread house, but I really don't think we're going to be able to. Look at the state of this stuff.'

'Nanna always made a house,' says Dylan sadly.

'Shhh,' says Patti, elbowing her brother in the ribs. 'Mum's tried her best. Maybe we could trim them down to look like snowmen.'

Joanie's rubbing her eyes with the backs of her hands, gingerbread batter all down the front of her jeans. 'I really am. The snowman biscuit idea is great, Patti. Thank you.'

Wendy watches the younger woman flounder for a moment before regaining her poise. She wonders if she could confide in her. Everything she's seen so far today suggests she could, but she mustn't rush anything. Some things take time.

The limp cheque sits in the centre of the kitchen table, on the plastic Christmas tablecloth covered in little curves of mistletoe. Wendy doesn't want to touch it again, as though there's poison pressed into the ink.

'I'd better get back to it,' the man says quickly. 'I'm still donating to the Feel Good but really don't want to be away from home on Christmas Eve more than I need to. My wife's already upset with me for putting this above her today. You'll be glad to know it's started off with a bang though. People are being really generous.'

'It looked like it was going well when that prat Euan Barratt knocked me flying,' says Joanie. 'Not on purpose, I'm sad to say. Wish I was the sort to lie, because he could do with a ticking off by the police, but he was in an angry rush and I just got in the way.'

'He should be barred until the New Year is what I think,' says the man, already at the door. 'I'll have a word.'

'Sue won't stand for someone like him ruining things,' says Joanie, admiringly, as the kids start pressing the snowman biscuit cutter into the warm, soft, not-very-well-baked dough and the man leaves, giving Wendy one slightly too long, last look.

I'll show you, she thinks, clear-headed and strong, feeling like she knows exactly what she needs to do next. *Don't you worry. I'll not let you get away with this. I'll show you.*

4.00 p.m.

Christmas Eve

Tash Blake

The Stop Shop

Tash's fingers are sore with paper cuts and scabbed over from endless tearing open of the plastic wrapping from delivery containers, but she doesn't want her shift to end because she doesn't want to not be with Rocky.

'Merry Christmas,' she says to the box of rotting clementines that are too far past their best to put out with the other stock. She'll have to explain how they got to that state, and, as usual, there'll be a passive-aggressive note in reply from Head Office via an embarrassed-looking Nadia, explaining targets, windows of opportunity and markdown pricing.

They were like this when they arrived, Tash writes on the waste note in her most sarcastic handwriting. It looks the same as her usual handwriting, but she's satisfied that she can see a difference.

'Ho, ho, ho,' Rocky appears at the entrance to the stock room with his elf hat at a jaunty angle and his elf shoes jangling as he goes. He somehow makes this look attractive.

'You do look so . . . Christmassy?' she grins at him. 'I presume you've seen the state of these clementines?'

'*Easy peelers,*' says Rocky.

'Yeah. Easy peelers because the skin rolls off as it rots. *Really* easy.'

'Ha! Don't worry. I'll explain. We'll sell enough booze today, so nobody's going to get in trouble.'

Tash smiles at him. 'Thank you. They really *were* like this beforehand.'

'I know. You know don't need to convince me. How are you feeling now?'

Tash wonders about this. She had thought her heart was going to explode out of her chest when the body in the ambulance might have been her sister. She knew she'd been hard on her over the past months. She just wished Joanie had fought harder to get her dad to stay. That's what it boiled down to.

'I feel better, but I feel awful for Mrs Finch. Imagine losing your husband on Christmas Eve.'

'It's like this street has a curse on it,' says Rocky, sadly. 'The amount of people who've been burgled too. What a lead-up to Christmas.'

'The clementines are a metaphor,' grins Tash, smiling slightly. 'It's all fresh shiny apples from here on.'

'You want to come to The Mariner in a bit when the others take over for the evening run, and blow our Christmas bonus?' Rocky gives her a look she doesn't quite understand. Is he asking her out? Is he being friendly? Is he inviting everyone?

'Maybe . . .' She keeps her answer vague just to be on the safe side.

'It'll be me, and you, and . . .' he pauses and picks up a crate of sliced bread. 'Anyone else who wants to come. Not that I've asked anyone else . . .'

'Not sure how easy it will be to blow a ten-pound Argos voucher in the pub . . .' laughs Tash.

'Bloody vouchers. Again,' says Rocky, rolling his eyes. 'We can blow it in real money, then replace whatever we were going to spend the money on with the vouchers. Mum and Dad owe me some drinks and a few packets of crisps anyway.'

'We can wear our complimentary elf ears,' says Tash, raising her eyebrows and trying to waggle hers independently.

'I'll keep mine on if you keep yours on.' Rocky strokes his own elf ears to the point with his spare hand. 'My mum says I make a handsome elf,' he says and starts laughing.

'She's your mum. She has to.' Tash isn't going to say, *Your mum is right.* She's been holding back telling Rocky how she feels about him for years. Since Year 8 at least. She isn't going to change that suddenly now. She wants to say, *In my opinion you'd look handsome in anything. Or out of it.* She stifles a laugh. Tash isn't shy. She knows how to say what she wants. But she's left it too long with Rocky, and now they have something she doesn't want to spoil. What if she said something and he never talks to her again? What if he laughs?

She'd always presumed her and Rocky would get together one day, she sort of lived her life by it, just waiting for the time to come when he'd spring it on her. 'Tash I'm in love with you!' and she'd say, 'Phew, at last!' and they'd kiss passionately against the coat rail outside the back office. But she doesn't really believe in all that anymore.

Maybe her dad moving on with Jen had broken her sense of romance? He'd always seemed so happy with her mum. They'd always seemed so right together. What Tash is really feeling about romantic love these days is that maybe it doesn't exist. Or, if it does, it doesn't last.

147

She realises she's gone quiet and is staring into space because Rocky is looking at her and waving.

'Hello! North Pole to Tash.'

'Sorry,' she says. 'Just thinking.'

'That's what I was worried about.' He smiles. 'Can you do the price reduction on that bin of Yule logs by the till? And then we're done, basically.'

'Yes,' replies Tash. 'You got it!'

Rocky turns and leaves to go to the shop floor with a crate of plastic-wrapped heat-up baguettes. 'You going to keep your elf costume on then?' he says with a wink.

'I will if you do.'

'Well, I think I've got to wear a different costume, if Mum has her way . . .'

The door swings shut behind him and Tash takes her time following him out. She enjoys walking through the trail of his aftershave.

You've got it bad, Natasha, she hears her mum's voice in her head. *Just tell the boy.*

As if it's ever that easy.

On the shop floor, Lou, one of the sales assistants who's agreed to work on Christmas Eve evening, is here for her shift and is accepting a thick stream of compliments for her elf costume and long plaits. She's put unwound wire through them so that they curl upwards, like she's someone from Whoville, and it really suits her. She'd got on shorts and striped tights and drawn freckles on her cheeks with brown eyebrow pencil. Tash wished she had the knack of looking like Lou. People always fancy Lou. Not that she ever notices. She's far too into the much older, rich boyfriend she's always talking about but has to keep secret because people would judge. And he has a wife. 'He's got posh houses all over the place,' she says enthusiastically.

'Last week, he set up candles and rose petals all around the hot tub in his cottage near Burnham Market.' Tash has given up telling her that anyone who wants to keep her a secret isn't worth it, because Lou always laughs and says, 'You'll know what I'm talking about when you have someone totally mad about you like he is me.' Tash let this, and her interest in hearing about the mystery man, slide.

She's relieved to be in the warm of the shop floor, and double relieved to see Rocky standing by the doorway with a mug of hot chocolate for her.

'Thought you might need this before we go,' he says and passes it to her with a big smile. Rocky's smile makes her feel funny. 'This Christmas must be so hard for you.'

'I'd rather stay out here, with you,' she says, then tries to swallow the words back immediately. 'With people, company, you know, *not by my myself*. I really hope Euan isn't in the pub,' she adds quickly, changing the subject.

'Ever again,' says Rocky, who seems to have missed her confession. 'I didn't know your sister had it in her.'

'Neither did I,' says Tash. 'Goes to show . . .'

'People are never what you expect?'

'Something like that. Next time I complain about her, can you remind me about how she stuck up for that bloke, despite the danger. When nobody else did.'

'I might . . . but when you're in one of your moods with her, nobody's going to stop your ranting. Least of all me.' He raises an eyebrow at her, but his expression is kind, and it makes her smile. 'Also,' Rocky continues, 'I hate to remind you of this, but I thought you said he was a weirdo.'

'I did . . . but . . .' She feels sheepish. Even this morning she was thinking that very same thing. 'Even weirdos deserve to be stood up for when being picked on by the

149

friendly members of the local EDL, or whatever they're calling themselves these days.'

'Urgh.'

'Urgh.'

'To be fair to you, maybe he *is* a weirdo.'

'Joanie's invited him for Christmas.'

'Well, let's hope he's not a weirdo then.'

'Thanks for the support.'

'Any time. Obviously.'

'Maybe I should try and be a better person,' she says, shrugging.

'Don't,' replies Rocky. 'I like you how you are.' He says this quickly, then turns around immediately to make his way to the little kitchen, so Tash can't read his facial expression. 'And,' he calls out behind him. 'Your sister is ace. Don't forget.'

Tash is left staring at the swing door wondering if Rocky really did say what she thought he did, or whether he was just being polite. Tash, the feisty one, the one who stands up for everybody, who doesn't worry about causing a scene for a good cause, can't say a simple thing to a boy she likes. She's not been as feisty this past year. It was like when her mum was in the world there was a rod of strength inside her, that's buckled now.

She shakes her head at herself. *Nobody has everything.* That's what her mum always said. Tash changes that slightly at the memory of her past, more forceful self. *Nobody is everything.* She finds that comforting. What she doesn't find comforting is the fact she looked out of her bedroom window at about 1.30 a.m. last night to see Rocky's dad walking an invisible dog along Newbury Street. She'd thought nothing of it at the time, but as the day's gone on she's started to wonder. The first burglary was John and Cynthia Ellis's house, and he and Larry Winters are always in competition with each other. Larry seems to have more money than usual. The burglaries have brought him lots of good publicity.

Tash, stop, she tells herself crossly. Larry Winters has no good reason for taking part in petty theft. He's a successful businessman with a happy family. And he's Rocky's *dad.*

So what was he doing out near the time her dad's house was burgled? She wonders, as she nips in behind the till to serve her last customers of Christmas Eve.

'It must be one of those from Victory House, is what I think.'

Tash is jolted from her worries about Larry by one of the women from the middle numbers of Newbury Street, talking to someone from one of the posh houses up the road, right in front of the newspaper stand.

'Or one of those houses split into flats,' says the other woman. 'Electric toilets that churn up all the waste, some of them have. In the corner of the bedroom, with a little partition.'

'So they steal from those who've saved and made good decisions.' The woman picks up her broadsheet and brings it to the counter. 'John always says jealousy is the destroyer of good things.' Then, in hushed tones, 'I think that's the problem with Cynthia, you know. She's the jealous type. Doesn't let him breathe without pestering him for all the details of his day. Poor man.'

'Such a *nice* man,' says the other woman.

Tash thinks of Cynthia Ellis, who the two women are talking about. She likes the woman, when she sees her, which isn't often. She's polite enough, and always asks after Patti and Dylan. Her mum used to say that there was more to Cynthia Ellis than meets the eye. Tash agrees, although

151

she has no idea what. But there's something about Cynthia Ellis that is strange. She's always wearing clothes that are several sizes too big for her. Expensive clothes, clothes from department stores and boutiques, but *way* too big for her. *One day I'll have the guts to ask her why*, thinks Tash.

'Why couldn't they have built Victory House somewhere else? The terraces were here first. It was quite a lovely area, back in the seventies. Clean. Going places.'

'Property prices in the area are still high,' says the other woman. 'We're still in the top ten places to live in the UK.'

'Yes, there is that,' the woman takes her purse out of her handbag. 'I hate those houses turned into flats even more. There's something not right about carving up a beautiful home like that. Invites the wrong kind of neighbours. John says you can't sell them like that. They need a lot of work before they can go back on the market. And, oh my goodness,' she leans one gloved hand on the counter, 'I think I'm in shock about poor Len Finch. Can you believe it? Today of all days!'

Tash feels her hackles rising. Victory House has been her home her whole life and she feels sick to hear it under attack. But then she remembers that man Isaac staring out of the top window of Number 127 and feels bad for thinking ill of him for basically the same reasons. 'Merry Christmas Eve to you. A terrible thing about Mr Finch. Truly terrible . . . Are you ready for it all? Are you going to Sue and Larry's Festive Feel Good at the pub?' She bombards the women with questions.

'We haven't quite decided. We might just donate money instead. In fact . . .'

Tash zones out, knowing she's only got ten minutes left of her shift, as the woman starts telling her all about her three-bird goose from a butcher just outside Holt, and feels an overwhelming fondness for her sister's efforts with crepe paper streamers and a plastic bin full of soaking turkey. Tash is ready to go with Rocky to his parents' pub and to let herself have a lovely time.

5.00 p.m.

Christmas Eve

DC Crane

The Mariner Pub

'Feeling Christmassy yet?' DC Crane turns to DC Ado as they do another turn of The Mariner. She intends to leave this place in the next half an hour and do some paperwork before she heads home.

DC Ado laughs. 'The more you ask me that, the less Christmassy I feel,' he says dryly. 'You're like the opposite of Father Christmas.'

'Unfounded,' says DC Crane, smiling.

'Fair, actually,' argues DC Ado, also smiling.

'Right. It's time,' announces Sue Winters excitedly, leaning over the bar and bringing out an old-fashioned handbell that she rings as loudly and grandly as is possible. The music has been turned off, as well as the fruit machines and the jukebox and anything else that might make bleeping noises during this special occasion.

To Sue Winters' obvious delight, and with a wink from Larry, everybody seems to stop what they are doing immediately, so she stops the ringing and places the bell carefully back down on the wooden bar.

'Hear ye, hear ye,' she says, loudly and with a broad smile. 'We are gathered here today, not only to celebrate Christmas Eve in the manner to which we've grown accustomed.' There are a few cheers and whoops in the background. 'But also to show the world that Newbury Street isn't going to sit on its backside and be blue when all this bad luck comes our way.'

Cheers in the background again.

'Larry and I wanted to do something for all the people who've been affected by these burglaries, so imagine our delight when we ended up with all this lot!' She nods at the big pile of presents under the over-stuffed tree, and then nods at her bucket of raffle ticket stubs. 'We wanted to make sure that nobody went without, and we've got enough to replace all the stolen presents, several times over. Local care homes for children, and the elderly, will be taking the extra gifts at a time of year youngsters without families of their own can really feel a sense of not belonging, even with the best will in the world by the authorities and those who look after them.'

'The *authorities* and *best will in the world* is not always a compatible sentence,' says Irma under her breath, although DC Crane is near enough to hear her. She watches her twisting a wet beer towel from the bar back and forth between her fingers, like it would hurt to be still. She keeps looking at her watch.

'And so,' says Sue, with a little curtsy and another ring of the old bell, 'I declare this Festive Feel Good well and truly open. Laura! Dan! Bring out the pastries!'

People cheer at that, as the two very busy kitchen staff from The Mariner Pub come out with tray after tray of sweet and savoury pastries. Who cares if they'd just heated them up and sprinkled a bit of icing sugar on top? As the trays of Prosecco come, and people swap ordering drinks for as many free drinks as they can get away with as they buy more raffle tickets, the evening seems to move into a sort of Christmas karaoke session. DC Crane and DC Ado wander over to where it's happening.

There's a little wooden stage, set up over towards the far back of the main bar, surrounded with lots of fairy lights, and a big microphone twisted about with silver tinsel. The lyric screen, rather like the old TVs and stands that used to be wheeled out when DC Crane was at primary school, is set up in front of the stage, covered in baubles and tinsel around the edges. The DJ, obscured in obligatory Santa hat and full costume fiddles with the plastic-sleeved books as a man and woman in their fifties wearing matching Christmas jumpers begin singing the original version of Band Aid, badly, into the microphone, occasionally stopping to call out.

'I'm *Bono*,' says the man.

'No, *I'm Bono!*' says the woman, making DC Crane think of a sort of very wrong version of *Spartacus*.

'Rocky!' She realises the karaoke DJ is in fact the youngest Winters brother.

'Merry Christmas, DC Crane,' he says from behind a nylon beard. 'Fancy a go at "Lonely This Christmas"?' Beside him, Tash Blake is sorting out a book of song lists. She's still dressed as a Christmas elf. Both of them are eating handfuls of peanuts and crisps and have pints of Coke with ice and paper straws.

'Urgh, no,' DC Crane replies. She can't think of anything she'd rather do less than Christmas karaoke. *Any* karaoke when it comes to it.

'I love karaoke,' says DC Ado. 'But we're on duty. It might not really give the right impression.'

Santa Rocky laughs. 'Hopefully later I'll be able to wear something that's not fancy dress, but you never know. Mum probably has more plans for me. And maybe you could come back and do karaoke when you're not on duty.'

DC Ado nods, non-committal, but keen, thinks DC Crane, noting his enthusiasm.

'Your brother seems to have avoided the whole dressing up thing,' she says, spotting Tim Winters standing at the bar with his boss John Ellis, the two men laughing raucously.

'Uh-huh,' nods Rocky, turning back towards the music system with a roll of his eyes. 'Thing is,' says Rocky, 'I don't mind helping Mum and Dad out. It's OK with me. Tim prefers . . .' He shrugs and goes back to his duties, sorting through the names that have been written down on pieces of green paper in the shape of holly leaves, all people who want to have a go, and the numbers of the songs they've found in the plastic-sleeved folders that are spread out around the tables, while Tash Blake sneaks adoring looks at him when she thinks nobody is looking.

DC Crane watches John Ellis holding an unlit cigar, with the top button of his crisp white shirt undone and his hair flopping in that bright white, silky fringe that hangs in a way that makes him look like the well-scrubbed boy he must have once been. The two men are talking to two of the daughters of one of the families who live at the far end of Newbury Street. Both must be in their early twenties, are pretty, and the intensity of John's conversation is startling. John's giving the shorter one his full attention, and as she throws her head back and laughs, he slides his hand into the small of her back and, for just a moment, DC Crane sees the older man's fingers rest at the base of the woman's spine. She jumps, at first, and then settles back into his palm. She must be at least forty-five years younger than him. She's drinking some kind of pink cocktail in a champagne glass. But she's not drunk . . . not yet.

DC Crane looks about for Cynthia, but she's nowhere to be seen. *Not your place to judge, Lucy*, she thinks to herself. But it's one thing to fall in love with someone people think you shouldn't and quite another to *cheat*. DC Crane has some simple morals. *Don't get anything from anyone if you wouldn't get it if you told them the truth. Cheating is for cowards.* Maybe John and Cynthia Ellis have an open marriage. They wouldn't be the first. *Maybe she turns a blind eye. Or maybe she's so awful to live with John has no choice.* DC Crane shakes her head at the last one. Maybe that's what John wants people to think.

'This song,' says DC Ado, interrupting her thoughts, 'is not good.'

'No,' agrees DC Crane as the man and woman on stage both sing Bono's line.

DC Ado pulls a face, which transforms into a smile, which soon transforms into a frown when he sees the conversation at the bar become heated, as Sue Winters approaches her eldest son. Tim Winters turns away from the woman he's talking to and begins waving his hands around.

'Fancy listening in on what they're talking about?' DC Ado says to DC Crane.

'I certainly do,' replies DC Crane. 'For research purposes.'

They edge slightly around the bar, making sure they're within earshot without disturbing the flow of conversation. Tim Winters is shaking his head, pulling his mum away from the women and John Ellis, and Sue's shaking her head back.

'I don't believe it,' she says firmly. 'I can't see how it could be her. She's my best member of staff.'

DC Crane's ears prick up.

'You've got a blind spot when it comes to her,' says Tim forcefully. 'I was just talking to John, and he thinks he's seen stuff going on at Number 127. That maybe she and that Isaac Whatsit who lives upstairs are doing it together. Somehow. I bet if you got the police to go in and look, they'd find the whole lot.'

'You can't just send the police into someone's home on Christmas Eve based on a tip-off from your *boss*.' Sue Winters says the word boss like she's saying something that disgusts her and, once again, DC Crane finds herself wondering what made the Winters and the Ellises frenemies in the first place. Money? A woman? A family secret?

'Oh great,' says Tim. 'Here we go again. It's obvious you and dad haven't forgiven him or me for me taking that job. I don't care if you believe me or not, it's true. Irma Woźniak is up to something, and I think it's to do with the missing presents. How late does she have to be after a break on the busiest day of the year? It's not like she's working late anyway . . . Ah, DC Crane!' Tim swivels round and smiles at her and DC Ado. 'DC Ado! Gone online and bought those trainers yet?'

'I'm on duty, still,' says DC Ado, not as friendly as before.

'I know this isn't the place for it,' says Tim. 'But maybe you can help me solve an argument.'

DC Crane doesn't say anything.

'It depends what the subject is,' says DC Ado, neutrally.

'I was talking to John, Ellis, you know, my *boss*. And he was saying how he has his suspicions about what's going on at Number 127, and I said me too. I used to go to school with Irma, and she wasn't right then. And then she got taken into care because her parents couldn't deal with her behaviour. She was all over the place. A bully, at school, to some of the younger girls. Rumours about her shoplifting make-up from Superdrug. All that. Not that Mum listened to me when she employed her, so it's no surprise she won't listen now.'

DC Crane isn't certain, but it looks like Sue Winters rolls her eyes. 'You'd never know he was the apple of my eye, would you, the way he goes on after a few?'

DC Crane doesn't think Tim looks like he's had too much to drink and wonders if his mum is making excuses for him.

'Tell her about the time Irma's till was down, by nearly one hundred quid . . .'

'Well,' says Sue carefully. 'It was, but that was a complicated situation. Plus, we'd had other people on and off the till that day, including casual staff. I didn't want to accuse anyone unfairly.'

'That's her problem,' says Tim. 'She won't accuse anyone unfairly, so she lets people walk all over her.'

'Urgh,' Sue sighs. 'This is the worst bit of Christmas,' she says brightly to DC Crane and DC Ado. 'The bit where the drink's settled in a little too much. Tim, darling, you know I adore you, but today is not the time to talk about this. Or do anything silly. Let the police do their thing.'

'If I'm right, I'm going to claim my reward,' says Tim, laughing now, easily. More gently. 'And spend it all in someone else's pub.'

'I don't think your dad will give you the ten grand reward if you're the one who gives information that leads to a prosecution,' smiles Sue. 'Sharing that information would be the very least he'd expect you to do. And me. It's how you've been brought up.'

Now it's time for Tim to roll his eyes. But the affection between the mother and son is plain to see. DC Crane thinks again of the phrase apple of my eye, but for some reason this comes with the vision of a pair of eye sockets with thin, twisting apple tree branches coming out of them, so she shudders and blinks this unwanted image away.

'So you think there's nothing in what your son is saying?' she asks.

'Of course not,' Sue snaps. 'I mean, Irma's had a good year. She's got a lot going for her. Even if I did believe she'd take the presents and the money, I just can't see . . .'

'Maybe that was Isaac . . .' says Tim, pulling an *I'm-right-and-you-know-it* face. 'Are you one hundred per cent sure though, Mum?'

DC Crane waits for the emphatic yes that she's sure will come, but instead she sees Sue Winters' eyes flick over to Irma behind the bar and then back to her son. She brushes something DC Crane can't see from the wool of her Christmas dress and straightens her hem. 'Not one hundred per cent sure, obviously,' she says. 'But nobody can be one hundred per cent sure about anyone, can they?'

Tim nods as though this proves his theory beyond doubt, 'There we are then,' he finishes. 'I'm glad we had this conversation.'

DC Crane and DC Ado nod and say thank you to the mother and son.

'Enjoy the rest of Christmas if we don't speak again,' says DC Crane.

'I hope we do speak again,' adds Tim emphatically. 'When you come and tell me I'm right.'

'You have a lovely Christmas too,' smiles Sue Winters, not responding to her son. 'Doing anything nice?'

'Family,' say DC Crane and DC Ado at the same time. They both smile at this, because they both have different ideas about what family means.

As they walk away, someone is singing 'Santa Baby' in the most unsexy voice that's ever been used for any song since there were songs.

'Ouch,' says DC Crane.

'Indeed,' agrees DC Ado.

'What do you think about what Tim Winters said?' asks DC Crane. 'A possibility?'

'It's not impossible,' says DC Ado. 'But I really hope it's not the case. I like her. I mean, I'm rooting for her. You know what I mean?'

'Look at you being *biased*,' she teases 'That's not you at all. You're the *don't-judge-until-you-know-all-the-facts-and-still-don't-judge* guy.'

'Funny what seeing some people behave like utter penises over the period of a day at Christmas can do to you,' he says quietly. 'I think it's time we get out of here, don't you?'

'Yes,' replies DC Crane. 'Absolutely.'

Outside, the cold air is refreshing and makes her mind whirr. Could it be the inhabitants of Number 127 had organised the burglaries? She doesn't think so, but it wouldn't hurt to take a look. She sees Nathan Patterson come out of the pub behind them, tucking his camera and folded-up tripod under his arm, pulling his coat collar up and wrapping his big scarf about him.

'Right,' he says to the detectives, affably. 'Home now for me. This is one of the best stories I've ever got round here. It's got intrigue, loyalty, betrayal.'

'What story is that?' DC Crane says, sternly. 'If it's something that will help with solving the burglaries, you should really talk to the police.'

'I'm aware of that,' says Nathan. 'I have done things like this before. And I am aware of the law. Wishing you both the best luck in catching whoever's behind all this. Merry Christmas.' And with that he heads off.

She watches the man she's seen on TV numerous times walk away along Newbury Street, his icy breath puffing out in front of him. DC Crane is formulating another theory at the back of her brain. There are a few details she would need to check, but, as far as she's concerned, Nathan Patterson is up to something, even if it's not the burglaries, and she intends to find out what.

6.00 p.m.

Christmas Eve

Sue Winters

The Mariner Pub

Sue is annoyed at Tim. It's not OK to tell the police things you don't know to be true; she wishes he hadn't been drinking. Tim's never been very good at holding his drink. It's why all the exercise he does gives her a great sense of relief. He doesn't often drink too much anymore.

She watches John Ellis blatantly flirt with Lily Smith, who's back from university, as her sister drifts away now she'd lost Tim's attention. The young woman doesn't seem to mind, which startles Sue because when she was her age, she'd have done anything she could to avoid being in close proximity to a flirty man in his sixties. She observes him for a moment. To see how he does it. It's all in the eyes. He's looking at Lily, directly, not looking away. He's looking at her like she's the only other person in the room. There's something wildly alluring about that. About being *seen*. *Clever bastard*, she thinks. And then thinks of Cynthia and feels a jolt of guilt. *If we all know what John's like, why do none of us say anything to her?* If it was Larry messing around with other women, possibly giving her diseases and lying to her daily, how would Sue feel?

Don't be silly, Sue. Larry would never do anything like that, so it's not a sensible comparison.

But still. She feels like she must do something, in the New Year maybe, to befriend Cynthia, to see what she thinks of her husband's behaviour. John has said many times before, at the bar with a whisky when he and Larry have been doing *their keep your enemies closer* version of friendship, that she's cold and cruel and would not be able to cope if he ever left her. He stays with her for her own benefit because she can't look after herself. *You could almost say it's a good deed.* Ha!

Why have I ever listened to five seconds of his crap? Sue realises she likes John Ellis even less than she thought she did. And she will befriend Cynthia properly, and even help the woman, if she needs help. Because seeing John with Lily Smith has made her blood boil. She thinks maybe that's partly why she didn't want to listen to Tim. Tim thinks the sun shines out of John Ellis's arse. Why should she trust someone, even if it is her beloved, beautiful son, who thinks living the way John Ellis does is something to be admired?

As the karaoke is in full swing, and while the bar is having a quiet moment, Sue decides to go out back to do some subtotalling. It takes a lot of effort to be switched on all the time, and sometimes she craves time and space to herself, not another person in sight, not even Larry. The worst thing about being a landlady isn't the long hours, it's the having to be polite, friendly and interested in people you'd not sit near on a bus in real life. *That's me*, she thinks. *The eternal actress.*

Sue eases out the till roll and her book of sums, staring at the figures in disbelief. It's actually *amazing*. Never have they made so much money at a charity event in The Mariner's history, and as she does the subtotal so far, her eyes widen with every calculation. She knew they'd got lots of people involved, she knew they'd get some nice things together to take to people in the area, but the amount was ridiculous. Over £24,000 – £14,000 of that in cash, plus all those gifts. *How is this even possible?*

In the back room, she has to think twice before she gets the right pin to open the safe. The combination is changed so often that she has problems remembering it. But you can never be too careful, especially since the spate of burglaries. When they'd started out in the pub business, she and John had slept with the cash takings rolled up in pint glasses hidden under their double divan. How times have changed.

There's a miaow at the back door, and without thinking, Sue puts the money in the safe and opens the door. Standing there, looking as though he has urgent business, is the tabby cat the regulars call Lord Nelson. A nod, somewhere, to the pub, and the city, and the admiral whose name adorns the county signs, as though he sailed the land into place at its corner of the United Kingdom himself.

'Hello, old man,' she says, reaching down to run her hand along the length of his spine. 'Fancy some scraps?'

Lord Nelson only likes food with fish flavours. Sue had tried him on others over the past few months, but it was only the fish he ever actually digested.

'I think I've got a can of tuna in here,' she says, taking out her phone to google *Is it safe to feed a cat tinned tuna?* and scrolling through the results, although her mind is elsewhere.

She can't get Tim's words out of her head. The whole while the Feel Good's been going on, she's had a creeping sensation, that somebody is betraying her. It makes no sense it's Irma, does it? Her best member of staff. Her listener, cocktail maker, favourite of the older generation who feel they're seeing one of their idols from the Golden Age of Hollywood come to life. But she's sure Irma *is* hiding something. Even before Tim had suggested it, if she's honest with herself. And Sue's afraid it's something to do with the burglaries.

She opens the back door as Lord Nelson decides he wants to go back outside, so she closes the search engine on her phone. *A little tuna once in a while should not hurt kitty, but it will be nutrient-lacking.* Who even refers to a cat as kitty?

'Fickle little git, aren't you?' laughs Sue as he pads out.

She's not going to let Tim's words ruin what's been a brilliant day. There's nothing she'd have done differently, no organising, no decoration, no tiny bulb out of place. If she could change one thing, it would be her dress, which was itchy now. And her shoes, which were new and nipped her small toe on her left foot. But, really, personal discomfort was better than customer discomfort. She could always have a long bath before she finally got to bed. Or a few gins.

As she watches the cat leave, she realises there's already another person out there, talking furtively into their mobile while smoking a cigarette. Sue can't see who it is at first, just hears the urgent murmur of the voice, notices the hunched-over body language, a secretive silhouette in the security light.

Of course, it's Irma.

What's she doing out here? Why's she whispering into her phone, out back, in secret?

People are allowed private lives Sue, she tells herself. But . . . Why is Tim so off with this woman? He has a good

167

ear for bullshit, and for betrayal. Forgetting his blind spot when it comes to John Ellis, she'd trust his opinion on a person before she'd trust her own, or even Larry's. Time and time again, he's been proved right about dodgy staff, bad traders, and women too. Their discussion earlier set off alarm bells in her head despite her telling him otherwise. And now this.

'We should go there. What I've got might be worth something,' says Irma into her phone. Sue is behind her and knows the younger woman doesn't realise she's there. 'Although I know Christmas Eve isn't ideal, but I need to do it today. I'll chicken out otherwise.'

Sue feels her heart plummet as she listens until she's totally sure. The air outside is cold and it's dark now, the sound of someone singing terrible karaoke from inside the pub so loud, there would probably be complaints from somebody. She makes a note to tell Rocky to change to disco mode when she goes back in.

When Irma has finished the call, Sue steps out of the shadows towards her.

'Irma,' says Sue, making the younger woman jump, 'I think you'd better tell me what's going on.'

Irma swivels and Sue finds herself face to face with a wild animal. Her eyes are blazing, and the careful eye flicks she's so neatly inked onto her eyelids make her eyes look like pure rage.

'What are you doing listening to my conversation, Sue?' Irma looks guilty, there is no other word for it. Her eyes are wild, and Sue suddenly has the feeling she's never really known anything about this young woman at all.

'I need you to tell me what is going on,' says Sue, firmly.

Irma looks at her, her face expressionless at first, and then her eyes flicking back and forth like she's trying to think of a good story, trying to make something up that will sound convincing as long as she doesn't have to tell the truth.

'Why?' is what she says in the end. Sue stares at her. She can't help feeling like she knows nothing about her at all.

'Because I've got people telling me I need to be careful when it comes to you, and you're not giving me any reasons to disagree with them.'

'You've never had any reason to doubt me,' says Irma. 'I'm good at my job. I'm loyal.'

'This isn't a job interview Irma,' Sue almost growls. There's an anger in her, rising, and Irma's face looks so blasé, like she has no respect for Sue at all.

'I'm giving you one last chance,' warns Sue. 'Explain to me what's going on, or I'll have to ask you to leave.

'I don't think,' spits Irma, 'that a boss has the right to probe into private conversations an employee is having on the phone. Do I need to talk to my union rep? Wait there, *I'm* the union rep.'

Sue had encouraged all her staff to join a union, so to have this used as a threat is a step too far.

'I don't think that's the conversation we need to be having right now, Irma, do you? How about you go? And I mean leave. I can't have staff I can't trust working here, can I? You leave me no choice.' This has all escalated too quickly and Sue hates the words, even as they leave her mouth. But what else can she do? Tim is certain, and this scene does nothing to aid Irma's cause, she's not even tried to explain herself.

'Sue!' Irma's tone changes, to one of pleading. 'I need this job. I love this job. But I don't have to tell you what I'm talking about on the phone on Christmas Eve. My own private conversation. On my own break, after I've worked my arse off.'

Sue knows what Irma is saying is true. There's no reason she *has* to share what she's talking about. Just as Sue didn't have to share what she's thinking now. That Irma has had something to do with the burglaries and is passing on stolen goods to someone she's just been planning with on the phone, in Sue and Larry's pub. *In our home.*

'You were on your break for over forty-five minutes. And now this. Just get out,' says Sue, firmly. 'I don't trust you. I don't want you here. Just go.'

Irma's eyes are full of tears, but she doesn't say anything else. She turns, fast, unlocking the bolt on the back gate and runs. Sue can hear the clack of her shoes as she goes.

Why does something always have to ruin a perfect day?

Back inside, Sue picks up the receiver to her landline. She still has the card DC Crane gave her earlier, so she pulls it out and types in the mobile number she's been given.

DC Crane answers after only a couple of rings.

'DC Crane,' says Sue, urgently. 'I think Tim is right when he says you need to look further into the comings and goings of the two people who live at Number 127 with regards to the burglaries. Especially Irma Woźniak. But Isaac Iwu too. I just heard her on the phone arranging *something*. When I asked her what it was about, she refused to tell me, and just seemed sneaky. Then she ran off. If she's innocent, what's the harm in telling me, is my thinking?'

DC Crane says thank you for the information and hangs up. Sue is shaking. She's hot in her knitted dress, and several of the sequins have fallen off so the pattern doesn't sit right. Her tights are sagging too, at that uncomfortable end-of-day not-quite-staying-up stage, and she notes there's nothing quite as disappointing as dressing up in your finest, to feel it all falling apart later on.

She hears a noise behind her and swivels round to see her eldest son filling out the doorway.

'Where's Irma?' asks Tim, grinning at his mum.

'She's gone,' says Sue firmly. 'And she won't be coming back here again in a hurry.'

Tim seems satisfied at that, holding his glass up high to toast an invisible companion. 'This day just gets better and better,' he says and Sue pushes any doubts about the situation far out of mind. All is settled now, and even if Irma's innocent, well, she's certainly up to *something*. And, when it comes down to it, you always choose family over anything else. It's Sue's first law of survival. *Family. No matter what.*

Just as Sue thinks the day can't get any worse, she goes back into the office and realises she forgot to lock the safe. She's hardly been gone for five minutes. Of course nothing will have happened to all that money. But Sue already knows, as she looks into the space where all the cash should be, that it won't be there. And the gaping black hole staring back at her proves she's right. The money, all of it, is gone.

6.30 p.m.

Christmas Eve

Frank Blake

118 Newbury Street

When Frank gets home, slightly drunk, slightly pissed off at Jen for not showing up or texting back, the house is in total darkness, not one light on and no sign of Jen or the boys. At first, he feels confused rather than worried as he reaches into his pocket, realising he's left his keys inside the house, because he hadn't thought he'd need them.

Tutting, he stumbles back out of the front gate, and round the side, to make his way to the back of the house. He remembers Jen saying she always left a spare key under the stone gnome. He'd told her it was a bad idea, even before the burglary. It wasn't safe, he knew, because how many times in his past life had he helped someone redecorate their interior when somebody's house had been broken into after some thief had found out, or guessed, about the spare key hidden under a pot plant, or an ornament, or a welcome mat by the back door?

He picks up the key and puts it in the lock. All he really wants is to lie down, with his head in Jen's lap, and have her stroke his hair. His conversation with Irma is fresh in his mind, and he can't wait to tell someone about it. Not just someone. Jen. Always Jen now.

Inside, the house is cold, and smells of . . . nothing? No food, nothing on the hob, no steam, or kettle. Unusual. He still feels calm, just a bit disappointed. It'd been a long day, a long few days, and he kept thinking about how it had felt when he'd come downstairs this morning to *all that*. Or a lack of all that, even. To everything taken away, and the tabby cat that he always knew as Spock at home, sitting in the living room licking his paws. *This* is *home now*, he reminds himself. *He's Valentino here.*

He puts his hand on the doorframe that leads from the kitchen to the dining room. The wood is newly painted. A sort of peach, lilac, grey. The name of it on the tin was Summer Dusk. He had thought it romantic when he'd picked it from the shelf in Homebase.

It *is* romantic. It's just Christmas was always going to be different without Allie. They'd woven a whole life together, for better or worse, through sickness. You don't just move on from that as though nothing happened. Even when you're happy.

He remembers Jen and Craig after their honeymoon, when she became Mullany. Both far blonder than they were before they left, with sea-cracked faces and salt-burned ears. They had a lightness to them, the sort of happiness you get from the simplicity of loving someone and them loving you. Frank knows he's been lucky to have it twice. He remembers his and Allie's honeymoon. They took pictures of each other by blinking. *I'll remember you like this for ever.* Frank feels his stomach lurch. He can still see her face on the pillow, the orange light from the bedside lamp, the silk nightie her mum Grace had bought for her. Allie laughing because it wasn't her and putting on

173

one of his T-shirts instead. And him thinking she looked perfect that way.

Stop.

It has to be OK to remember her. Even when it hurts. But this is too much. And the house feels . . . wrong. His head hurts. *Why didn't you stop after a few? Why can you never stop after a few?* He can't wait to give Jen a cuddle, and to remember how his life is now.

Frank pulls off his tan leather shoes and lines them up neatly inside the shoe rack by the back door, turning on the kitchen light with his elbow as he does so. The kitchen is clean, neat, tidy, as always. There's no note on the counter to explain why Jen or the kids aren't there, although there could be many reasons.

He opens the fridge and sees the food has been replaced, all of it, and inside the door stand champagne and orange juice for tomorrow morning's Buck's Fizz. Christmas is heavy with memories of Allie. She always bought Buck's Fizz too, but it was the pre-mixed stuff that they sell for £2, cava and a too-bright orange juice, laden with strands and powdery clouds. He feels embarrassed and doesn't know why. The fridge heaves with pickles, salad, hams, pork pies, salami, brie, chocolate mousse, pâté, everything. There's a Christmas pudding in a red plastic tub tied over with a tartan piece of cloth and a red bow. Santa's been already.

He walks over to the kettle and thinks better of it. He needs a proper drink. *'You always choose alcohol over me and the kids. And then you get cross and say I'm ruining your fun. Is this fun, Frank? Is this fun?'* Not Jen saying this, but Allie. Not long before she found out she was ill. He tries not to think about those conversations. They are still too raw. And they don't fit with how he remembers the two of them. How *everyone else* remembers the two of them.

Maybe the kids are still with Jen's parents and she's fallen asleep upstairs. She does nap in the day sometimes, when work's been too much, or when she's just overdone things. Jen's a great overdoer of things, always thinking she has more energy than she does. Always thinking she can fit more into twenty-four hours than is possible, because she forgets she needs to sleep, or eat a sandwich.

When Jen told him that she'd ended her marriage because she had feelings for him, they'd been in her car, and he'd found himself thinking, *I want her*, without thought to the consequences. It was a thought that thrilled him enough to lean over and kiss her. They hadn't been able to stop. No, that's not true. They had *chosen* not to stop. Afterwards, she'd carefully pinned her long hair back up into a bun and had caught his eye in the wing mirror, without turning to look at him.

'I think I'm falling in love with you, Jen,' he'd said.

'I think I'm falling in love with you too, Frank,' she'd replied, talking as though they were a couple on a radio drama, which also thrilled him. Later, as he'd taken a shower and thought of all the times he might be lucky enough to enjoy her body in future, he had no regrets. Despite the guilt. Despite the memory of Allie, soft in the dark. Frank had always been a one-woman man. He'd thought that was it, after Allie. And now this. All this. All this at its best is like a wonderful dream.

He could do with going to bed with Jen now. To feel alive. To leave death at the door with his over-polished shoes.

He flicks on the heating at the boiler in the cupboard, and feels a strange coldness that is to do with more than the weather.

I hope Tash is ready to take Love, Actually apart xxx

He sends the text to Joanie without thinking. He wants Tash to live with them. It's not right she's at the other place, Joanie's place now, when he's only up the road. He should listen to Jen more, he knows. Teenagers are her expert subject. He just likes to think he can sort these things out himself. He remembers how proud the girls were of him when they were little. A flashback to a *Comic Relief*, in 2005 – a memory of Allie and the girls pouring baked beans over him and him appearing in the *Evening News* and on local television pops into his head. The laughter. The girls, 'Ewwwww, Daddy!' but tipping more and more into the bath, so he'd sat there, in tomato sauce, for several hours, as friends and family had visited, and he'd proudly and patiently made £584.

'Jen!' he calls out. The house begins to blaze with light as he walks through, turning on anything that gives out light and has a switch. He doesn't want any dark corners. He suddenly feels . . . scared. Who had been lurking about in the dark in their house last night? Why hadn't he heard them? He wants to curl up on the sofa with whisky and the smell of Jen's lovely hair.

He pours a whisky from the decanter. A funny thing, a decanter, but he'd always wanted one after seeing an episode of *Minder* where Arthur Daley had poured one from it, or was it Del Boy on *Only Fools and Horses*? Maybe both. Anyway, he'd bought it when he'd moved in with Jen and had always made sure it was filled since. She'd found it funny and teased him gently about it for days.

As he takes his first sip, he notices something that cools his blood. Jen's handbag is on the bookshelf.

'Jen?' he says slowly. She never went out without her handbag. Not once. He remembers him, Allie and Craig laughing at *her*, the sort of teasing all four shared with each other back in the old days, when she'd once taken it out with her to clean the inside of the wheelie bins. If her bag is here, it means Jen is here.

She *has to* be upstairs asleep. He can hear his heartbeat, heavy in his chest and loud in his ears as he climbs the staircase. The landing light is off, all the lights still out on the second floor, and as he turns it on as he steps towards their bedroom, his mind flashes with an unwanted image of Jen's body, crumpled, broken, a spread of dark blood around her head, one single crack along her forehead running from her crown, and he bashes the bedroom door open with huge, unnecessary, yet urgent, force, feeling he might throw up. Those TV dramas have a lot to answer for.

He flicks the light switch, his entire mouth dry, and his fingers still pinching at the glass in his hand. The bedroom is exactly as they'd left it that morning, before they'd realised they'd been robbed. Neat, tidy, the purple and gold patterned duvet spread neatly over the bed, smoothed out, and the scatter cushions in their usual position that he'd joked he'd have to crack the Enigma code to recreate it the way Jen does. But no Jen. No anything.

He feels angry then. Why is she causing him this unnecessary panic? He needs her, and she isn't there.

That's not fair, Frank. She's given up a lot to be with you. You're being a dick. Maybe something's happened . . . No, of course nothing's happened. Jen's just had to pop out and forgotten her bag, that'll be all.

He goes back downstairs and sits on the sofa, moving the decanter to the coffee table, and turns on the TV.

Picking up his mobile he notices there's a message from Joanie, not Tash, of Tash holding a thumb down at the TV to the opening credits of *Love, Actually*. **You'll be pleased to know the tradition is alive and kicking . . . x**

That's my girl xxx he texts back. He wonders if Tash knew her sister was sending the photo, and if she'll text him herself. Just like Joanie to make it look like Tash was replying in her own way. *Joanie is always papering over everybody's cracks to the detriment of herself.* A teacher had written that on her school report. Neither he nor Allie really understand what that meant. Not then, anyway.

I love you Jen, he thinks, leaning back, sat with his whisky glass in one hand and the other stroking the mustard and cream patchwork throw. Who should he ring? Her mother, who hates him? Her friends from work, whose names he can't remember? What would he say?

It's then he hears the sirens, loud as warnings, screeching down the street, and the turn of the blue lights through the curtains. His heart is in his chest, his mouth like iron. Something's happened to Jen, he thinks, it must have done. The universe is never going to let them be happy. And before he knows it, he's up at the door and out on the street, ready to confront whatever it is.

7.14 p.m.

Christmas Eve

Wendy Finch

The Mariner Pub

Wendy stands, triumphant, in the doorway of The Mariner, holding tightly to the wooden walking stick that Allie used in the last weeks of her life and Joanie had kindly gifted her. She feels invincible. *I did it*, she thinks, watching the faces stare back at her. Her legs are shaking, and her thin arms seem heavier than they've ever been, but she feels triumphant. She did it. She's here. *I'll show him*, she thinks.

Her body might be shaking, but her brain is clearer than it has been in months. She knows what she's going to do. And it will start with entering the pub with Joanie and her children, ordering drinks and toasting Len, the man she loved for most of her life, who she still loves, and who'd been taken from her far too soon through the acts of an evil man.

There are several police officers in the pub, and the cars outside had nearly put her off, but Joanie and the children had ushered her on. When she'd thought of that man's face, she pushed herself onwards, and now here she is.

'Mrs Finch! Oh, this is wonderful! Come in. Come in!' Sue Winters rushes over to the group at the door, her usual combination of kind, brash and enthusiastic. Wendy notices her earrings, big diamonds, flashy, and the sequins on her dress. 'You're the last person I expected to see here. But I'm so *glad* to see you here. Gosh. Come in! Come in! Make way will you, Gary,' she shoos away a group of regulars at the table nearest the door, picking up beer mats and ripped-up tinsel as she goes. 'We've got a special visitor.'

'What's going on . . .?' says Joanie. 'Is it safe for the kids to be here?'

'Of course it is,' says Sue. 'We just had an incident. Not violent. A theft. I rang them immediately.'

'Where's Irma?' Joanie asks, looking worried.

'Have you not seen her?' Sue pulls a sheepish expression.

'No. I thought she'd be here. Working.'

'She . . . er . . . went home. We'll talk about it tomorrow.' Sue turns her attention back to Wendy. 'Now to our special visitor!'

'I'm not a special visitor. But I would like a glass of Babycham if you have it, and a glass each of whatever these three are having. I hope you don't mind, but I thought I'd like to drop by.'

'Oh, goodness, of course I don't mind. I don't mind at all. Now, kids what can I get you?'

'Grapefruit juice with ice please,' says Patti, seriously.

'Mum, can I have a Coke?' asks Dylan, turning to Joanie, who's shaking her head.

'You're still too young.'

'I'm six years old! Everyone I know drinks Coke.'

'How about a lemonade? There's no caffeine in that.'

'A lemonade with ice in it please,' he says in a grown-up voice.'

'A Coke for me please,' says Joanie. 'Ice too.' Wendy can see her looking about the pub for evidence of Irma.

'Come on!' says Dylan. 'That's so unfair!' and they all laugh. Wendy thinks how nice it is to be here with this family, even though the circumstances that brought them together were so terrible.

'Of course. Of course!' Sue manages to part the punters in the main bar with such ease, it's like she's walking through ghosts in a cartoon.

Wendy sits at the table, too warm in her leopard-print coat, but not wanting to take it off, aware that lots of eyes are upon her. The pub is loud. The Christmas disco continues. Even though it's in the side room, the door is open and the coloured lights make bright splashes across the carpet of the main bar. The children chat excitedly.

'Do you think we're the last children to not be in bed yet?'

'Do you think we'll see Father Christmas?'

'Look there's Tash. Dancing!' Their aunt is jumping about and pulling silly faces in the disco room, laughing and smiling and sipping from a pint glass of Coke. She waves at them as she moves. They wave back.

'Well, that's the best thing I've seen in a long time,' says Joanie, a big smile on her face, which falls quickly when she takes out her phone and sees there's no messages or calls from Irma. 'I hope Irma's all right.'

Wendy sits, regal, and takes it all in. 'I'm sure she is. She's a lovely girl.'

'She is. It's just Euan Whatsit said something today that I can't stop thinking about. That she was looking elsewhere.'

Wendy shakes her head. She knows love when she sees it. 'That girl is mad about you. Honestly. There'll be a good reason she's gone AWOL. Maybe she's picking up a special Christmas gift . . .'

'Maybe.' Joanie puts a bright smile on her face and starts pointing people out to the children. 'Look! It's Mrs Young from your school! Look, that's Solomon Dash who went to school with me. There's Tash dancing like a robot to eighties classics!'

'Can we go and dance with her?' asks Patti.

'I don't see why not. If she doesn't mind.'

Wendy looks over to see Tash furiously waving the children over. Before long all three of them are being robots, and Rocky's joined in too, the four linking hands and turning round in circles, laughing as Shakin' Stevens comes on, doing some strange actions that Wendy can only imagine is them pretending to be snowflakes. She admires their confidence. When she was a girl, she stood nervously at the side, waiting for permission. Len's love of dancing was something he passed to her. Before then, she'd been quite the wallflower.

When Sue comes back, she's full of apologies. 'Sorry. It's so busy! And with the police. And sorry about the mess. I'm trying to keep it pristine in here today. Special, you know.' She artfully clears the table in a few movements and rearranges the decorative candle holder in the centre. Holly berries, sprigs of spruce, golden pinecones entwined around a red candle.

'Please don't apologise,' says Wendy. 'You know, I've just realised I haven't been in here in over five years.' This fact swamps her. She remembers when the Winters' took on the pub, both their boys little, one still in nappies. She remembers them standing out the front having their photo taken for the local newspaper. It was big news then. The Mariner had been run by the same family for twenty years beforehand. People were suspicious of Sue and Larry. But, in time, that changes. Things do. People get used to it.

Wendy hears his voice before she sees him. Loud, laughing, with not a care in the world. She shuffles across the bench to face inwards, so she can see his expression when he sees her there. How good an actor is he? *Let's see, shall we,* thinks Wendy. *Let's see.* He has his back to them and hasn't noticed that she's there. There's time for that. She doesn't need to be there long, just long enough for him to wonder what she'll do next. To *worry* him.

She closes her eyes and think of Len, back when they first started spending time together. It's easy to remember how she felt, when they first went out for the afternoon on their bikes. There was sky like the end of the summer pears, streaked green and red, and the day was turning to charcoal at the tips. The sun was a stamp of approval, low, gold with rewards. Wendy stood next to Len as they both watched a plump bird in the reeds with its ridiculous legs, a neck like a brachiosaurus, feathers a shamble of knotted stalks.

'It's a butterbump,' said Len. 'A sign of good luck. They're rare.'

'Who calls a bird a butterbump?' Wendy laughed.

'It's as good a name as any,' Len was smiling. 'Some folk call them bitterns. But I think butterbump suits them better.'

'So do I.'

'Let's rename everything!' said Len, taking both her hands in his. 'To what suits it!'

'You think you know better than *God* now?' She was teasing. They'd already had the conversation that neither of them believed in God, despite church every Sunday, and their neatly bound prayer books, and their knowledge of the Psalms.

'Ha!' Len laughed. 'I think every man has his own language, inside him. Different from everybody else.'

'And woman,' said Wendy.

'Them too.' Len winked.

Wendy liked how Len stood, like he wanted to hear everything, see everything, touch everything. He moved all the time, twitched with the brilliance of everything. He made her want to jump into the sky and scoop handfuls of it around her like water and air and eiderdown. It was as if something about the way he merely existed touched a piece of her that nobody ever tells you exists. He lit something.

Mostly, they liked to kiss. Behind trees, beside the river, under old bridges, by hidden campfires in hidden places. She wanted to feel him against her all the time. She liked the smell of him, she remembers clearly. His skin. His hair. Even his breath. *Was it really so long ago?*

Their first Christmas, he presented her with the painting of Cromer pier and he asked her to marry him. How could she not fall in love with a man who unrolled a map of all the future moments she'd dreamed of before her like a patchwork stitched with promise, every second spent together a place of note, a stud throughout her life's timeline; a rivet of something solid and shiny, well-made and true. She'd said yes immediately, without hesitation. And had never regretted it. Not once.

The children come back from dancing as Sue delivers the drinks on a shiny tray.

'Now, you enjoy,' she orders. 'You all deserve a lovely Christmas.'

As Sue moves away slipping between the customers with ease, Joanie and the children talk excitedly. They are such a beautiful family, and Wendy feels a surge of good feeling towards them.

She sips at her Babycham and watches the back of the man carefully. She wants to make sure she's looking him straight in the eye when he sees her. He laughs again. Loud. Unafraid. This only makes her more determined. Ordering brightly coloured drinks in martini glasses, laughing, reaching out to put a piece of the young woman's long hair behind her ear. *All the moves*, as she and her friends would have called them at the same age. Of course, this isn't his wife. His wife is a very different sort of woman, although Wendy hadn't often interacted with her. Where is she now?

She wonders what it would be like to be this man's wife, and her heart floods with Len. He was an innocent, really. It hadn't occurred to him that this man, with his good hair and his shiny car and his briefcase full of important documents, could ever do anything that wasn't totally above board. Those things made Len trust him more, not less. Watching him now, Wendy knows she never trusted him. Not even in the beginning. She trusted Len, and that's why she never said anything.

Len. The boy she'd first loved that golden summer and who had filled her life with the sort of quiet happiness a man like this could never imagine.

Wendy is overcome, suddenly, by an aching tiredness. *I could sleep for ever*, she thinks. *But I must not.*

She wills the man she considers her enemy to turn around so she can go back to Joanie Blake's, get into her night-dress and climb under the reindeer-patterned duvet cover. Tomorrow is Christmas Day, and so much has happened today, it almost feels like it might never end.

She stares at the back of the man's head, narrowing her eyes and trying to bore right into him. He reaches up and smooths out the back of his hair, and she wonders if he can feel the anger in her, the need for justice, the fact she *sees* him, as he is, not as who he presents himself to be.

185

He turns then, quickly, as though he's heard something, almost twisting right off the stool he's leaning on.

She stares at him.

He stares back.

He raises a hand, as though to say hello. Their eyes are locked. Wendy can't hear the Christmas music, the talk, the noise of anything else. She stares at him and doesn't blink. She doesn't smile either, nor anything else. She just stares. Their eyes locked together.

John Ellis lowers his hand but doesn't look away.

Wendy doesn't look away either.

Eventually, he turns his head back to the woman he's with. She sees it then, as his face turns. His expression changes. The brightness of his fake hello drops. Only for a second. He's a good actor, and he knows how to hide his feelings. But Wendy sees it. A brief but very real moment of 'What's going on . . .?' It's a look of fear.

He doesn't come over, doesn't turn back around to look at her, and carries on as though nothing's happened. Anybody else watching would think he's having a perfectly lovely time. But Wendy sees a difference in him, very subtle. He's slightly hunched over. The worry travels through his body and down to his smartly shoed feet. *Right*, she thinks. *Now it's time.*

'Could you get that DC Crane to come over here and talk to me,' she says, turning to Joanie. 'There's something I want to tell her.'

'Of course,' says Joanie, looking concerned. 'Is everything OK?'

'More than OK. How about you get the children to have one last dance with their aunt before we go home? What I'm going to say isn't really for small ears.'

'Good plan,' says Joanie. Wendy watches the mother lead her two children onto the dance floor where they link arms with Tash and start doing a rather wobbly version of the can-can.

DC Crane and Joanie sit down at the table together and Wendy waits to make sure John Ellis has seen them sitting together. She sees a creep of red along his neck. Good.

'You are one amazing woman,' says DC Crane, smiling. 'Don't take this the wrong way, but you're the last person I thought I'd see out here this evening.'

'I wanted to tell you something,' says Wendy, brushing aside her compliment. 'About how me and Len got into the state we did. It wasn't because we're not good with money. We've been careful with money our whole lives.'

'I wouldn't judge you if you hadn't,' smiles DC Crane.

'I'm sure. But the thing is we were careful because we wanted to move to the sea. Before we died. We were careful so we could do that.'

'I love the sea myself. I get that,' says DC Crane. 'Nothing quite like it.'

'But . . .' Wendy pauses, taking time to choose the words for what comes next. It's crucial she tells it right.

DC Crane and Joanie lean forward at the same time.

'Someone came into our lives who tricked us into releasing equity from the house directly to them. I wasn't sure at first. I thought maybe the money was still out there somewhere. But it's not. He tricked Len into passing over money directly and that's why we ended up living in poverty.' She says the words quickly before she changes her mind.

'What arsehole did that?' Joanie looks genuinely shocked. 'I . . . can't believe people do stuff like that. It's evil.'

'That's the word I would use,' says DC Crane. 'Who was it, do you know?'

'I do know,' says Wendy calmly. 'It was John Ellis. And I'm afraid he's going to do something to stop me from telling anyone about it. But it was him. And I'm telling you now, so I don't have to think about what to do about it.'

Joanie pushes her chair back from the table. 'Why, that absolute monster,' she says. 'I'll give him a piece of my mind.'

'Sit down, Joanie, please,' says DC Crane. 'I believe you, Wendy, and we're going to investigate and make sure we do everything to support you. But I need to deal with this in a way that means chances of prosecution are high. I need to talk to some people. We'll make sure you're safe.'

'Thank you,' says Wendy as DC Crane moves away across the pub, with her mobile phone in her hand, gesturing to DC Ado who was in conversation with Sue Winters and two uniformed officers. Wendy is trembling now, not quite believing she managed to get the words out.

There we go, Len, she thinks. *I should have sorted this out sooner, then you'd be here with me. But, it's done now. Merry Christmas, John Ellis. I hope you like your gift. I've got plenty more of those for you, as it happens. I'm not going to let you kill both of us.*

She feels tears in her eyes and is suddenly very tired.

'I'd like to go home now,' says Wendy to Joanie. 'Isn't it about time those two put their stockings out and got into bed?'

'Kids. Stockings!' calls out Joanie. 'I cannot believe that slimy bastard,' she says to Wendy quietly. 'How much of his money comes from stuff like that?'

'I dread to think,' says Wendy, but in reality it's the first time she hasn't dreaded to think in a long time.

Tash brings the two excited children over to the table.

'Ready to hang out your stockings, you beautiful loves?' says Joanie.

'Yes!' The two children head towards the door without being asked a second time. 'Will you help us put out the mince pie and the sherry Mrs Finch?'

'Of course,' says Wendy. 'But please do call me Wendy.' She feels so tired, like she could sleep for a very long time.

'And the carrot for Rudolph. Although, Mum,' Patti turns to Joanie, 'can we put out nine carrots?'

'Nine carrots? Um. I'm not even sure we've got nine spare carrots. Most of them are sitting cut up in a pan.'

'We'll need nine carrots. It's not fair that only Rudolph gets a carrot. Santa has eight other reindeer. I wonder how many treats get left out for them?'

'We'll have a look and see what we've got. I wonder if they like sprouts . . .'

'Can we look up what they eat? When we get in? Before we clean our teeth?'

'Yes, of course. Come on then! It's Christmas Eve! What time will you be back, Tash?'

'Do you mind when?'

'No,' says Joanie, smiling. 'As long as you're safe.'

'I'd like to stay and dance till the end.'

Wendy sees the grin on the girl's face and remembers the feeling perfectly. The start of love when the flame's first lit.

'Have a lovely, lovely time,' says Joanie, squeezing her sister on the arm. 'You deserve it. I'm so proud of you.'

'And I'm proud of you too.'

Tash skips back to the disco and Joanie smiles at the others.

The four of them move carefully through the crowd of people to get to the door. Wendy uses the stick and feels an ache at the base of her spine. She also feels elated. Like she's taken back a power she never meant to give away. She looks over her shoulder at John Ellis one last time. He's staring back at her, but she doesn't blink and doesn't turn away immediately. Instead she smiles at him. And nods. Then she turns away and doesn't look back.

'Will you do it with us, *Wendy*?' Dylan asks, reaching out and taking her free hand. 'Will you set out the food and drink for Santa and the reindeer with us?'

'Yes of course,' says Wendy, the warmth from the little boy's hand in hers spreading throughout her. 'I'd like that very much.'

Just as the four of them go to leave the pub, Frank Blake appears in the doorway.

'Joanie. Thank God. Have you seen Jen?'

'No,' says Joanie, looking panicked. 'Why?'

'Because the kids are still at her mum's and she hasn't come home. She's gone missing! When I saw the sirens, I thought . . .' He slumps forward and Wendy can see he's been crying.

'You all right, buddy?' the leer of Euan Barratt staggers across their path. He reaches out to put his hand on Frank's shoulder as Joanie pulls the children to her, as far away from him as possible.

'I reckon we can conjure up nine items worthy of Santa's reindeer,' she says enthusiastically to the children. Wendy admires how the younger woman calmly takes them out of the situation.

'I'm fine,' says Frank. 'Would you mind? We're having a private conversation. I need to get back to Jen.'

'Oh, that's funny,' says Euan, very obviously enjoying his moment of glory. 'Because I saw her speeding off in that Irma's Ka half an hour ago. They looked very cosy, I can tell you. Holding hands they were . . . tried to tell you earlier, Joanie, but you didn't want to listen. I've seen your missus standing outside Number 118 staring

190

through the window plenty of times. Proper obsessed, she is. Maybe they've eloped for Christmas.' He laughs then, a cruel laugh. A drunken laugh, and then staggers off in the direction of the bar, leaving them all staring after him.

'That can't be right . . .' says Joanie. 'Can it, Dad?'

'Of course not,' says Frank. 'How could it?' But neither of them look very convinced, and the conversation as they walk over to Victory House is just Wendy, Patti and Dylan talking about Santa and carrots and reindeer.

7.30 p.m.

Christmas Eve

Irma Woźniak

The A11

Irma has never felt so angry.

She crunches the gears on her Ford Ka, a fury at Sue, and at Tim especially, that she had managed to hold inside her for a long time. This evening was supposed to be the opening of the door to the mystery *and* she had been excited about picking up Joanie's gift. She'd been looking forward to it, had spent time and care choosing it in a way she'd never really taken care over a gift before. Well, not before – or since – Klara.

'How dare she accuse me of being responsible for the robberies. Me!' Irma mutters as she drives out along Earlham Road and joins the A11 towards Elveden. It's not like she's ever done anything to make Sue doubt her. It was just Tim. Constantly sowing little seeds of doubt in his mum's mind. And, of course he did. It didn't suit him to have Irma around. Even at the time, back then, his biggest concern was what his mum would think. Tim must have said something. It would be just like him to twist something she'd said or done to make her look guilty, or worse.

When she'd taken the job at The Mariner, she had known Sue and Larry were Tim's parents, but she needed the money and just had to hope he wouldn't be around most of the time. The first time she'd seen him, popping in for some home-cooked food, still in his running shoes, she'd set solid, fixed in the past.

He hadn't recognised her at first. She had changed a lot since she was fifteen, and Tim had never had a big imagination. But then he'd realised and ever since he had been doing whatever he could to make his parents doubt her. So much of her teen years she'd blocked out of her memory, through trial and error technique. Through necessity.

She puts the radio on and it's 'Driving Home for Christmas'. She's doing the opposite. Driving *away* from home, for a reason she's not even sure is the right one, yet. She turns to the passenger beside her.

'I'm sorry for the shouting. I'm not really a madwoman. Well. I am. But my intentions are good.'

Jen Mullany seems calm when she speaks. She's sitting in the passenger seat with her hands in her lap, and her navy tailored jacket neatly in place. 'It was my idea to come, Irma,' she says softly. 'And it would be odd if you weren't feeling frantic. Don't worry about your job now. Let's see if this woman can help you learn more about what happened to Klara.'

'I'm sorry I was sort of stalking you,' says Irma. Embarrassed, even though she'd been proved right. Miss Bray, or Jen Mullany as she was now, had been a woman she could trust. Even after all these years.

'It's not a problem,' says Jen, smiling. 'Just don't do it again.'

The A11 is a mystery of a road. It never takes the same amount of time to get to the same place twice. Irma's purposefully avoided driving this way since she learned to drive. It was almost a case of if she never went there, it never existed.

It takes her twenty-five minutes. The journey is unrecognisable from that last and only time, when she sat in the passenger seat and watched dark snow flick upon the window like ink from a pen. She had felt Christmassy then. Excited, because if the baby came on time, it would be her first Christmas with a baby of her own. It was mid-December. It made her think of the song.

Snow had fallen, snow on snow,
Snow on snow,
In the bleak midwinter,
Long ago.

With Google Maps on her phone, she follows the blue line and arrow into the little row of houses, where she parks on the gravel path. The row of dark trees are like giants with open mouths, the shadows nodding in the darkness.

'We're here,' she says quietly.

'It looks like the place,' replies Jen. 'Don't worry. I did ring beforehand. The people here know we're coming. I can't believe they sent you here to have a baby. It seems . . .' she trails off.

Irma imagines she's seen a lot of stuff in her time in her work. How does someone live with all that stuff inside their head?

'But what are the chances they are the same people?' wonders Irma.

'We won't know until we talk to them properly, will we?' says Jen calmly.

Irma locks the car behind her and walking away from the building towards the stream with Jen following behind her, she remembers, watching rain fall into the water,

194

making small ripples like complacent shrugs towards the deep black of whatever was out there. It made her want to be near the sea, to watch sprays of foam, pops of froth and whole worlds that would never meet the land, never be known, never been thought of, nor understood.

Irma kicks off her boots and stands in her bare feet with that childlike and vaguely hopeful idea people have; that by standing in water, wet-footed, trousers rolled up, all would suddenly be forgiven, all would make sense. That clarity is just a question of the right vista and location.

A baptism.

If only.

Irma dips one bare foot into the icy water, thinking of all the times she'd made choices that confirmed she was the worst person in the world. For so many years, she'd unravelled all the things she'd hated about herself, the lengths and coils that made her wonder if she was simply bad, irredeemably broken, a fault in the womb, and she presented them to the world like a dog begging for kind treatment. Dropping the worst of her at its feet and waiting for the world to pet her. Or kick her in the guts.

Jen coughs, just a little.

'Sorry. I'm being weird.'

'It's not that,' says Jen. 'I just didn't expect to be here tonight. It's been an odd year.'

'It really has,' says Irma, trying to see the humour in it, but failing. She'd never returned here since Klara had been taken away, in part because she didn't know if she was allowed to go back, almost like she'd done battle with the place, huge cracks of lightning in the sky, the stream parting, her skin falling away like a fish caught and scraped, and this place, its vast face, never changing, always as it was and would be, had won.

195

Irma pulls out her phone. There's a message from Joanie from earlier that's just come through.

Just sent a text to Dad with a photo of Tash yesterday, pretending she's at home watching Love, Actually. What's wrong with me? Please remind me to let the two of them sort their own shit out. Btw. I love you xxxxx

I love you too xxxxx she types back. She really does.

Irma turns around, nods at Jen, and they both walk back towards the row of houses, up the steps and along the front. This quiet row of unassuming, pretty houses near the forest and lake was the place her mum and stepdad sent her to have the baby. To give away the baby, it turned out, although they said it was just a hospital for young mothers and that she'd be bringing Klara home. She feels content, almost. The anger at her unfair dismissal and the claustrophobia of The Mariner at Christmas somewhere out there, far away. Closed up for Christmas.

I'm not closed up for Christmas anymore, thinks Irma, which produces her first proper smile since this morning. When she'd had Joanie's kids at her table eating breakfast, chattering about Santa and stockings and *What do you want for Christmas, Irma?* she'd felt like she was a real person. An important person. Like she mattered.

Irma knows which house it is, easily. It's called The Glades now, a big white, pebble-dashed terrace, with great bay windows, ivy up the side and a gravel drive. The front garden has an unexpected, lit-up, life-size nativity scene set out, like you see in American movies. There's a sign next to an empty wooden box that says:

All herbs £1
1/2 dozen eggs £1
Cut flowers £1 a bunch

Irma knocks at the door and Jen squeezes her arm.

The man who answers wears a hand-knitted Raymond Briggs *Snowman* jumper, jeans and wellies, and is very tall. He's got an earpiece in one ear, attached to a small plastic device clipped to his belt.

'Hullo there!' he says. Friendly. 'You must be Irma and Jenny. Merry Christmas. Come in. Come in.'

Irma hesitates, before stepping inside. Is this the right thing to do? Does she want to be here? She looks up the stairs in the hallway and notices two bedroom doors. The one on the far right had been hers. She gasps then, because that door is the portal to the only place she'd ever held Klara.

Irma steps inside, with Jen close behind her and the man closes the front door and points to the door to the kitchen which is open. 'She says to go through,' says the man. 'I won't come with you. It's not my business. Lovely to meet you.'

He wanders off to the other side of the house, talking to himself and leaving Irma standing in front of the open kitchen door.

Of course, the place has been redecorated and is nothing like the vague hospital interior of Irma's memory. It's a very beautiful home, all exposed wood, patterns, textures, books, books, books, and shelves right up to the ceiling.

Irma and Jen step into the kitchen where a woman Irma recognises immediately is wearing a Christmas apron and waving a spoon in and out of a glass jar of dark mincemeat, then smoothing the mixture out into little shells of raw pastry cupped neatly in a bun tin.

'Hello,' says the woman. Then, 'Gosh, you look so different! But I'd recognise you anywhere.'

'You haven't changed a bit!' says Irma. The woman looks exactly the same. Long brown hair tied back in a ponytail, freckles, even the way she holds the spoon hits Irma with the immediacy of the past. Fiona Long. The nurse who'd helped her with Klara after she was born. The woman who'd shown her great kindness.

'Tea?' Fiona asks.

'Yes please.'

'Do take a seat both of you,' she says, gesturing to the wooden benches that follow the line of the table. 'I'm so glad you got hold of me. I was so shocked. You were one of the happy stories, I told myself. I felt relieved when I thought they'd let you keep the baby,' says Fiona, flicking on the kettle. 'I thought you were a natural.' She smiles at Irma.

'A natural?' Irma speaks slowly.

'A natural *mum*,' Fiona smiles. 'It was obvious you adored her.'

An entire unlived life comes at Irma like a wave. She can see it. Her thirteen-year-old daughter and a twenty-eight-year-old her, a whole life of stories, memories, moments. Photographs in album after album. Her first day at school. Her first lost tooth. Her first favourite thing, her first word, her twenty-thousandth word. All the words and all the touches, the hugs, the holding hands across roads, the little steps towards autonomy, all the smiles and sometimes the tears, but all the kindness, all the kindness, Irma knows – has known throughout her entire self since the moment Klara was taken away – she could have given her. A mother to her daughter.

Fiona sets out the tea things, and sits down so the two women are next to each other, opposite her. Irma appreciates Jen being there, quietly, to support her.

'How did you end up living here?' Irma can't believe the good fortune of finding out Fiona is still at the same place. Incongruous. Yet here she is.

'It's silly really,' says Fiona. 'Although seeing you at my table, like this, makes me know it wasn't silly. Not silly at all. I always felt . . . guilty. That my nursing work went in such a . . . *wrong* direction back then. I wanted to help and it didn't always feel like helping . . . When Mark and I married, and we saw this place for sale . . . I thought, and I know this sounds ridiculous, I do, but I thought I could be a sort of gatekeeper to the past. That I could be here. In case any of you came back.'

'Really?' says Irma.

'Yes. Doesn't it sound so self-important?' Fiona laughs. 'What could I really do? I didn't know the half of it. What can I tell you? What can I do? Nothing when it comes down to it.'

'Yes, but imagine,' says Irma calmly. 'Imagine how I'd be feeling if Jen hadn't found out you were here.'

Irma's past and present horror at the loss of Klara is split through with a clear thought: *there is kindness in the world. This woman is kind. Jen is kind. Joanie is kind. Patti and Dylan are kind.* All around the world, right now, there are awful things happening, terrors, fears, indescribable pains. And yet, somehow, people continue, and give each other hope, and find ways to be kind and make a difference. This thought makes Irma's eyes hot with tears. All those years she'd tried to put up walls to protect herself, kindness found a way in anyway.

'We were told we were helping young women who didn't want abortions but couldn't look after the children. The thing I noticed most in time was that the girls who came had no independent means, no money of their own, no support. And the people – often kind, lovely people in truth – who adopted their babies *did* have those things. That was the difference. It didn't seem right to me. It doesn't seem right to me.'

Irma had only ever thought of this happening to her. The idea of others is mind-boggling. 'Do you think any of the girls wanted to give their children away?' she asks.

'I've thought about this,' says Fiona. 'When I was young, starting out, I didn't know about life much. I think some of them did want to give them away. Of course, some did. But nearly all of those ones, the minority of girls who came here, they'd have had abortions if their families had allowed it, not go through childbirth and all the rest, you know? I think they would have kept them. No doubt. Lots of them. I saw plenty. It made me feel . . .' She shakes her head. 'I was told I was doing the right thing. It was supported in law . . . and there are all these people who can't have children. Hard-working people, who deserve children . . . and that's it, you see. It came down to some idea that we get to choose who deserves to have children and who doesn't. Those girls, the ones who wanted to keep them, the only reason they couldn't is that there would be nowhere for them to go. Society wasn't going to look after them; often, their families wouldn't, because of all the shame. So, their bodies, still full of hormones and memory, were expected to fall back into old lives as though nothing had happened. It was worse in the decades before you, far worse, but . . . It was a very dark time. I heard a lot of young women cry and cry and cry. It happened far less often by the time you came. But I don't think I'll ever make my peace with it.'

Irma has never thought of herself as part of a group of women before. She's always felt slightly outside the clusters that naturally gravitate to each other, and has never quite been an easy fit. But there are thousands of women like her, of all ages, throughout history, who've been forced or coerced into giving their babies away.

I was made to feel like I'd done a terrible thing, she thinks. *But it was* them. *They were doing terrible things.*

'And then,' continues Fiona, softly. 'And then, something worse than the crying was when they stopped crying. Something would happen, and they'd stop. A shield would come down over their faces and they'd find whatever it was inside, that hard, cold, hidden place they needed to reach in order to continue. I've thought about that, often. Who they became afterwards.'

'My whole life I've hated myself because I wasn't good enough to be her mum.'

Fiona looks Irma directly in the eye. 'You, Irma, were plenty good enough. Most women are, with the right support, the right help, with the right kindness. If that's what they want. That's what I believe now. I've seen it with my own eyes.'

'Even someone like me?'

'What on earth do you mean? There's nothing wrong with you that some consistency, some tender loving care and some understanding wouldn't have fixed.'

Irma doesn't know what to say to this. In a few sentences this woman from her past has changed everything. What had Irma thought, that the women who worked there thought she and the other girls were monsters? Perhaps so. *There's nothing wrong with you.* She tries to really listen to the words, to feel them working inside her.

'It's never too late to find her, you know,' adds Fiona.

'I'd help you,' adds Jen, reaching out and putting a hand over Irma's. 'I'll help you find her. There are registers you can put yourself on that would show her you are happy to be contacted if she goes looking for you. I looked it up after you came this afternoon.'

At those words, Irma leans forward, puts her head in her hands and cries, unabandoned, fully, yet with a sense of safety too, for what feels like for ever. It seems such a simple idea, one she's had hidden away in her own head for years, as though it wasn't within her power to even hope for it. But now it's like she's been given *permission* to look. That she's not silly for holding onto all these feelings.

Klara, I'm going to look for you. She says it to the big sky, and to the lake, and to her daughter, who could be out there somewhere, waiting.

8.15 p.m.

Christmas Eve

Craig Mullany

118 Newbury Street

The sky is Parma Violets.

Upstairs, the boys are asleep after stockings were hung, excited babble about listening out for sleigh bells, the usual *I'm not going to fall asleep this year, am I?* then that lovely sound of the catch of their breath as they fall asleep. Mouths open, their freshly brushed teeth puffing out long breaths of minty air. The gurgle of life. Getting to put them to bed was his own kind of Christmas miracle.

He moves through the house to the back door, through the new utility room, which has been added on to his old terrace at great cost. He stands at the back door looking out across all the other long, narrow gardens that run beside theirs — Jen and Frank's, not Jen and his. Lots of them at that end of Newbury Street still have the low fences so as not to cut off other people's light, an unwritten neighbourly gesture to save on heating bills, and sunlight. There are the memories of the summer flowers, and vines and frosted-over vegetable plots, carefully tended laws, swings, trampolines, potted herbs, patios, decking, chairs, tables, damp parasols, bunting, fairy lights and, further along, a group of people in the cold dark, drinking wine, smoking, huddled laughing, enjoying the last of the day.

All these things are familiar to Craig, but he doesn't feel like he misses them. He misses something else – a life unlived. He knows these gardens. He knows some of the people, but he definitely knows the trees. He's seen them grow, since she was young and this was his parents' house when people's gardens were merely separated by wires; easy to slip in and out of, to go and see your friends without ever leaving your front door. He had seen the flourishing of magnolia and roses. The withered and reignited clematis, hidden now through winter, while the spruce and the conifer and the artificial lights dominate the darkness. Even though he can't see the beans that sometimes forgot to turn from red petals to pods, he knows they're there. He'd heard the arguments. He'd seen various children grow. They were all part of the same thing. A lot can happen in fifteen years.

And . . .

So much in his life has changed. He'd never have predicted Jen would live in his childhood home with another man and their children. Life. A mystery from beginning to end.

He looks up at the children's bedroom window. The soft light from their green and blue nightlights escapes gently through the edges of the curtain. He can still, in his dreams sometimes, hear the beep of Allie's medical equipment, the whirr of the syringe driver, even now she isn't there. He'd sat with his best friend's wife for hours, holding her hand, talking of all she had to look forward to. Had he really believed she'd die?

No.

Yes.

Maybe.

He isn't yet at the point where he can talk freely about Allie, even though there was often so much he'd like to say. *There needs to be a better language of loss*, he thinks. *We need to use it before we lose things. Find the shape of the words, so we can describe it when it comes. We need to be able to say, 'This person matters to me, and so does this sky and so does this shop window and so does the colour of that front door that I've passed on my way to work every morning for the past nine years.' Maybe if we talked about things and people that really matter, and explained why they mattered at the time, without shame, there wouldn't be this nasty seep towards the sort of nostalgia that excludes people. If people could say, 'I want things to stay the same because I have lost people that matter to me, because I feel things deeply, because I'm looking for a way to make sense of all I've lost.'*

Hold on Craig, he laughs at himself. *Slow down.*

Ever since the moment the front door had opened earlier and Craig had seen Frank standing there, shrunken, vulnerable, he's felt different somehow.

'Thank you for coming. The boys are home and would like you to put them to bed.'

He has the strange, under-the-skin feeling of knowing it is time to tell Frank and Jen the truth, and that he can't put it off anymore.

He has an image at the forefront of his mind. A swimming pool. An *empty* swimming pool at night; a public one, with everywhere shut up, locked, and low lights in the ceiling. No splashing. No swimming. No floating plasters. No people. Just a clear stretch of water and the smell of chlorine, an echo of other people's fun. The promise of it too, but him, alone, standing in a big empty space, where nothing is happening, nothing will happen. Where he stands at the side waiting to know what to do.

Craig Mullany had always known what to do. This new feeling scares him.

On the patio Frank has set out snacks, two wine glasses and a bottle of Rioja. One Craig is fond of.

'Thank you.'

'No problem.'

'Thank you for letting me put the boys to bed.'

Frank shakes his head then as he pours wine into both glasses. 'You shouldn't need to thank me for letting you do anything. They're your sons.'

'Well, thank you anyway,' says Craig. It's hard to believe, from this conversation, that the two men used to be best friends.

Even though it's bitterly cold, they sit on the wrought-iron chairs, looking out along the length of lawn to the trellis with its curled leaves; to the pond a few gardens along, in John and Cynthia Ellis's garden. Their fountain backcombs the water into air and the statue of Asclepius reaches over, catching droplets in his stone cup. John had loudly told Craig at The Stop Shop that he'd had it commissioned from a sculptor in Holt. The statue had come in a crate with Epione, who lived much further down the garden, long coils of stone hair wrapped around her body, right down to her feet. Everything John Ellis does is the wrong side of ostentatious, but he somehow makes it seem like it's perfectly humble. Clever, really.

'Who'd have thought we'd be doing this?' says Craig, eventually.

'I know. It's good,' says Frank. 'Even Steve and Natalie said when they dropped the boys back that they think you're a great dad.'

'They did?' This surprises Craig as he'd always thought Jen's mum and dad hadn't really liked him.

'They did.'

'Do you think Jen will mind me being here?'

'I don't know,' says Frank plainly. 'Her text said she would be late home because she was helping someone. There was no detail. I'm not a jealous man, so I accept that. I'm also helping someone. I'm helping a man put his kids to bed on Christmas Eve.'

'Ha. Yes I suppose.'

'I've missed you,' says Frank. 'Ridiculous but true.'

'I've missed you too.' It's true. Craig hasn't only lost Jen, he's lost his best friend. And he's lost Allie, which seemed worst of all. He takes a big breath, thinks of all those thoughts about having words for things that matter, and for loss, and decides to say exactly how he is feeling. 'I miss Allie,' he says, the words coming out of him like air from a hot-air balloon.

'So do I. So much. I hadn't realised how much I talked to her on a daily basis. She was just always there. I don't say all those words now. They stay inside me. Bubbling.' Frank sighs and takes a sip of wine. 'I am happy, in so many ways. But.'

'Everything was different when she'd gone,' agrees Craig, allowing himself to say what he really should have said months ago. 'It was like the world was painted in different colours or something. I think we all think we know how we'll feel or what we'll do in certain situations. Then they happen, and we're completely different people than we thought we were.'

'That's true enough,' says Frank.

He'd thought of this, a lot, recently. He thought he knew, fervently and outspokenly at times, what he believed about

207

things, about what he'd do in certain situations. And then something happened, like Allie becoming too ill to talk, to interact, and it's as though he'd had another personality entirely. A body hiding inside the one that walks about and talks, and cuts the grass, and does the laundry. He'd realised he knows nothing, and all those firmly held opinions and beliefs were a way of holding himself together, making himself a cohesive person in the face of the disquiet, all the fear, all the endless ticks of all the endless clocks that will continue long after your preferences, your ideas and your projections have disintegrated into nothing. It's too much. Death. You have to do something to feel alive afterwards, otherwise you'd shed all your skin and there'd be nothing left.

The water rises from the Ellis's fountain with an awful chugging sound. Craig puts both hands around the wine glass like he's holding a cup coffee. The sky is never totally black in the city, pockets of light reflected from the ground up. He wants to say so many things but doesn't know where to start.

Frank beats him to it.

'I'm sorry I hurt you,' he says, sipping his wine. 'I know I've said it before, but I wanted to say it to you like this. What I did was, while technically not wrong – we never cheated on you, or anything like that – it hurt you anyway. And I'm sorry.'

'It's OK,' says Craig. He's shaking, like he's nervous and his knee is jiggling up and down so that the wine in his glass nearly sloshes over the top and onto his jeans.

'It's not OK. You were married. You had children. I didn't stop to think.'

'Death makes everybody act differently,' he says.

'I *am* sorry though.'

'I know, but I don't want you to be. That's what I've been trying to say to you. For a long time.'

'I can't help it.'

'Do you remember,' Craig says slowly, 'when the four of us went on that boat trip, on the Broads, and we were all laughing so much? Allie was beating everyone at Scrabble, as usual.'

'Ha,' laughs Frank 'Yes. She was unbeatable.'

'Always.' Craig pauses. It's now or never. *Don't chicken out now. Say it.* 'Something happened that night, that I've never told you about. I should have told you, but I couldn't quite . . . there was never the right time. And then Jen left me. Cruelly.' He says it in a joking voice, to try and lighten the tone.

'What happened?' Franks asks.

'It was innocent enough,' Craig says. 'But . . .'

'What was it?' Frank's losing his patience, Craig can hear it in his tone.

'If I don't say this, I might never say it,' Craig starts, taking a deep breath. 'And as time goes on, it's less likely I'll say it.' He's mumbling and stumbling over his words, but he can't stop now. 'I had feelings for Allie, and I told her. And then she got sick,' he says, the words tumbling out of him like shaken up Scrabble letters from the bag. He's so surprised he's actually said them that he puts his hand up over his mouth and holds it there, feeling his breath on his fingers.

Frank stares at him with his mouth open, like a person in a comic book waiting for the speech bubble to be filled with words.

'I had feelings for Allie,' Craig repeats. 'And I haven't been able to talk to anybody about it and it's making me sick. Not you being with Jen. Not the divorce. Not even not being with the boys. None of that. My feelings for Allie, and how I can't talk about her all the time like I want to, how she's gone and I see her everywhere. On the street, in doorways, carrying a bloody trifle out of Victory House.'

Frank still stares at him with his mouth open.

'And I feel guilty every time someone says how awful it is for me. How badly you've treated me. I try to stand up for you, but people just think I'm being nice and are even more against you.'

'Yes,' says Frank, finally. 'I know.' His hands are shaking now.

'The worst bit,' says Craig, holding the wine glass to his lips, 'is that, just before she got that diagnosis . . .' He pauses, looks at the floor and up at Frank. He's never seen him like this, in all the years he's known him. 'We went into the city for the day. We had a meal. We had some wine. We sat by the river at The Adam and Eve, talking, you know, about a possible future. I've never felt so nervous about anything in my life.' He shakes his head.

'And what did she say?' asks Frank. 'Was she nice to you about it? Knowing Allie, she was. Did she tell you to go home and sleep it off?'

Craig looks guilty. 'No,' he says simply.

'*What did she say, Craig?*'

'She said she felt the same and had for a while.'

'What?' Frank's face falls.

'She said she felt the same and had for a while, and then we sat looking at each other until one of us, I can't remember who, said, "So what are we going to do about it?"'

It's only then Craig realises the light from the house has shifted, and that the two of them are in shadow. He turns round to see the silhouette of Jen in the doorway. She's breathing loudly and slowly and rubbing her eyes with the back of one of her hands.

Frank jumps up and rushes over to her, lacing his arms around her. She lets her arms hang limp at her sides.

'I've been standing here for the past ten minutes and . . .' her voice is low. Almost a growl. 'And, what the *actual fuck* did you just say about Allie?' Jen releases herself from Frank's arms and walks towards the table jaw set, fists still clenched. Craig's never seen her so angry. Her whole body is almost pulsating with rage. 'And what *did* you do about it, *Craig*?'

Craig looks at Frank, who seems to crumple slightly, seems to lose the fight in him, then he sits back down in the chair and starts to cry.

8.55 p.m.

Christmas Eve

Joanie Blake

Flat 5, Victory House

Joanie listens to the children trying to explain to Mrs Finch how Father Christmas gets into the flats when there are no chimneys and feels the space where her mum's body and words and laughter used to be. The flat was usually so full of her on Christmas Eve. Her food and preparations, her little tricks for making each and every one of them feel special. Even last year, when she was ill, and knew it, she'd done stockings for everybody, grown-ups included, made wreaths for the Christmas fete at Patti and Dylan's school, made food parcels she'd got Frank to deliver to those who needed them, and then seemed to lie down for a long time to recover.

Joanie wants to live up to her mum, but it seems impossible. Still, the children are laughing, and are happy. People always say they are. She, and their dad – now happily married and living in Nottingham, but a regular part of their lives – must be doing something right. But, right now, Joanie feels exhausted, and like maybe she's doing everything wrong, especially when it comes to Irma, which is confusing as if anyone had asked her earlier, she'd have said without hesitation that her relationship with Irma couldn't have been going any better.

Why has Irma gone off with Jen Mullany? It makes no sense.

Joanie has never been the jealous type, more an if-you-love-them-then-set-them-free kind of person. She taps out a message.

Whatever's going on with you, I'm here for you. You don't owe me anything. I'll always be here for you xxx

She doesn't want it to be over. Irma features so strongly in her idea of a future, it's sometimes like it's happened already. But . . .

She looks at the turkey, cooling on the side, and shakes her head. Her mum always cooked the turkey the night before, so there'd be room in the small oven for all the trimmings on the big day. *'You never know the difference when you've poured the gravy over it,'* she'd say, always smiling. *'And you can cut it really thin, rather than have it fall off in chunks. Plus, you can't fit all the other stuff in the oven. That's the main thing. Unless you don't fancy pigs in blankets . . .?'*

Joanie can see her, now. *Feel* her there in the flat. Why does that short bit of time, when she was in pain and disintegrating, take up so much of the memory. Will it change, in time? Will her mum go back to being the woman she was, big, bright, shy at times, but full of life?

'Right,' she says, distracting herself. 'That was a fun trip out, but now it's time for PJs and clean teeth and bed.' She looks at the faces of her two children and feels her heart soar. *How lucky I am, to be their mum,* she thinks. *How lucky I am that Mum met them. How beautiful they are.* She resists the temptation to hold onto them, tightly, and never let go.

'Yes!' says Dylan. 'Are we three still sleeping in the living room?'

'We could make beds on the floor. With our duvets and cushions from the sofa,' adds Patti.

'Of course,' says Joanie. She loves it when they camp out in the living room. Their faces look the same as they did as babies when they sleep. Their easy breathing and warm breath, and she gets to lie with them and take it all in. Her own pot of happiness there.

'Right, PJs on first, then teeth. Go, go, go!'

The children run off to their bedrooms to get their new Christmas pyjamas. Angels for Dylan and snowmen for Patti, just as they'd chosen. Joanie cleans up on the side and puts a foil helmet over the turkey.

'I'm sure it will taste lovely,' says Mrs Finch, kindly.

'Did *you* used to do the veg the night before, when you cooked Christmas dinner?' Joanie asks, turning to look at her guest, who this morning was a stranger and now. Well. The amount of admiration and respect Joanie has for Wendy Finch is indescribable. What an amazing woman she really is.

'Yes. Always peeled and sitting in cold water on top of the hob. Although, I never did a big dinner for lots of people. Not after mine and Len's parents passed away. It was often just Len and I. And he helped me peel the veg.' She laughed. 'Or at least tried to.'

'I've always been a crap cook. Honestly. I'm going to do it differently next year. This year it seemed important, but I'll not do all this again.' Joanie gestures to the piles of food preparation that threaten to take over the kitchen. 'And, by the way, that was impressive you know, going to the pub like that.'

Mrs Finch shakes her head. 'Not really. I just had the feeling that I should. So I did.'

'Are you glad you went? Are you glad you talked to DC Crane?' asks Joanie.

'Yes I am. Yes . . .' She pauses and lets out a long breath. 'I really am.'

'I'm sorry for all you've gone through.' It doesn't sound enough, all things considered. But Mrs Finch smiles.

'And I you. The kids seemed happy at the pub.'

'Oh, they love any opportunity to pretend they're little adults,' smiles Joanie. 'And to listen in on adult conversation.'

'Ha! I think I was the same when I was young. People didn't say much in front of children then, but, also, I spent a lot of time playing just out of sight but within ear range.'

'People don't give children enough credit.'

'That's true.'

Joanie hears the children laughing with each other and her heart swells. They're singing the Christmas song from their school Christmas play. They'd both played the part of the inside of a cracker. Their teachers had written the play with the children and there was a note on the programme saying the point was to get people thinking about what's *inside* Christmas. The show was brilliant, but the songs have stayed in her head all week: *Look inside yourself this Christmas, you may find a surprise. Make sure you're kind to others as you're tucking into mince pies.*

Ha! What lyrics! But Joanie's eyes well up. *What is it about Christmas?* she thinks. *All these feelings that we manage all year burst out like water from a badly fixed tap.* It's because of the memories. Joanie understands why some people who used to do Christmas don't do Christmas anymore. Why pick at scabs and bruises? But to her, it's one of her favourite times of year. Even when there's not much money. Even, no matter how much it hurts, with her mum not there. Her mum had taught her to love Christmas, and she'd never let that go.

'Ta-da!' Patti and Dylan knee-slide into the kitchen from the hall, both adorable in their new pyjamas. 'We are clean and ready for Christmas!' says Dylan.

Patti does a big gappy smile. 'Look. Two minutes and they're super shiny.'

'Wonderful,' says Joanie. 'Have you got your stockings?'

'Obviously!' They both hold them up towards her. Her mum had made them, when they were born, little robins in a nest stitched carefully into green and red felt with white fake-fur tips. They were older now. Some of the felt was gaping. But they'd never had a Christmas without them.

'We've already dragged our duvets into the living room,' says Patti. 'I told Tash earlier she could keep ours to herself. Just for once. Is she going to come back before we go to bed?' Joanie wonders if they'll ever live somewhere the girls can have separate bedrooms and where she wouldn't have to sleep on a futon in the living room. Would she want to leave here which had so many memories? She isn't sure.

'You won't see her before bed, no,' says Joanie. 'I've told her she should do exactly what she'd like for Christmas Eve. But she'll be here when you get up. Now let's get you to bed.'

'It's more fun in the living room!'

'Can we have a story?'

'I don't see why not. Which one?'

'*The Nutcracker*!' says Patti. 'Grami's copy. Like always.'

'Of course,' says Joanie, smiling. 'It's already on the side ready, see.'

'Can Mrs Finch read it to us?' says Dylan, and Patti nods enthusiastically. Joanie smiles at how much of a shine they've taken to her.

216

'Only if Mrs Finch wants to,' says Joanie. She'd never read them *The Nutcracker* herself, it was always something her mum did with them. She's touched they want their guest to read it, but turns to Mrs Finch. 'Please don't feel you have to.'

'*The Nutcracker*!' says Mrs Finch, grinning. 'I love *The Nutcracker*. That evil mouse king. Have you ever seen the ballet? I did once, many years ago. Oh, you must. I love the dancing toys!'

'Is that a yes?' says Dylan, nodding.

'It's a yes. Come on then. Lead the way.'

'Thank you,' says Joanie. She feels a sort of relief and gratitude that sweeps right through her. 'You've been so wonderful today.'

'And so have you. I wasn't expecting to have such a nice time.'

'You'll come in after the story's finished, Mum, won't you? To kiss us and everything before we fall asleep?' Patti says, quickly.

'To give us a huggle?' adds Dylan.

'Of course I will. That's the best part of the day.'

'Yay!' The children skip off to the living room, and Mrs Finch follows after. When they've gone, Joanie sits down at the kitchen table and breathes slowly. They've nearly done it. Nearly got through their first Christmas Eve without Allie. Now there's only Christmas Day and Boxing Day and that strange week between Christmas and New Year where everything feels like you're looking at it in a fairground mirror. Then . . . all of the days. *For the rest of my life, I'll never see you again.* It seems too awful to be true. How can people just end? How can her mum just be gone, when the evidence of who she was, and the effect she had, is all around them, all the time?

Joanie is startled, then, by a knock at the door and when she goes to open it, there stands Irma with her perfect timing, a bunch of flowers and an overnight bag.

'Merry Christmas,' she says as Joanie rushes towards her. 'If it's all right with you, I thought I'd quite like to stay somewhere people love me this Christmas.'

Joanie bursts into happy tears. 'Oh, this is the best Christmas present ever!' She throws her arms around Irma and kisses her all over her face. 'Thank you, thank you, thank you! Euan Barratt told me and Dad you'd run off with Jen Mullany.'

Irma laughs. 'He couldn't be more wrong, the prat. All right, all right, let's not go over the top. Are you actually going to let me in?'

As she enters, the tabby cat comes in behind her.

'Spock!' says Joanie, leading the way. 'You should come and try the turkey. I could probably strip you off a bit, just a little piece.'

'You know very well that's not Spock, that's Hedy Lamarr,' laughs Irma, coming up behind her and putting her hands around Joanie's waist. They always play-argue about the name of the cat.

'That is most certainly *not* Hedy Lamarr,' laughs Joanie, stepping back so Irma can come into the kitchen. 'You can tell it's Spock. Look at his pointy ears.'

Joanie feels like her heart might burst. All day, she's tried to keep herself together. Cleaning at the Pattersons', asking Mrs Finch to stay, trying to bake things to make the children happy, finding a voice inside herself to shout at Euan Barratt. But now, this. Just for her.

'Don't tell me I've missed saying good night to the kids?' Irma asks.

'Nope. Mrs Finch is reading them *The Nutcracker*.'

'Wonderful!' Irma lets her head fall onto Joanie's shoulder. 'By the way,' she says softly, 'I've lost my job.'

'You what? Who dare sack you on Christmas Eve?'

'Don't worry, it's OK. I've already got a new one.'

'What?!' Joanie gets the tea things from the cupboard and gets out the pot so she can use her mum's Santa tea cosy. 'Sit down and tell me all about it before we go in the living room and kiss the kids. Want a piece of mum's Christmas Eve cake?'

'Obviously,' says Irma, and Joanie feels so happy she has to do a little skip as she cuts a slice and carries it over to the kitchen table.

10.46 p.m.

Christmas Eve

Cynthia Ellis

121 Newbury Street

The Festive Feel Good fundraiser seems a success.

Cynthia knows this because if she leans the right way out of the bedroom window, she can see people congregating outside the front of the pub around the benches, smoking, vaping, laughing. There were police there earlier, but that seems to have calmed down too. John is outside, smoking a cigar. She doesn't even need to see him to know it.

She hasn't taken her sleeping pill and doesn't intend to. How many nights has she popped one under her tongue at 8 p.m. and drifted into one of those strange dreamless sleeps which, when she wakes up, feels like she hasn't been asleep at all? How many times has she just assumed John has come home when he said he will, and been too fast asleep to notice if it's true or not? Come to think of it, why exactly did she start taking the pills in the first place? She can't remember any long periods of insomnia.

Cynthia slides the sash window down slightly, quietly, so she can hear what's happening. The voices are meshed together, happy, full of alcohol and cheer. She should be

there. She is never at these things. Always at the last-minute, John thinks of a way to make her decide not to go.

Yes, that's what it is. He makes *her* decide. So if anyone asks why she's not there, he can say it was her idea, and she would usually *think* it was her idea, but, really, it never was.

None of this is your imagination, she tells herself. You must know this by now. It's like there have always been two voices inside her, ever since they married. The one who knows what he's like, who he is, and the other one who knows what she wished he was like, who she thought she was marrying, and could not match those feelings with what she experienced on their wedding night and every day after, so just pretended none of it was even happening.

She can hear him talking, laughing, and she leans towards the open window a little further.

'You never bring your wife to these things, John,' says a woman's voice. A kind voice. She can't quite see through the net curtain who it is, but it might be Sue. 'You should!'

'Ah, come on, Sue, you should know me a bit better by now. Not all of us are lucky enough to be married to a woman like you.' His voice is dripping with charm, the sort she'd heard all their married life, and, until now, always responded to by giving him what he wants.

'Ah, come off it,' the woman laughs, but with a tone of warning. 'You've got a loyal one there.'

'Loyal yes. But you don't take a sandwich to a banquet.'

His words are like an axe to the middle of her and Cynthia slumps over like a falling tree. There's no rearranging his words to make the meaning different. There's no way she can misunderstand, like he so often says she has. *You can't take a sandwich to a banquet.* She is the sandwich and John's whole *life* is a banquet. *How did I get here?*

She is glad she didn't take her sleeping tablet. What else has she missed with her early nights? Does she even know what's in them? She'd lied to the detectives earlier about Lois Rowntree getting her her sleeping pills. It's always been John. She can't remember ever asking for them.

Cynthia feels in the pocket of the outfit she'd put on especially to go to the Festive Feel Good and finds the card she was given earlier. She looks at DC Crane's telephone number printed neatly in dark blue ink. She could call her at any time, the woman had said so herself. But what would she say? How would she even begin to have the conversation when she hasn't even had it with herself.

Cynthia doesn't want to hear any more. She leaves the window open but steps out of her bedroom and goes downstairs. In the living room, she pours herself a glass of John's favourite single malt, in his favourite glass, and she holds it to her mouth like she's taking the sacrament. When it's gone, her throat burns, but she knows what she wants to do next.

She holds the cordless phone in her hand and taps in DC Crane's number. Above her, the beautiful Christmas tree heaves with the decorations she's collected over the years. Beautiful glass and china ornaments, piped and shaped with all sorts of festive patterns and creatures, and a whole nativity, set out in bright reds, and yellows and blues. The dove at the top of the tree made of white marbled glass, with its silver beak and golden eyes and feet, held tightly around a golden branch. Every year, the ornaments matter to her when she hangs them so carefully. With each bauble, each wise man, each lamb or icicle or star, she has imagined the life she thought she'd have. The life she was promised.

He shouldn't have left me alone on Christmas Eve, she thinks angrily. *He really shouldn't have done that.*

He probably doesn't think she can do anything for herself. Well, she'll show him.

DC Crane's phone goes straight to voicemail. *Please leave a message after the tone.*

Cynthia Ellis clears her throat. It feels dry, like she hasn't had anything to drink in a long time. Like she's coming back from the desert.

'Hello, Detective Constable Crane,' she says, sounding more formal than she'd intended, as usual. 'This is Cynthia Ellis, from Number 121 Newbury Street. I would like to report something. I don't want to say what over the telephone. But I'd appreciate talking to you in person as soon as you're free. Many thanks. Cheerio for now.'

She pulls the phone away from her face and presses the button to end the call. She couldn't think of what to say when it came to it. Maybe when DC Crane calls back, she'll think of how to word it. She panics then, and realises she hasn't left the proper instructions. She looks at DC Crane's number again and taps it in. It goes straight to voicemail again, but this time she's prepared.

'Hello, DC Crane. It's me. Cynthia Ellis again. From 121 Newbury Street. When you call me back, can you not say I called you. Can you pretend it's about something you want to talk to me about? I don't want John to know I've called. I'm sorry I forgot to say that, but please know I wouldn't say that unless it was really important. Many thanks. Bye bye.'

She ends the call and her skin pricks with adrenaline. She hears 'Last Christmas' blasting out from the pub and people singing along, so loud it's like it's playing in their living room. What was she thinking, calling DC Crane? What on earth will she say?

She picks one of the marbled glass baubles from the tree and holds it between her fingers. It really is a beautifully decorated tree. Could she really give all this up and start again? She squeezes the glass too hard as she feels her heart beat fast in her chest. The glass of the bauble cracks, and as the sharp shards dig into her palm, she watches the crimson blood drip in thick drops onto the cream carpet.

It's only then, when she's still feeling brave, that she rushes to his office. She doesn't know what she's looking for. It's the act of looking that seems important. *This is my house too and I will look at anything I want.* She recognises the voice in her head, but it's one from long ago. From before she met her husband, when she thought she'd *become* someone. When she didn't doubt herself any more than the next person.

On the desk, John's tortoiseshell reading glasses are still set neatly, arms carefully tucked under. The library book he was reading, *Victorian Medicine* by Ely Butterworth in hardback, is where he left it, the spine-attached navy ribbon hanging from the closed pages. He is two thirds of the way through, and the ribbon droops like a banner at the end of a party, as though it knows nothing will be the same in the house again. His moleskin jotter still open, and the yellow 2B pencil with the rubber at the end mid crossword calculations. Words and anagrams in his exacting letters. GOTINANE. NETNAGOI. ATONING-E. ANTIGONE. BRASIL SCRIPTURE? PORCUPINE. UNDILUTED. ARAMETHEA. Cynthia has never been clever enough to do the crossword. Or, at least, that's what he'd said. She realises now, looking at his neat work, that she's never even tried.

Cynthia carefully pulls the top drawer of the filing cabinet open. She flicks through the dark green drop files, not knowing exactly what she's looking for, but knowing it's *something*. She feels an out-of-character thrill of wrongdoing. John has always made it clear that privacy is highly important to him, as is trust. Women who go trawling through their husbands' pockets and phonebooks and, these days, their emails and their text messages, have always seemed pathetic to him. To trust, even when the less good parts of you are telling you to do otherwise, is what love is, she'd thought. She'd never pried. She'd never asked him to explain.

The papers in the drop files are all contracts. She supposes for houses. A, B, C, D, E, F. Finch. There. *That's the one*, she thinks, not sure how she knows, just that she does, and pulls it out of the drawer, then slides it shut on its metal rods. She can't make sense of the figures, but one piece of paper seems to say that John Ellis Homes owns Len and Wendy Finch's house in entirety. *That doesn't make sense*, thinks Cynthia. *Why would they have given him their house?* She wants to read the file properly, so she takes it with her as she goes downstairs to the kitchen to make herself a mug of tea. Her heart is still racing at John's words, at her calling DC Crane, at the drop file in her hand. *Sandwich. Banquet.* To hear herself talked about this way, it's cracked open her life and the yolk of her is sliding about, with nothing to contain her. *I can do anything I want. And John can't stop me.*

In the kitchen, she feels calmer. It's always been her space, her own version of a study. It's the one part of the house John's never had any input, nor cared about, and for that reason it's held its own secrets, like the food for Sir Tom, or the dark, beautifully wrapped chocolate hidden in the cookery books, and the pictures she's cut, for years, from magazines, of streets and bars and cafes and beaches and cities around the world that she lies in bed and imagines herself visiting. In her imagination, she's always a much younger version of herself, wearing a swingy pale cotton dress and turquoise sandals. Her fingers are covered in gold rings. She's wearing an anklet and carries a parasol. This is her most calming and much-returned-to fantasy.

Cynthia pours fresh water from the filter jug in the fridge into the kettle, returning it to its spot inside the door shelf. Somehow she's nudged the magnets out of place. It disturbs the rhythm of the kitchen. Everything is carefully positioned, to flow and, well, feel right.

Each magnet is from a place she and John had visited on their holidays each year from the 1980s onwards, so many coastal towns and cathedral cities across the United Kingdom. How she longed to go to Venice, but John always reminded her that her sea and air and travel sickness would not allow a city on water, let alone the getting there. She's never left this country and had always thought John was so patient. How lonely he must have been, she'd always thought, travelling the world without her, for the good of the business. She'd always believed the measure of love is how much a person is willing to give up in order to be with you. She'd always believed John had given up so much for her. This makes her laugh now, a laugh she's never heard before, as she spoons two sugars into her mug, not a cup.

The kettle bubbles as she puts the magnets back into the diamond formation that looks just right. Land's End. Chichester. Bournemouth. The Isle of Wight. Canterbury. Windsor. Herne Bay. Plymouth. Durham. Liverpool. Rochester. Ely. Firvan. Margate. Weymouth. St. Ives. Salisbury. Great Yarmouth. York. Clacton-on-Sea.

She pours the water into her mug and feels better, when she thinks she hears something, like the letterbox clattering. She breathes in the steam as she walks back through to the hallway and looks at the door. Waiting for her on the mat is a postcard of the Norwich Lanes at night, at Christmas. Fairy lights and shop windows and gentle snow. She puts the mug on the telephone table and reaches down to pick it up.

How magical Norwich is, she thinks, as she looks at the shimmer of night on the cobbles. How like a city that hides under mists of history, only to be revealed to the rest of the world when the sun shines. And then she turns the postcard over and reads the writing.

I need to talk to you about your husband.

11.30 p.m.

Christmas Eve

Rocky

Tash is watching Rocky's dad as he takes the mike and shushes the pub quiet. It takes something to work the room the way his parents do. Rocky's seen them do this hundreds of times, maybe thousands over the years, and here they are again, rallying the troops, making money for good causes. For themselves too. Sometimes it feels like it all blends into one.

'Time for our last raffle prizes of the evening, for the late crowd, and, yes, I'm afraid the disco is over,' his dad says, holding up the raffle bag. 'We've got our big prize of the evening: a long weekend for two at The Gauntlet, a beautiful home from home in the North Norfolk countryside. Four-star grub. Um,' he squints at the ticket as though he can't read it. Rocky shakes his head. He's seen his dad do the 'I'm too old and past it to read the name that's written on the ticket' thing during raffles. It suits him to seem a bit confused and doddery, even though he's anything but. Punters like to tease him. It's part of how it works. Rocky sometimes wonders what his dad is like, when there's nobody watching him. Larry pulls out the ticket and calls out enthusiastically.

'Lorraine Kingdom! Congratulations, Lorraine! We hope you enjoy your stay. It says here on the ticket that she won't be here at this last bit, so we'll contact Lorraine on the number she's written down and give her the great news!'

'Your dad,' Tash smiles, 'is funny.'

'Yeah,' says Rocky. He doesn't need to say anything to her about the fakeness of it. If you don't know, it's endearing. And Larry is a great dad, so Rocky forgives him his little flashes of showmanship.

He turns to look at Tash and pulls off his fake beard. She's got a glass of alcohol-free punch and is smiling. She's still got her elf shoes on, although the ears are tucked in her handbag. Her glasses are fogged up around the edges and she pulls them off, wiping them clean on the corner of her waistcoat. *I really like her*, he thinks, and he feels even more nervous than he did before.

'The next is six PT sessions with my eldest son, Tim Winters! That's that one over there. Handsome fellow, not sure where he gets *that* from.'

'Oi!' Rocky's mum calls out from the prize table, pouting and shaking her hair out with her fingers. The crowd laughs.

'From my wife, *obviously*,' says Larry, smiling. 'We all know I've always been punching well above my weight there. You don't need to be polite.' There is a murmur of agreement and Rocky smiles. His mum and dad are a proper team. And, the truth is, when you see them behind the scenes, they are very much still in love. That's not faked, not ever. 'So, six PT sessions with my son over there goes to . . . Euan Barratt . . . !'

A groan goes around the room, and Rocky watches to see what his dad will do.

'Couldn't have happened to a nicer bloke,' says Larry, pulling a face. 'Still, maybe a few gym sessions might, um, help. All's fair in this raffle, as you can see!'

'Are you fucking kidding me?' Tim sinks into one of the bar stools and doesn't look best pleased. Rocky presumes he was hoping for someone of the opposite sex to win. He can't help but find it funny. He and Tim couldn't be more different if they tried. They used to get on when they were younger, but something changed when his brother started high school. Tim used to pretend he didn't know Rocky on the way home from school when he was with his cool mates. Bastard.

His dad puts away the mike and the music turns to that from the jukebox again, softly, to show the punters it's nearly time to leave.

'I'm freeee!' Rocky jumps up and punches the air. 'I've been dressed up like a Christmas card all day, so now I get to be me!' He pulls the Santa suit off and then he's there in his hoodie, tracksuit bottoms and his black trainers. He was hot in the suit, and can feel beads of sweat on his neck and forehead. What next? He's been looking forward to this moment all evening – all day, in truth – when he doesn't have to be part of parents' event and can hang out with Tash, just the two of them.

Before he's decided what he's going to ask her to do next, Tim comes over, holding a whisky and a bellini cocktail. Rocky wonders which one is for him, but he's already decided not to drink this evening, because even though he's nineteen, Tash is seventeen and he wants to do everything by the book. And growing up in a pub, you either go big on the drink or see it as being inside a cautionary tale. For Rocky it's the latter, he doesn't care. He's seen too much stuff that would put a person off for life.

'Merry Christmas, Tash,' says Tim, smiling. 'You want one of these?' He holds out the bellini and she frowns at him.

'Won't your mum and dad get in trouble if I drink that?'

'Nobody checks on Christmas Eve,' Tim says and shrugs. 'Treat yourself!'

Rocky feels the anger in him. His brother is a prize bastard. Every time he meets someone he likes, in strides Tim and shows Rocky she would choose him if he wanted. He hasn't admitted it to anybody, but it's why he's never told Tash how he feels. Because he's so used to Tim being the best Winters brother. And because Rocky doesn't want to *get*, or *have*, or *do* women. But here is his brother now, with Tash, bringing her bellinis in his tight T-shirt and his neat haircut and his . . . essence of Tim.

'Well, I don't drink,' says Tash. 'I got myself an alcohol-free punch and it's nice thanks.'

Rocky looks at her. Did she just roll her eyes at Tim?

He leans forward, the sound of his dad chatting loudly with punters, talking about how awful it had been to those who'd been robbed, and how hopefully this evening would bring some comfort, and the sound of people clapping and laughing and more drinks being poured, loud, in the background.

'Why don't you drink?' Tim has put the bellini down but hasn't given up. He's stepped nearer to her. 'Are you a good girl?' Rocky tenses. He knows this style of chat from Tim is about chatting women up. Rocky hates it enough at the best of times, but now his brother is pulling that crap on Tash, he feels sick. He wonders what he should say, when Tash smiles sweetly and replies.

'Well, I'm not a dick who tries to force drink on underage girls,' she says clearly.

Rocky stares at her in awe. He knows Tash has a mouth on her. It's one of the things he likes about her. But this. This!

'And when you've grown up watching someone who's wonderful the rest of the time be a prick to everyone they

231

love when they drink, and hear them say sorry a zillion times, well, you know, it's not that appealing.'

Tim stares at her and Rocky laughs, which causes his brother to turn on him.

'You're laughing at a woman's story about having someone in her family having a problem with drink, *Sylvester*. Classy.'

'He's not laughing at that, and you know it,' says Tash. 'And I know his real name's Sylvester, so calling him that isn't going to make him look stupid to me, though it might make you look like a dick. Again. So.' Tash picks a sausage roll from a bowl on the table in front of her, pops it into her mouth and turns to Rocky and gives him the hugest grin. 'Shall we do something different?'

'Very good plan,' says Rocky. 'What do you suggest?'

'Anything away from here,' she says, looking Tim up and down like he's something unpleasant, and then she reaches over, takes Rocky's hand and leads him away from the table. All the while the bells on her shoes are lightly jangling, as is his pulse at being hand and hand with her after all this time.

When Rocky looks over his shoulder, he sees Tim seething, almost vibrating with the anger of what's just occurred. Nothing like this has ever happened between the two of them before. This is new. But Rocky doesn't even care about Tim right now. He looks at Tash's face and his heart swells.

Outside, the two of them stand by the benches and look out along Newbury Street. It's like something in a Christmas card, lights strung between the houses, the flashing ones, the subtle ones, the huge Santa and Rudolph ones.

Rocky is breathing fast. What just happened in the pub was something he'd never dared dream of. He hadn't had to do anything either. He'd just sat there, while Tash picked his brother's flirting technique to pieces. And she'd taken his hand. They're still holding hands now. He can feel the warmth of her blood in her veins, trying to hold off the cold. Nothing is better than this. This night can't get any better, but then . . .

'Can I kiss you?' says Tash. 'Because I'd really like to.'

'*Can* you?' he laughs, putting his hands out and holding onto the collar of her coat. 'I'd say from where I'm standing, it's obligatory.'

She tastes of punch and salted snacks and blackberry lip salve, and it's wonderful. He doesn't think of anything, just about the kiss. One of those kisses you forget yourself in, and then have to repeat over in your head, again and again. Until it's morning. Until you have to do something else but really don't want to.

'I could make a lifestyle out of this,' he says grinning, as they pull away.

Tash slides her arm through his and rests her head on his shoulder. 'I can think of a zillion worse ways to spend my first Christmas Eve without my mum,' she says happily.

He feels a lift to know he's made her feel this way. Sometimes it's easy to think he's not important. But, right now, he feels like the most important person in the world.

'I'm glad you're spending it with me,' says Rocky.

And the two of them stand in silence, staring into night, squeezing each other's hands and tracing their thumbs over each other's skin.

'I've got an idea,' he says suddenly, wondering why he didn't think of it sooner. He pulls her with him as he starts to walk.

Newbury Street is beautiful in the dark, the ice in the air makes it look like a mist is setting in. He can't believe she's walking with him, holding his hand. His thumb is rubbing circles into the back of her hand, and, in her elf costume, she shivers, but not from the cold.

He quickens his pace and keeps looking over his shoulder. His black trainers and black trackies make it look like his body doesn't exist in the dark. 'Have you noticed this mist and the dark are making us invisible,' she laughs.

'Good thing I've got candles,' he says, tapping the pocket of his coat. 'And something to light them with.' She doesn't ask him why he's got candles in his pockets, and he's relieved about that.

'Where are we going?'

'You'll see,' says Rocky, his breath fast ice and his smile wide. They both can't stop grinning at each other.

When they are far along Newbury Street, right at the other end, Rocky stops walking and puts his hand in his pocket.

'We're here,' he says.

Tash looks about her, obviously confused. 'We're going to light some candles outside Number 45 and 47 Newbury Street? It wasn't *quite* what I was thinking.'

'Of course not,' says Rocky, leading her along the path of Number 47. 'We're going to do that *inside* Number 45 and 47 . . .'

As Rocky pushes the key into his brother's empty mid-renovation house, he feels the excitement of doing something he shouldn't be doing, at being alone with Tash, at last, and at the pure romance of it all on an icy Christmas Eve. Some things are just meant to be.

'Should we really be doing this?' says Tash, sounding uncertain, but still grinning.

'If you're not sure, we don't have to. I mean, it's Tim's house. He's knocked the two together to make some kind of uber-bachelor pad. You know what he's like. He probably wouldn't like us being here, and he doesn't know I took his key. So . . . Shall we turn around? I suppose leading you to breaking into to someone's house on our first proper date is probably a bit shit. I wasn't thinking . . . And, you know. We're just going to hang out . . . I'm not saying we have to . . .' he stops as Tash holds a finger up to his lips to stop him talking. 'In any other circumstance breaking into someone's house isn't something I'd do,' she says. 'So long as you understand that.'

'Well, that's the same for me too,' says Rocky. 'This is the first and last time. Next time, we'll go somewhere lovely. If you'd like there to be a next time.' He squeezes Tash's hand and shuts the door behind them. As he pulls her towards him and puts a cold hand to her face, he feels the beat of excitement in her heart as their lips touch and they kiss.

'Of course I do,' she says and kisses him again.

'I could just stand here and do this for the rest of my life, just so you know,' he says.

'So could I, as it happens,' says Tash, and Rocky feels, for this moment at least, perfectly happy.

But when he opens his eyes, he realises they're not alone. Tim has let himself in behind them and is now standing behind them with a look of pure rage on his face. Before Rocky's had a chance to say anything, his brother has locked the door so all three of them are trapped inside the house together.

11.45 p.m.

Christmas Eve

Frank Blake

118 Newbury Street

Frank looks at Craig, now sitting on the armchair opposite their new sofa and has no idea what to say. He doesn't know if he's supposed to feel angry, or devastated, or *what*? For the moment, it's anger. Still. Even though they've been talking for hours.

Jen's in the kitchen now, making them mugs of tea and arranging mince pies on a plate. She's gone into Stepford Wife mode, trying to make everything OK by excelling at the domestic.

Craig's still wearing his coat, it's still done up, right to the top, and his hands are cupped over his knees, like he doesn't know how to sit comfortably. *Or*, thinks Frank, *like he's about to spring up and knife me and watch my innards bleed onto the carpet*. He knows this is ridiculous, but he just wants to go to bed with Jen and forget today with all its break-ins and revelations.

I don't want anyone in our home other than us.

'Is there any point still talking this out?' says Jen as she walks through with the pies and tea on a tray. 'None of us can

236

say we're perfect. None of us can say we've always behaved the way we should. We're human. That's it. Humans are a bit shit sometimes. And a bit wonderful at others.'

'There is a point talking it out,' says Frank, standing up, unable to bear sitting opposite his once friend. 'He's waited ten months to tell us this. We've agonised over getting together, taken shit from every corner. I want him to talk *that* out. Why he did that. Why he let that happen.'

'I didn't want that to happen,' says Craig. 'I wasn't sure what I was letting happen, to be honest. I had rather a lot on my mind. I felt guilty myself, you know. And broken-hearted . . . because . . . who could I talk to about my feelings? Nobody.'

'Poor you,' Frank scoffs.

The two men glare at each other.

'Tell me one thing,' says Jen, sitting down now Frank is standing up. She's calm now, almost a different person from when she'd first appeared in the doorway to the garden. She's never angry for long, and she's been listening, carefully, to everything that's been said. 'There's still the matter of whether anything ever happen between you and Allie,' she says clearly.

Craig takes in a deep breath and shakes his head. 'No! That's the point. All this over words and feelings. Nothing happened. We didn't do anything. Other than talk over all the things we could do . . .'

'Uh . . .' says Frank, tensing.

'Jesus, Frank, not like that. Just . . . how we'd live. If we told you both and decided to make a new life together. *You* know.'

Frank knows. He and Jen had what seemed like hundreds of conversations like that. Never with an outcome that left everyone happy. Somebody always got hurt.

'People always *did* say they couldn't tell who was married to whom when we were together,' says Craig.

'That was just . . .' Frank stops. It's true. People did say that. When they went to a pub, when they went to a restaurant, when they went to a funfair, or The Norfolk Show, or any of those things. The boundaries between who was with whom were always blurred to people on the outside. Allie and Craig, gentle and serious, talking about whatever it was they talked about. Things that made Frank feel he was thick, or insensitive, or that just bored him. And he and Jen, loud, roaring with laughter, finding the humour in everything they shouldn't. He'd never taken what people said seriously. They all congratulated them-selves on finding friends and partners who fitted so neatly together. A collage of happy photos through decades of friendship.

'Shit,' he says.

'Exactly,' says Craig.

'Do you think . . .' This is almost too painful for Frank to think, let alone say. He has a slideshow of Allie in his head that he plays on loop: her at school, her on the bus, her at the registry office in her blue and yellow dress, her on the day Joanie was born, her on the day Tash was born. Her smile, her hair, her baking. Her whole self, next to him at night, with her arm over his side, snaked up his chest, and her breath on his back.

'I can't wait until tomorrow,' he'd say.

'Why?' she'd say back.

'Because I can't wait to see you again.'

It was their bedtime script and the thought of it crushes him on the inside. When did that stop? Would it have stopped permanently, if the cancer hadn't got to her? Did that matter now?

'Look. Do you think the two of you would have got together if she'd not got ill? Do you think that?' Frank asks.

Craig looks down at his feet and then back up at him. 'That's the thing,' he says, shaking his head. 'I don't know. I can't know. We'd only just started talking about it. My heart and head were full of it. And the guilt. Sometimes I think we wouldn't. She was concerned about Barnie and Ray. She was concerned about you, Jen, and you Frank. She loved you. And about Tash. Not so much Joanie. The two of them . . . they were like . . .'

'Soulmates,' says Frank.

'Yes,' Craig nods. 'I don't think she was the sort of person to end a marriage, even when she had feelings for someone else. But maybe I'm putting her on a death pedestal. She'd never have cheated. I know that.'

'We're all guilty of doing that,' says Jen. 'To make the story work in our favour. Truth is, we'll never know.'

The two men nod.

'And we can spend the rest of our lives trying to work it out, trying to work out who did what to who, who betrayed who, when things went wrong, when they went right, and what would it all be for?' Jen smiles at both men.

Nobody says anything.

She continues. 'Nothing, that's what. This may sound cold, I don't know. But my feeling is, it's Christmas Eve. I'm in love with you, Frank. I have two wonderful children with you, Craig, and I loved you for years. I still do, in some odd way that's inexplicable really. And, Allie was my best friend. We went through everything together. If she was alive, would I be with Frank? Would she be with Craig? I don't care. I really don't. I loved her. I'll always love her. And I love the both of you too. In different ways now.

And I just want to move forward. And live life without berating myself every morning for daring to be happy.'

'I agree,' says Craig. 'I want to be happy, and I want to grieve first. For what I lost. The idea of what I lost. And the two of you . . . you should get to have what you have. Because if one of you died, you'd regret it. Believe me.'

'Craig . . .' Frank moves towards his friend. 'I honestly didn't mean to fuck you over.' He's not angry anymore. He feels an odd sense of calm, like Craig was holding the missing piece to them all moving forward.

He looks around his and Jen's newly decorated living room, at the Christmas tree covered in silver and orange lights, at the new presents Jen has bought during the day to replace the stolen ones, pushed underneath, bright, wrapped beautifully, and he thinks, *This is it. This is my life now.* And this thought brings with it a warm feeling that he supposes must be happiness.

'I know. I know,' Craig says. 'People can't help what they feel. It's what they do that matters. If the two of you had had an affair behind my back, it would be different.'

'I'd never have done that,' says Frank.

'And you know I wouldn't,' acknowledges Jen.

'I know,' admits Craig. 'I'm just angry at the universe for the unfairness that you two got to give it a go and me and Allie . . .' He shakes his head. 'I'm going to go home now. Let you have some of Christmas Eve to yourselves. I have a house full of unmade flatpack furniture and no desire to do anything about it.'

Frank feels very tired all of a sudden. And calm. He'd thought he was going to rip Craig's head off when he heard him talking in the garden, but now all he feels towards his friend is love and sympathy.

'Right,' says Jen.

'Right,' says Craig.

And then Frank's phone makes a beeping noise to mark the arrival of a text. It's Tash. *Better late than never*, he thinks. Today has been too much, but seeing his youngest daughter's name flash up on his phone screen unprovoked is the best Christmas present he can think of. He opens it, still smiling.

Help dad im in trouble

That's it. Frank's stomach is stone.

He immediately taps the call icon on her number. It doesn't ring and goes straight to voicemail.

Where are you? He taps a message and sends it.

He jumps up from the sofa and grabs his coat from the back of the front door. 'Tash is in trouble and we need to go and find her.'

Craig jumps up immediately and joins him at the door.

'What is it?' Jen rushes over to him and touches his face.

'I don't know. But Tash needs me.'

'I love you,' she says, face etched with concern.

'I love you too.' He blows her a kiss.

And then Frank and Craig are out of the door.

Midnight
Christmas Day

Tash Blake

17 Newbury Street

Everything had happened so quickly.

One minute she and Rocky had been kissing in the hallway, and the next Tim had locked them in, and his booted foot had come at them, and Rocky had been kicked right in the stomach. He's lying on the floor, holding onto his belly, as Tash looks about her for a way to get them out. With the mood Tim seems to be in, who knows what he'd be capable of.

'What I really want to know is, what the fuck did you think you're doing, Sylvester?' the voice snarls with the sort of anger you only hear in documentaries about wild animals.

'I'm sorry, OK!' Rocky is sitting on the floor of the empty living room, with Tash the other side. She's looking for a way to use her phone again. The message she'd managed to send to her dad hadn't been of much use if he didn't know where she was. If only she could distract Rocky's brother, so she could text him again.

'This is my house,' says Tim, looming over his younger brother. 'I've bought it with my hard-earned money, while you prance about at art school making sculptures of people's feelings or whatever it is you do, and then you bring a girl here to impress her . . . and just help yourself?'

'It was a stupid idea. I'm sorry. I wasn't going to take anything. I was just looking for a bit of privacy.'

'Well, you very well may be sorry, but that didn't stop you invading *my* privacy, did it?'

Tash has never liked Tim, even though people always go on about him being a dreamboat. She never liked the way he put Rocky down. She never liked the way he spoke about women in front of her when he came into the shop. She never liked the way he made a performance of running, either, as though he was the only person to put on a pair of trainers and make use of the pavement.

'Now I've got to work out what to do with you,' says Tim, pacing the empty room.

'Kick us out and tell Mum and Dad about it tomorrow?' suggests Rocky. 'Just let us go now, before this gets too weird.'

Tash notices Rocky is cradling his stomach and she's worried Tim has really hurt him.

'I need the toilet,' she says suddenly, going to stand up.

'Tough,' says Tim.

'I'll have to wet myself on your nice polished floor,' she says.

He looks at her. He's dressed all in dark clothes, and still has his hood up.

'Do that then,' he says, and laughs.

'Tim!' Rocky raises his voice. 'Enough is enough. We're going now. We're not going to be kept in here like hostages. It's weird. Let her go to the toilet.'

'Hand me your phone,' says Tim, and Tash knows she was stupid to think he'd fall for such an obvious trick.

'Here you go,' she says, handing it over, glad it's got thumbprint recognition as part of its features.

'The toilet is next to the kitchen. Don't go doing anything silly. I've still got your boyfriend in here.'

'Tim,' Rocky's tone is firm. 'You're being out of order.'

'*I'm* being out of order. You were the one about to start shagging in my hallway. Don't you think that's a bit weird?'

'I wasn't. We weren't going to do that here.'

Tash gets up and goes to the toilet. They *might* have been about to, she's not sure. She'd have liked to. Every moment she's spent with Rocky since they kissed had felt like a wonderful dream. Until this bit. Which is more like Jack Nicholson in *The Shining*.

She stands in the bathroom with the door shut. Tim may have her phone, but what could she do instead? The bathroom doesn't have anything much in it. Just a roll of toilet paper, a magazine and a hand towel. There's a small window, the sort that opens out and is kept open with a metal bar. She'd never fit out of it, even if she tried really hard. She opens it quietly, trying to look out onto the street.

It's then she realises that the cat, Spock, is on the windowsill, miaowing.

'If this was a movie,' she says, 'you'd go and fetch help. The Cat Who Saved Christmas. You know the sort of thing. Do you think you could do that? For all that Felix I've given you? Hey? Spock?' She makes a kissing noise with her lips, the way people do when they're trying to get a cat's attention. She can see the shape of him through the bobbled glass window.

It's then she hears voices.

'Dad!' she whispers, loudly, not caring that Tim might hear because what harm could he do in the few seconds it would take her dad to get over to her and, with his strength, into the house. 'Dad! Come and help me!'

But the voices and the shadows disappear.

Shit.

Tash washes her hands and leaves the toilet. What can she do? Nothing for the moment. She just hopes her dad realises which house they're in.

In the main room, Tim has thrown a pile of money on the floor. There's loads of curled-up five-, then twenty-, even some fifty-pound notes. He's laughing and has moved his foot down Rocky's back.

'What's all this?' She feels frightened now. Tim isn't acting like the Tim everyone knows from the pub. Yes, he's always been a ladies' man. Yes, he's always treated Rocky like a piece of rubbish. But he's decent, isn't he? The scene before her suggests even that has been an act.

'I'm teaching my little brother about success,' says Tim smugly. 'About taking what you want when you want it and not wasting your time being nice.'

'You're teaching him about capitalism then,' she says. 'I guess the three spirits haven't visited you yet.'

'What?'

'Never mind.'

'She's too smart for you,' says Rocky from under Tim's foot.

Tim laughs then. 'Mum's never going to press charges about this.' He gestures to the money. 'She's got me out of trouble before. That's what mums do. Isn't it, Tash?'

She shakes her head, looking for something heavy to grab and whack him over the head with. She had wondered about just rushing at him, but Tim is strong, and fit, and physically she's no match for him at all.

'I could just squash Sylvester's head here, splat it to the ground.' Tim's smirking, his whole face seeming to show a delight in the situation they find themselves in. 'I'm not usually a fan of violence. But I can be convinced if the occasion is right.'

'Don't!' Tash calls out. She can see the pain on Rocky's face and realises Tim's foot is pressing harder.

'He wouldn't be missed,' says Tim, laughing again.

'Yes he would,' says Tash defiantly. 'He'd be very missed. He's kind. He helps people. He remembers things about the customers that make them feel special, just because it makes them feel special not because it will get him something. He's funny and brilliant and makes the best hot chocolate. He never takes more than he needs . . . yes, you may laugh at that, it may sound stupid to you . . . but it makes him a very wonderful person.'

'Well, that's touching. In case you noticed, being a nice person doesn't get you anywhere.'

'I feel sorry for you,' she says softly. 'And just in case you didn't realise,' she says, looking Rocky firmly in the eyes, 'I'm in love with you.'

She sees him smile, despite his face being squashed beneath Tim's boot. She sees the smile reach his eyes, and his face light up. She's scared, but totally calm.

'I'm in love with you too.' Everything she'd ever wanted to hear, in totally the wrong circumstances.

Tim is about to say something else when their conversation is interrupted by loud banging on the door. Banging so loud, Tash thinks it might come off the hinges. Tim lifts his foot from Rocky's face.

'Tim, you need to open up. Are you in there? What's going on?' Her dad isn't going to stop banging on the door, she knows that. Tim knows that too. He stands looking from her to the door, and back again, as though he doesn't know what to do.

'I should have let you piss yourself,' he says, angrily.

'I think you should open the door,' she says, feeling braver.

Tim shrugs and pulls a strange face. 'I suppose I should.'

Rocky is up on his feet and standing behind him now, holding out his arms, his hands up like he's walking cautiously towards a ticking bomb.

'Tim, mate.' Her dad's voice comes from the other side of the front door.' I can see Tash is in there from her Snapchat map. Unless you've nicked her phone. So let me in.'

'You were free to go all along. It was just a silly misunderstanding,' says Tim quickly. His whole body language changes, becomes meeker, less aggressive. Tash has to admire his acting ability. It has been wasted.

When he opens the door, Frank and Craig nearly go tumbling over onto the hall rug.

'What the fuck is going on?' says her dad.

Tash runs towards him and throws her arms around his neck. She's never been so relieved to see somebody in her life. 'Dad!'

'Tash!' He holds her tightly.

'Tim . . .?' Craig is standing face to face with Rocky's brother.

'I just caught these two over-amorous teenagers going at it on my newly polished hallway floor,' he says, his tone totally different than it was before the door was opened. 'You should have a word with your daughter, Frank mate. Make a habit of this type of thing, does she?' he jokes.

'We were not *going at it*,' Rocky is in the hallway too, still holding onto the side of his stomach where he'd been kicked. Tash thinks he looks like he's in lots of pain.

'We weren't,' says Tash. 'We were kissing. And grinning at each other, ridiculously.'

'You don't need to explain yourself to me,' says her dad quickly. 'You're both old enough.' He turns to Rocky. 'I know she likes you. What she does with her body is her business.'

'How very *modern*,' says Tim. 'You do realise they broke into my house, and I caught them, and then they protested when I said I'd call the police.'

'Is that right?'

Tash looks at the ground and back up again. 'We did let ourselves into the house. With a key. Yes. That bit's true.'

Her dad shakes his head. 'The rest of it, I don't care about. But you need to say sorry for that.'

'I am sorry about that,' she says.

'She shouldn't be sorry,' says Rocky. 'That was my fault and I shouldn't have done it without asking. No excuses.'

'So, all's well that ends well,' says Tim. 'I'll forgive you kids this once, but just this once. You can't go letting yourselves into other people's houses without permission. It makes you no better than the thief.'

Tash can't believe Tim's tone has changed so easily. It's like he's a different man than he was just a few minutes ago.

Her dad straightens himself out and looks between Tash and Tim. 'Well, I'm glad we've sorted that out. For one awful moment I thought you were up to something terrible, mate. I'm sorry I thought ill of you. Funny what stress will do to the brain.'

'I forgive you,' says Tim, smirking. 'When I've got kids of my own, I'll probably be the same.'

'You will,' says Frank and the two men lean over to shake hands.

Rocky and Tash hold hands and look at each other. She knows something's off with Tim, but how to convince Dad and Craig.

'I'd love to offer you all some refreshments,' says Tim. 'But, as you can see, I've got nothing in . . . as soon as I've finished the glow-up you'll be the first round.'

'We'll take you up on that. Come on, Tash, let's go.'

Everyone moves to the open door to be on their way. Tash wants to scream that Tim is no ordinary man but an actual psychopath who only moments ago was threatening to crush his own brother's head beneath his foot.

Just as they've all nearly left, Craig spins round, is distracted, peering over Tim's shoulder to something he's spotted on the stairs. 'Tim. What the hell is this?' He's holding up a little gingerbread man, decorated badly with a striped icing scarf and out of place features.

'I . . .' Tim doesn't answer quickly enough.

'Wait there,' says Frank. 'I saw Barnie and Ray decorate that yesterday. That's . . .' Tash watches her dad's face crumple, then rearrange itself with shards of steel. 'That's one of the gingerbread people the burglar took from our house last night. I'd recognise it anywhere. What's it doing here?'

'I don't know,' says Tim. 'I think I was given it. Yeah, that's right. Euan Barratt gave it to me earlier. To say sorry for going for it in the pub.'

'Did he now . . .?' Frank's tone changes as the realisation begins to kick in.

'Yeah. Creepy bastard. You don't think he's the one who's behind all the burglaries, do you?' Tim pulls a shocked face and Tash knows immediately he is acting. He's got his arms crossed in front of him, biting his top lip, trying to make himself come across as concerned, but she sees straight through him.

Rocky stands open-mouthed. 'Tim, what's upstairs?'

'Don't you dare go up there. This is my house and you're already testing my patience.'

'It was you, wasn't it?' her dad says slowly. 'You've been robbing people's houses and . . . what? Storing it here where nobody will look? What would we find if we went upstairs, hey?'

Tim doesn't answer, instead he turns and runs out of the back door and off into the dark. Craig and Frank start running after him.

'Don't worry,' her dad calls over his shoulder. 'You get Tash home safe. Rocky, call the police. I'll get him.'

The three men disappear into the dark of Newbury Street. Rocky types in 999, and when he's finished reporting what's happened, he hangs up and goes over to Tash.

'I'll walk you home, if you'd like.'

'I'd like,' she says.

'I meant what I said,' Rocky says shyly.

'I meant what I said too.'

'Best Christmas present ever.' Tash sees his face light up, even though it's obvious he's still in pain.

Tash pulls out her phone and taps out a text.

Merry Christmas Dad xxx

A text comes back almost immediately.

Don't worry Tash. We got him. Merry Christmas to you too xxx

She squeezes Rocky's had as they walk, and it feels like the sky's sparkling.

1.00 a.m.

Christmas Day

Cynthia Ellis

121 Newbury Street

When John gets in, Sir Tom follows behind him and gets tangled in his feet as he takes his shoes off.

'For fuck's sake, cat,' says John, trying to push him back out with his foot, not quite a kick, but Cynthia breathes in at the wafer-thin difference.

'He doesn't mean it,' she says, calmly. Sir Tom weaves his way along the hallway, despite John's efforts, and she feels relieved.

'It's a greedy bastard, is what it is,' says John. 'In and out of everyone's houses like . . .' he pauses and shakes his head. 'What are you doing up? Didn't you take your tablet?'

'Well, this is his home,' says Cynthia, ignoring his question, trying on a bit of the confidence she'd felt earlier.

John snorts. 'It's not even our cat.'

Cynthia decides not to argue with him. She knows better than that.

When they first met all those years ago, John had seemed like he was interested in everybody because he was just a really lovely person. It was one of the things she fell in love with. Now it seems different, like that interest was purely about getting people interested in *him*, that after the initial bit, after the initial care and attention, what he needs is some kind of continuous applause.

Maybe he was always like that, she thinks sombrely, *and I just didn't notice because I felt so happy that someone was paying me attention.* This isn't an easy thought to have, but it rings true.

Once he's inside and the front door is closed behind them, John turns towards her and put his hands out to take hers. She lets him, and then squeezes them. Maybe this will all be OK. They walk, like a newly married couple, into the middle of their living room in front of Cynthia's majestic tree, holding hands and looking into each other's eyes.

'I'm glad you're up,' John says softly. 'Because I wanted to talk to you about how often you belittle me in public.' His face is fixed, his eyes intent on hers. It's the last thing she's expecting, and it throws her.

She stares back at him, blinking, unable to form an answer. Her skin creeps with red heat. She's heard this tone in his voice before. The bravery she felt earlier falls onto the carpet. In their earlier years, he mentioned her belittling him in public so often she started to wonder if the words coming out of her mouth were the ones she thought they were. She'd never belittle him. What was he hearing in her words that she didn't mean to be there. *Maybe he was just trying to get you to stop talking*, she thinks. *Maybe he wanted you to doubt yourself.*

'You can look at me like that all you want,' he raises his voice just a little bit. 'But we both know you've always thought you are too good for me and take any opportunity to remind me of it. I'm here to say it's not good enough.

I'm here to say I'm *onto* you.' She feels his hand tighten around hers.

'That's not true!' She blurts it, like she's being sick. Loud. A shout. A loss of control.

'Come off it,' he says, smirking. 'You've never once supported me in my dreams. You've spent the past year looking down on me as I've tried to expand, questioning things you know nothing about. You're only kind to me when you want to buy something for the house, or want help with something. Your sense of entitlement really is quite something else.'

The unfairness of what he's saying rises up inside her. How can he say things like this, as they stand in their living room lovingly decorated for Christmas by her every year. The place she brings him cups of tea, asks him about his day, or gives him all the space he needs as he watches the news?

'How can you say that?' She tries hard to keep hold of the things she knows to be true, although there are tears now, that she can't control.

What is true? She goes over a list. The money her parents left her twenty years ago that she gave him, readily, so he could get a better car to use on work trips, because she believed him when he told her people laughed at his old Escort, that he just needed the chance to be taken seriously. The time she'd stopped going to netball because he said he felt she was more likely to cheat if he wasn't around and he couldn't sleep thinking of what he'd do if he lost her, and how that was affecting the business. About Lydia, and Jamila, and Sean, all friends she'd had since she was a child, who he, slowly but surely, convinced her were not good for her, or would embarrass or make uncomfortable, until she was too embarrassed to get in touch with them and she never heard from them again. And the times he'd said, 'You don't need anyone else, you've got me.' Or would present her with friends he found for her, who'd sit in her living room like CCTV cameras, watching her every move on his behalf without really knowing that's what they were doing.

Of all the times she'd had enough, and been ready to leave – so many, now she comes to think of it – and he'd sat crying, saying sorry, that he knew he was insecure, that he'd change, that he loved her, that he was sorry, but *please don't leave*. And she felt bad for him, felt bad that she'd misunderstood, so had stroked his hair and said, 'I won't leave you.' And the whole thing had started again, and again, until she thought she was losing her mind. He always feels better so quickly. The tears stop as soon as she did whatever it was he wanted her to do. Like, they weren't real tears at all.

He's standing over her now and he doesn't look sorry. He looks angry. She'd never seen pure, unadulterated anger until she knew John. It comes from nowhere, escalates in just a few moments. He's never hit her, which he reminds her on the few occasions she's managed to put forward her case that he's mistreating her. He shakes with fury at the slightest of things, the most unexpected of things. Once again, she feels nervous. What she's noticed, since the children left home particularly, and what she notices now, is that she only ever feels like this when she's around him. Just him. The rest of the time she's a different person. Happy, mostly. Silly. Caring.

It isn't me. It isn't me. She repeats this to herself, now, in her head, to the tune of 'O Christmas Tree' to try and keep herself grounded, to make herself remember all the things she is, not all the things he says she is.

'It's true, Cynthia,' he says. 'You've held me back and controlled me ever since I met you. All I ask is for some support and you can't even give me that.'

She wants to scream, then. She wants to scream 'That's all I've ever given you!' But she knows when she behaves like that he holds it up as proof there's something wrong with her. That she has an anger problem and that normal woman wouldn't behave like that. *I hope our children don't inherit your temper,* was one of his favourite lines, that left her with nothing to say, because anything she did say would be used against her as proof he was right.

'You should see a doctor again,' he says now, beginning to pace the living room. He's out of place in the glow of the tree lights, the beautiful decorations and all the cards, so many cards, some with her name, and some *To John Ellis and wife*. She thinks, as his body casts an angry shadow against the far wall, *Why doesn't he have any real friends?*

'I don't feel unwell,' she says. She hopes that if she sticks to calm, general statements this situation won't escalate and then she can go back to her Mum's and feel safe and happy and pretend none of this has even happened.

'I still think it's worth checking about personality disorders,' he says. 'You flit back and forth between being the kindest person in the world and a total cow, you know you do.'

She flinches at his use of the word cow.

He leans in to kiss her now, on top of her head, like she used to kiss the children, and she pulls away. *I don't want you anywhere near me. Ever again.* The sentence is so clear in her head, she knows it's true. She's not sure how she will make this happen, because she's sure he won't let her go without a fight. But it's true. She doesn't want him anywhere near her.

255

He raises an eyebrow. 'See what I mean? I'm so loving and you can't even give me that.' He pulls a really strange face then, one that looks like features on a wooden puppet, a fixed smile. 'But I love you anyway. So what does that say about me? That I put up with all the abuse you throw at me, the lack of care, the belittling . . .' his voices gets louder.

Cynthia knows it's not good when he gets onto the topic of being belittled. It is the thing that makes him most angry, not being taken seriously, being spoken down to. He seems to think people do that to him a lot.

I hate you, she thinks.

Her mind runs through all the bits of her life she loves or is proud of. A slideshow of smiles, laughter, love. Sarah and James at the park or on the sofa when they were children, each with a head on her shoulder, listening to them read, tucking them up in bed. Her mum. Her dad. Her job, before he convinced her to leave. How she used to feel when she played netball, when she knew what she was for and for the first time in a long time, she knows what she wants now.

'Whatever I did or said, I'm sorry. I'm sorry I hurt you,' she says. Usually she is sorry, but this time she's just saying it to end the conversation and go to bed so she can make arrangements for her new life in the morning. To get Christmas Eve out of the way. She wants to get out of there. She wants to be away from this angry man who everyone seems to think is so handsome and charming and how lucky she is he even looked at her. She is aware he's positioned himself in a way that stops her from getting to the door.

'Ha!' He shouts it. He's becoming more and more agitated, and there's something about the way he's moving that scares her, like a big cat at the zoo, all the muscles in his body taut, like his whole self is on edge.

She sits down on the sofa.

Maybe I did do something, she thinks, the familiar doubt setting in. She can't help it. Why would he be so upset if she hadn't?

The Christmas tree looks too bright behind him.

He leans over her. She wishes she hadn't sat down.

'You can't even give me the courtesy of paying attention when I'm talking about my feelings,' he says. 'Do you know how that makes me feel?'

Yes. Yes I do, she thinks. But she doesn't say anything. She tries to make herself as small as possible, pulling her shoulders in, pulling her whole self deep into the cushions of the sofa.

'I *am* listening,' she says. 'I don't know what to say.'

'Ah, here we go,' he says, reaching out to the tree and putting his hand around the thin trunk like it's a neck.

'Here we go what?' Cynthia knows she's shouting now, she can feel the force of her voice through her body. She's trying to stay calm, but it all feels so unfair, everything he's saying and doing feels unfair.

He looks directly into her eyes and pulls that face she sometimes wonders if she imagines, so rarely does he show it. His eyes go dull, like he's dead, and his features drop, like there's nothing inside him, no brain or heart or guts or anything. Like there's no life in him, just hatred and rage. She feels her heart thump hard in her chest.

He shakes the tree with his hands round its neck.

For a moment it feels like the tree is her, that she can feel all the decorations, lovingly collected and cared for by her and the children all these years. She feels them, hanging from her body, on their delicate strings, trembling.

He shakes it and shakes it, all the while looking into Cynthia's eyes, with his dull eyes and his expressionless features.

The decorations fling off in all directions, the expensive ones, the old ones, the new ones, the little drummer boy James made in reception, the Christmas giraffe Sarah made of straws and tin foil with its ridiculous googly eyes, the knitted elf, given to her by her mother before she died, that she'd put against her face last Christmas and cried because she missed her, that still smelt of the rosewater soap, and the smell of her mother and father's house.

She watches the symbols of the life she has built for herself fly from the tree, and she forgets to breathe. For a moment, she thinks he won't stop. That he'll just stand here, strangling and shaking the tree, for the rest of their lives.

'Please. Be kind to me,' he says softly then. 'All I've ever asked for is for you to be kind to me.' He's still shaking the tree. His knuckles stretched white.

She's speechless, staring at him, and the discarded ornaments, thinking, *What do I say right now to make all this stop?* It's the way she lives, second-guessing what he wants from her, or what behaviour he'll respond best to. She hadn't realised just how much thinking of this went into her daily life, but it's there, threaded through everything, in such a way that, if she described it to anybody, they would say, 'Why didn't you just leave?' and she wouldn't be able to explain, and she'd always come across as paranoid, or ridiculous, or worse.

Eventually, John's face changes and he lets go of the tree. He slumps down on the floor at her feet then and he's that little boy again, the boy who says he was picked on at school, who says he doesn't know how to show love because nobody ever showed him love, just like he always tells her whenever she tries to stand up for herself.

'Please don't leave me,' he says, and his eyes are full of tears. 'I don't ever want you to leave me.'

For a moment she wants to comfort him, like she has so many times before. She always feels for him in these moments, usually enough to wipe out the memory of what has happened seconds before. But not this time. *Not this time.*

'I won't leave you,' she says, as meekly as she can. For the first time since she met him, this response is a lie.

'Will you promise to get help?' he says softly. 'With your temper and your cruelty and your unfair expectations?'

'Yes,' she says immediately. 'Yes I will. As soon as the surgery's open after Christmas. I will.'

She feels something new. *This isn't your fault. He'd be like this whoever he was with.*

Looking at him now, it's like he picks fights when he wants an excuse to do something he knows will upset her, so he can say to her, '*But you treated me badly. I felt like nothing. What choice did I have? What would anybody do in this situation?*'

'Thank you,' he says. 'That means so much to me.'

He stands up then, is a different person. Smiling, his eyes lit through with kindness. Another mask.

Cynthia gets up and starts to put the broken and far-flung decorations in a pile under the tree and, as she does so, John laughs, as though nothing has happened. Not a cruel laugh, a genuinely amused and gentle laugh.

'We'll tell people the cat did it,' he says, brushing himself down. 'It's the sort of thing it'd do. Ugly thing.' Sir Tom is at the door, scratching to get out.

If she hadn't witnessed what had happened moments before she'd have never believed it had happened. He's a different person again.

259

'You've got to admit,' he says, coming up behind her and putting his arms around her middle. It takes everything in her power not to flinch, not to let him know what she's really thinking. 'Some of those decorations were a bit crap, hey?'

'I . . .'

He puts his hands on her neck, lightly at first, and then starts to squeeze. 'Weren't they?'

Cynthia Ellis knows in her heart he's not going to stop. He's going to squeeze until there's no life in her.

'John. Please. That hurts.'

'Ask nicely,' he says.

'John!' She's starting to feel dizzy as she tries to gulp back some air. Just as she thinks he'll never stop, the doorbell rings and makes him jump.

'Shit!' he shouts 'Who could that be?'

'We'd better answer it,' she says, breathing heavily at having her airway free.

'At gone midnight?'

The bell rings again.

'It's probably kids playing a game,' he says, gaining composure.

Cynthia can still feel the throb of his fingers on her neck.

'But it might not be,' she says, suddenly hoping for some kind of cavalry, anyone who might be able to step into this house of soured memories, and actually help.

'So be it,' he lets out a sigh and goes to the door.

Cynthia follows close behind him, thanking God for this intervention that might just have saved her life.

Behind the door stands DC Crane and DC Ado. They are both lit up by the Christmas lights around John and Cynthia's doorway.

'Good evening,' says DC Crane, giving Cynthia a kind look. 'I'm sorry it's so late.'

'Late?' John says too loudly. 'Is it usual for victims of a crime to be woken up at one in the morning for a house call?'

DC Crane's face doesn't change. 'No, sir, it's not. But this really is quite important. May we come in?'

'Of course,' says Cynthia, beckoning the two detectives into the house with a sense of overwhelming relief. She's never been so happy to see anyone in her life.

9.01 a.m.

Christmas Day

Wendy Finch

Flat 5, Victory House

Wendy wakes up and for that awful first moment forgets where she is and what has happened. She reaches out to feel for Len, like she did for so many years, then opens her eyes to the strangeness of Joanie's bedroom and feels the loss of yesterday like the sky has been unravelled into a heavy blue thread, holding her to the bed like rope around a barrel.

Oh.

He's really gone.

She can hear the children running about excitedly, their footsteps and laughter and the sound of water from the taps and Joanie's voice. Warm. Full of care. She'll get up in a minute, and go and spend this unexpected morning with them. Of all the places she thought she'd ever be, here was not one of them. Life can still surprise you, even when you think you've created a life that can't surprise you.

Wendy reaches for her glass of water from the bedside table and takes a sip, then puts it back and pulls herself up into a sitting position. The room is warm. Joanie must have turned the heating on early, but she still pulls the blanket around her shoulders and wraps it about her a few times, just in case. She reaches to the bedside table and picks up the other thing she put there last night. A rectangular box, wrapped in silver Christmas paper and tied about with a red ribbon. She holds her gift from her husband carefully, putting her thumb slightly under the fold of tape, trying not to tear the paper. For a moment, she thinks, *I could just not open it, just keep it, for all the Christmases I've got left, and put it under the tree, so there's always something from him.* Her heart thuds at the thought he'd wrapped this for her, and it's here in her hands. *His fingerprints are still on here*, she thinks. *I could just leave them there.*

But Wendy Finch is not that sort of person. She wants to see what he'd wrapped for her, what he'd found time to wrap, when everything was going so badly, and all they'd worked for was falling away from them. The fact he found a way to give her a present touches her deeply. He was still the Len she'd fallen in love with. He'd just got himself into a terrible muddle and didn't know what to do.

You silly fool. You could have just talked to me and we could have found a way through. But if he'd done that he'd have been a different person than she married, and she didn't want that either. He was who he was, and she'd loved him. And now he was gone. It couldn't have been any other way.

The paper he'd used has little silver mistletoe printed all over it. Wendy has never seen it before. She usually knew where all the wrapping paper was, had been the one to send cards, to buy presents, to remember birthdays, anniversaries, important events, throughout their marriage. The paper is pretty and looks expensive. Like the sort of paper they use for the presents under the trees in expensive hotels, or upmarket department stores.

Wendy slides her fingers under the paper and slits the sticky tape. Her hands are shaking and there is that last moment, where she holds the gift and thinks, *This is it. This is the last present I'll ever get from Len*, and her brain runs a slideshow of all their other Christmases, the other presents: soft mint-green leather gloves, a brooch like an orchid, a fountain pen in a silver box, a sewing box, that year he bought her a Magimix and she'd stared at it in horror because she knew she'd never use it, and he'd looked at her face and said, 'Right, that's the last time I listen to a shop assistant about what my wife would like for Christmas,' and they'd laughed.

The paper falls away and, in her hands, Wendy holds a heavy little jar, the same shape as the perfume bottles they used to sell and she would always stop and look at in shop windows. The expensive kind. But it's not perfume in the bottle. It's sand.

One day we'll be sea people.

Wendy wraps her fingers around the smooth glass and listens to the beat of her heart. He hadn't forgotten their plans. He'd found a way to get the beach to her, somehow, even when their dream seemed further away than ever before. She cries then. For the first time since the police officer told her Len had died. She cries for all their plans and all their hopes and for their innocence when confronted with a man who knew innocence was a good way to make money.

She holds the bottle to her face and strokes the cool glass along her skin. *It's a gift, to have been loved*, she thinks. *It is a gift to love, too.*

She puts the bottle down on the bedside table, pulls back the reindeer duvet and swings herself out of bed. She wraps herself in Joanie's borrowed dressing gown and puts on the slippers. She then puts the bottle of sand deep into one of the soft pockets, and lets her hand stay there, turning it over in her palm. The glass is comforting to touch, the patterned ridges in its sides pleasing between her fingers. When she closes her eyes she can see his face perfectly. She's not one to believe in afterlives and heaven, but she can feel him still there with her. In the memories she has. In the hopes and wishes they had, that will never stop existing, whether they ever had the chance to come true or not.

When she opens the bedroom door, Patti is standing there, about to knock.

'Mum says would you like a cup of tea?' Patti says enthusiastically, standing in her new Christmas pyjamas and dressing gown and two huge fluffy slippers that look like polar bears.

'Yes please, Patti,' says Wendy. 'That would be lovely.'

'We got slime in our stockings,' says Patti excitedly. 'I'm about to put some on Dylan's head.' She runs off down the corridor, giggling.

'A nice cup of tea will do,' says Wendy, stroking the bottle of sand with her thumb. She strokes it with her thumb and thinks of the last time they went to the beach. They sat on a bench and ate chips, heavy with salt, as Len fed the seagulls and Wendy said he probably shouldn't do that, and he'd put his hand on her knee and said, 'You're probably right.'

She enters the kitchen, which is full of steam and bubbling pans and a table covered in pastries.

'Merry Christmas, Wendy,' says Joanie, smiling. 'Help yourself to anything you fancy for breakfast.'

'Merry Christmas, Joanie.' Wendy smiles back. 'This looks good. Did you make these?' she asks, nodding at the pastries.

Joanie laughs. 'Sadly, not. I wisely bought a load from Lidl.'

'Tissue kissed a boy last night and she can't stop going on about how dreamy he is!' says Dylan, sticking his tongue out at his auntie Tash. 'And I've got an Iron Man fist. Look!' He holds up a maroon and gold plastic arm in front of her and she nods approvingly, even though she has no idea what it is.

Tash smiles too. 'I did! I did! Guess what. Me and Rocky are together.' She looks so happy, Wendy can't help but feel her heart swell for her.

'Well, that's lovely Tash. He's a lovely boy.'

'He is! Did you know he makes these clay beads and makes sculptures out of them. Thousands of the things. Each one different, painted and glazed. They look like cherries and buttons and the brightest jewels!'

'She's been like this all morning,' says Dylan, rolling his eyes in a comedy manner.

'And so she should be,' smiles Wendy. 'Love is something to be celebrated. Never hidden. I'm very happy for you.'

'And guess what else?' says Patti, dangling green slime in front of Dylan's face, so he jumps off and runs off. 'They arrested Tim Winters for the Newbury Street burglaries. Craig Mullany chased him right up to the cemetery and *tackled him to the ground* until the police came. Like a superhero!'

'Well,' says Wendy, lifting the teacup to her mouth and sipping in the hot liquid. Proper milk. No floating powder bits. 'That is unexpected.'

'I know,' says Joanie, shaking her head. 'He always seemed so nice. But I've known for a while he's not what he seemed. Irma knew him when she was younger.'

'Well, he definitely wasn't nice last night when he trapped me and Rocky in his house and tried to squash his head flat under his shoe, I can tell you,' says Tash.

'He did what?' Dylan has wide eyes.

'No need to go into such detail,' says Joanie.

'He's not a nice person,' says Irma, who appears from the door to the living room, already up and dressed, with her hair and make-up set. 'Good morning, Mrs Finch,' she says. 'Merry Christmas.'

'Merry Christmas to you, Irma,' says Wendy. 'Oh! Who's that?' She looks at the cat in Irma's arms and feels her heart race. It couldn't be . . . could it? 'Is that your cat . . . because Len and I lost our cat a few months back. She never came home and we thought she'd been knocked over, or something . . . But your cat looks . . .' She stops. It would be too much of a coincidence for their cat to return today, like this, on Christmas Day.

'Well, this is a stray,' says Irma.

'Everybody's been looking after him,' adds Joanie.

'Competing for him, you might say,' continues Irma, putting the cat down onto the lino, where he immediately makes his way to Wendy and jumps up onto her lap.

'Oh my goodness!' says Wendy. 'It's him! It is! He had this pink splodge around his nose that made him look like he'd had his face in a packet of Angel Delight. That's nearly what we called him.'

'Angel Delight?' Dylan laughs.

'Well, Angel, anyway. Yes!'

'What *is* his name?' ask Joanie and Irma at exactly the same time, looking at each other and giggling.

'Sandy,' says Wendy. 'Because we always wanted to move to the seaside.' She strokes her hand through the fur of the cat she'd let out several months ago and who'd never come home. She'd not made a fuss about it as they hadn't been able to feed him and Len had said it might be better for Sandy to be taken on by people who could afford to look after him properly. But, as the cat snuggles down into the towelling of the dressing gown, purring into Wendy's legs and stretching his paws out, then tucking them under his warm body, she knows he'll be coming home with her when she returns. Len's gift, suddenly twofold.

'Well, this is just perfect,' says Joanie, slipping her arm around Irma's waist. 'Now tell us about this new job!'

'It's working with a woman who's set up a charity for people who were forced or coerced to have their babies adopted . . . not to help them find their children as such, but to get the message out that not all adoption is wanted adoption. And work therapeutically for healing.' Irma sounds so excited, it's impossible not to catch her enthusiasm. 'I start next week. There will be funded retreats and all sorts.'

'That's brilliant!' exclaims Joanie.

'Congratulations,' Wendy.

'We were just telling Mrs Finch about Tim being arrested for the burglaries,' says Dylan.

'Yes,' answers Irma. 'I must say that doesn't surprise me one bit.'

'I think,' says Wendy, feeling confident with her bottle of sand in her pocket and her cat in her lap, 'there might be somebody else who's been arrested on Newbury Street today. Joanie, would you mind terribly if I borrowed your phone?'

10.14 a.m.

Christmas Day

Sue Winters

Newbury Street

Sue Winters walks up Newbury Street carrying a trifle she would never normally be carrying outside of the pub, but she does so in her best shoes and Christmas dress and jacket. Despite the weather, she has no doubt in her mind what she needs to do. *Always admit your mistakes*, that's the first thing. *Always say sorry*, that's another. *Even though blood is thicker than water, don't wash other people in it.* That's a new one. She thought of that this morning.

As she walks, trying not to let the cling film ping away from the special dish, nor the custard and cream slosh over the top, she wonders what she regrets most. Blaming Irma. Blaming the Iwu boy. Telling DC Crane they might be responsible for the burglaries. She feels embarrassed. Some of the things she said were so hateful that she can hardly believe they came out of her mouth. She couldn't hide away though. She couldn't pretend she'd looked to every door but her own son's. He'd got into all sorts of trouble at school, but they'd always come up with reasons for it. It wasn't that he enjoyed it. They were sure of that.

But the evidence always suggested otherwise. Until the early hours of this morning when the police took her son away.

She knocks on the door of 127. She wonders who will answer, either of the inhabitants will do. She's trembling, and is hot, despite the cold weather. Newbury Street looks quite beautiful in the frost. She carries the horror of what Tim did inside her like she's carrying him again. She remembers the pregnancy well. It was easy. No pain. No suffering. Labour was easy too, unlike with Rocky. Like Tim was a blessing from the very start. Nothing is ever that easy. She should have known that.

Isaac opens the door. He's wearing jeans and a red jumper. He's got a smart coat on and looks like he's about to go out. He jolts at the sight of Sue, and hunches in on himself, almost as though he's going to close the door in her face.

'Hello, Isaac,' says Sue. 'I'm looking for Irma.'

'Hello, Mrs Winters,' says Isaac. 'She's staying at her girlfriend's. You know her? Joanie Blake. She lives in the flats.'

'Yes, I know Joanie,' says Sue.

'Is that for her?' he asks.

'Yes.'

'It looks good,' he smiles.

'Thanks! I actually made it for me and Larry. But . . . I need to say sorry for something.'

'Christmas is a good day to say sorry for something,' says Isaac. He's such a ridiculously polite young man that Sue feels the heat of shame at listening to any of Tim's bile about him.

'Yes, it is. I'll take it to her there, then,' says Sue.

Isaac steps out onto the path. 'Do you mind if I come with you. Joanie invited me for Christmas dinner, and a

270

good person told me, if I wanted to make my life better, I should start with accepting small kindnesses.'

'That's very wise advice.'

'I don't really like kindness,' he says seriously. 'It always feels like a trick. But I'll learn.'

Sue nods. It's a sad thought that someone doesn't like kindness, but considering how she'd behaved recently, is it any wonder?

The two of them walk up Newbury Street together. Sue thinks of all the Christmases when Tim was a little boy. When he and his brother would sit by the tree and open their presents, the feel of them in their pyjamas, bouncing on her and Larry's bed, ripping off the paper from their stocking presents, sucking on sugar mice, with the tails dangling from their mouths. She can see Tim so clearly, the year he got his Buzz Lightyear and he kept jumping off the bed shouting, 'To infinity and beyond!' and the photo she'd taken of him kissing Buzz on the foot. Did she imagine those times?

What had she got so wrong that he ended up taking presents away from other people, ruining other people's Christmas, and laughing about it? Could she follow a string right the way back to the point when he became the sort of person who would do that? Could she have guessed? Could she have prevented people getting hurt? *Could she have saved him?*

As they pass John and Cynthia Ellis's front door, Sue feels a shot of embarrassment about the card she'd posted there last night, and just as she's wondering how she'll explain it away, the door opens and there stands Cynthia, dressed beautifully in clothes that fit her perfectly, holding a bowl of batter and a whisk.

'Sue!' she calls out.

271

Sue takes a deep breath and waits for John to come out behind her. But there's nothing. Just Cynthia. Who's smiling and whisking as she stands there.

'Have you got time for a sherry?' she asks. 'Both of you . . . if you'd like.'

Sue looks down at the trifle then back up at Isaac, then at Cynthia.

'I can take the trifle if you'd like,' says Isaac.

'I need to say sorry to Irma personally,' says Sue, but the look on Cynthia's face suggests this woman needs her more right now.

'I can tell her you'll do that, and give her this as a start.'

'That's very kind. Yes please. I'd like that.'

Isaac takes the bowl of trifle from her and nods the two women goodbye.

They stand out on Newbury Street, both in their best clothes, and smile at each other.

'You'd better come in,' says Cynthia, and Sue follows her inside, where the smell of roast dinner hits her immediately. Michael Bublé is playing on the sound system. The house is full of steam and candles and it feels light, somehow.

'Did you put that card through my door last night?' Cynthia addresses her directly and Sue realises there's no point denying it. How had this Christmas become such a muddle?

'Yes,' says Sue, honestly. 'That was me.'

Cynthia sighs, but smiles. 'Can you tell me what made you do it?'

Cynthia can't, exactly. It was a feeling of injustice. A feeling that it was unfair that John got to have the time of his life while Cynthia sat at home unaware. It was a feeling of guilt in herself, maybe, although she didn't know it then.

'I know he has affairs,' says Sue plainly. 'He's always said you know, or that you're a nightmare to live with

272

and refuse to even kiss him. But I watched him last night and I remember you saying you were looking forward to coming to the Feel Good, and I just . . .'

'Decided to intervene.'

'Yes.'

'I appreciate it.' Cynthia pours batter into Yorkshire pudding tins.

'How many have you got for dinner?' Sue changes the subject. She suddenly wants to be home. There's something different about Cynthia today. She seems so happy. How could that be?

'Just me,' says Cynthia. 'But I'm going to have a feast.'

'Is everything OK? It's just I had a hard time of it myself last night and I think I'd like to go home.'

'I'm so sorry to hear about Tim. You shouldn't blame yourself. You know, John was arrested last night. For fraud and . . . well, other things. He's been tricking old people out of their homes, don't you know. Including Mr and Mrs Finch. It's why Mr Finch died, they think. He was so frail. They couldn't afford the heating.'

Sue stares, unable to say anything to this revelation.

'I didn't know anything about it,' Cynthia continues, 'but last night, I went looking in John's records. I called that nice DC Crane. Mrs Finch had told her about it too. And then I called my daughter Sarah in Australia and organised to visit her for New Year. I'm going to get my passport at the one-day service. Next week. Imagine me. With a passport!'

'Oh Cynthia . . .' Sue feels her stomach lurch. 'That's . . .'

'I don't know if Tim was involved, sorry,' says Cynthia suddenly.

'I wouldn't be surprised if he was,' says Sue sadly. 'The things he did were bad enough.'

'Can I tell you something I've never told anyone, Sue?' Cynthia asks. 'I feel like if I get this off my chest I can move forwards. I don't want to be a burden, I really don't, but there's nobody else I can talk to.'

Sue nods cautiously. The news of John Ellis's illegal doings has shocked her. Even though her and Larry always thought him a bit of a peacock, they'd never expected that.

'I'm thinking of all the colours I'll decorate the house,' says Cynthia. 'All the rich ferns and plums and olives. Skirting boards the colour of grass. Doors of dark orange. Did you know that all this time I've been wearing clothes too big for me because John told me clothes the right size were too tight. They've been hanging off me all this while. How did I not notice? I thought they were still too small. I was tempted to go up a size, recently. Did you ever notice?'

'I always wondered why, but I thought there was a personal reason for it.'

'No,' says Cynthia brightly. 'Just him tricking me into doubting myself. Clever, isn't it?'

Sue nods slowly.

'The night of our honeymoon he left a brooch on the nightstand. A swallow made of threads of gold – he was always buying me these ostentatious brooches as gifts in the early days – it has emeralds for eyes and sapphire on the tips of the wings. He attached a note: *To Cynthia, my wife now x*. The proof: our names signed together, and the gold ring on my finger, his initials engraved on the inside.'

Sue doesn't know what to say. This woman has been through so much, but nobody had even noticed.

'He went out for a walk. I was so excited, getting ready for our first night, like a maid in a movie. I spent a long time on my hair, even though it wasn't pinned up. I had it down over my shoulders, curled, long, and I was wearing the pale pink, silk nightgown I saved and bought with my own money. It was long, to the ground, and my hip bones stood out through the material. I remember how it sat across my collarbone, fragile lace at my throat.' She pushes the Yorkshire puddings into the oven and pours them both sherry in cut glasses. 'I felt like a mermaid with shimmering skin. Doesn't that sound mad? I was so young. So *in love.* I pinned two flowers at my crown, and one wedge of curls, so it sat higher and fell across my face. I spent a long time practising. The silk felt like a touch by moonlight. In the mirror, I shimmered. A star's kiss.'

'You have a very beautiful way with words, Cynthia,' says Sue. 'I can imagine that perfectly. I was excited like that on my wedding night, but . . . you know. We'd done it before. We didn't wait. It never felt like we should. But people did, and still do, obviously.' She's trying to think of Cynthia Ellis with long hair shimmering like a mermaid and she must admit she's struggling.

'Anyway. When he came back from his walk or wherever he'd been, he gave me a look up and down and told me he thought I should cut my hair,' she says. '"*I like short hair on a woman.*" I think that's what he said.'

'That's . . .' But Sue doesn't know how to finish.

'And he wouldn't talk to me. He said I'd put him out of the mood. That my selfishness had ruined our wedding night. So I did the only thing I could think of. I was only young, you see, and we were married, and I wanted to make him happy.'

'What did you do, Cynthia?' Sue feels a sort of horror building up inside her. It's Christmas Day. They're supposed to be celebrating.

'Well,' says Cynthia, sipping at her sherry, 'I held the lengths of my hair in my hands. It felt like old threads, tatty,

275

with a cheap shine, all of a sudden. My crowning glory, my mother had called it. I'd imagined John holding handfuls of my hair, scooping it up as he held and kissed me. I felt so embarrassed. Anyway. He passed me the nail scissors and I cut it all off. Then and there. Never grew it back either.'

The two women stare at each other.

'Oh, Cynthia,' says Sue, her eyes wide and her heart twisted. 'All these years, you've lived with a man like that . . .'

'It didn't seem so bad, lots of the time.' She shrugs then. 'Jesus Christ. I'm so sorry.'

'It's not your fault. It's not anybody's fault apart from his. But I wanted to tell someone. I wanted to tell you. So that it's gone. Buried, and I can start everything anew.'

'I appreciate you telling me. Is there anything I can do?'

'No,' says Cynthia smiling. 'Honestly, I feel great. I might pop into The Mariner later though, when you do afternoon drinks.'

'You'd be most welcome.' Sue looks at her watch. She must be getting on. There's still her own Christmas dinner to cook.

'I'm going to have to get going, actually,' she says kindly. 'Are you sure you're going to be OK?'

'Yes. Really. I am,' says Cynthia, leading Sue to the door. 'And thank you for the card. And thank you for listening.'

'Any time. Honestly.'

When the door shuts behind her, Sue walks home quickly, the brutality of the story sinking in, looking forward to putting her arms around Larry, and letting Christmas, whatever it would or could be after all that has happened, truly begin.

When Sue gets back to The Mariner, she goes into the kitchen to find Larry trying and failing to make Yorkshire puddings.

He's crying. 'I got it into my head if I just made Yorkshire puddings, everything would be OK.'

Gently, Sue takes the bowl from her husband and puts it down on the bar. She reaches for a napkin from the box on the counter, and takes one, dabbing it at his eyes.

'Where did we go so wrong?' says Larry, looking at her, confused and as hurt as she's feeling. 'I'd not have thought it was Tim in a million years, would have staked all my money and my sense on him.'

'That's love though, isn't it?' says Sue, putting her arms around him and placing her face in the dip of his shoulder, where it's always felt such a perfect fit. 'You love someone anyway, and you believe in them. That's what you do.'

'Not if they're bad,' says Larry, putting his arms around her.

'Sometimes love stops you from seeing that. I, for one am not going to spend Christmas thinking of every single thing I ever said to him that might have pushed him towards the life he chose. I'm just not. Are you?'

'Maybe we should. Maybe that's what we deserve?'

'What we deserve,' says Sue, leading her husband into a dance to 'Let it Snow', her arms tight about him, 'is to have a good Christmas day, no matter what. We've got another son, and he's wonderful. We can worry about the rest of it after.'

'What about the Yorkshire puddings?'

'Let's forget about them,' she says, as she kisses him. It would be her first non-perfectly orchestrated Christmas. But life wasn't always perfect, Sue was beginning to learn.

11.30 a.m.

Christmas Day

Joanie Blake

Flat 5, Victory House

Joanie's flat is full of steam and music and laughter. She's smiling at what it feels like to be part of it all, to let herself really belong there. She watches Dylan jump up on Irma's lap and put his arm around her.

'Thank you for my dinosaur!' he says. 'I love it! Can you help me put the batteries in?'

Irma nods, and smiles, untwisting the metal ties that hold the green plastic robotic toy in place. 'Has anybody got a little screwdriver?' she asks, tapping one of the battery backs that's screwed in place.

'Do I?' laughs Joanie, who already has a golden paper crown on her head. She reaches into one of the kitchen drawers and pulls out one of those kits of mini screwdrivers her mum had saved from a cracker another year. Her mum always knew what was worth saving and what was worth getting rid of. Joanie hasn't quite grasped that skill yet.

'You save the cracker gifts?' Tash stares at her sister, with a certain look. 'Who does that?'

'Mum!' says Joanie, gently. 'Because if she didn't, then we wouldn't be able to put all the batteries in all the toys people have bought these two for Christmas.'

'Ah . . .' Tash nods and Joanie knows she's thinking about their mum who made every Christmas full of care and love without any of them really noticing all the effort she put in.

Sue Winters' trifle doesn't fit in the fridge, so it's sitting on top of the chest of drawers they use for cutlery and plates and bowls that her mum covered over with acrylics and gloss. Isaac is sitting on the other side of the table from Mrs Finch, and the two of them are talking about their unexpected shared love of old photographs. Isaac collects them from charity shops and Mrs Finch says she's got boxes full of the things if he wants to go and see them.

'Nothing wrong with being prepared.' Mrs Finch smiles. She too is wearing a paper crown, silver, covered in dinosaur stickers. Joanie smiles. She'll miss her when she leaves. 'I was just saying to Isaac here, I will be in the market for the lodger, I think . . .'

'I would very much be interested if that's the case,' he says. 'Can you remember the first time you had your photograph taken?'

'I can as it happens. Gosh, my mother made a fuss of it. I had to wear this . . .'

Joanie feels her heart soar. When she'd seen Isaac standing at the doorway holding a trifle she was so pleased to see him. He's fitted in so easily. Like he's always been there. This is exactly what she wants. Everything that's here in this room right now. Like the future is opened up like the back of the dinosaur Irma's now slotting the batteries into. It's as easy as that. Get the right screwdriver, open it up, batteries in, off you go. It's not such a beautiful image, but it works for Joanie. She feels happy.

'Thanks!' Dylan grins at Irma and puts the dinosaur on the lino. He presses the big button on its back and watches it waddle towards his sister. It makes a noise that sounds like someone coughing. He's utterly delighted.

'Can we put my centrepiece on the table now?' says Patti.

She holds up the shiny paper, paper flower, and toilet roll masterpiece she'd so lovingly taken time over and Joanie says, 'Of course! That's the most important bit! Dad, could you help me with the table?'

Frank comes over to move things about. Jen stands with Tash over by the window. They're talking about Rocky and all the things Tash likes about him. They're talking about youth work too.

'I'd like to work in something like care,' says Tash. 'Something where I do some good.'

'I think you'd be good at it,' says Jen. 'And that's not me flattering you because I want us to get on.'

'I'm past hating you,' says Tash. 'You make Dad happy. Everyone deserves to feel happy.'

'Thank you,' says Jen. 'And I agree.'

They wave out of the window at Craig and the boys as they play on their new scooters. Joanie's glad they've all agreed to come round before they have their own Christmas dinner. She's glad everybody's getting along. It's better than she could have planned, even if the turkey isn't quite what it should have been.

Irma comes up beside her and says quietly, 'Do you think there's time for us to take a bit of a walk?'

'There's so much to do!' says Joanie, thinking of the food on the stove, the presents still to be unwrapped, glasses to fill, teapots to pour, all the comings and goings that make everybody's Christmas what it should be.

'Nobody will mind if you take some time for yourself. And there's something I want to ask you. I thought . . . we could go to the cemetery and visit your mum.'

Joanie leans against the wall for a moment. She's managed to put off going to visit where her mum's ashes are buried underneath their neat gold plaque for ten months. She's always had a good reason why she couldn't go. Work, a doctor's appointment, a school concert, anything really. The truth was she hadn't wanted to visit because as soon as she sees the plaque she will have to admit that her mum is never coming back. And she doesn't want to admit that. She wants to believe that one day she'll look up at the front door as it opens and see her mum standing there, pulling off her navy coat, hanging it on the brass hook, and saying, 'So, are you making a cup of tea or am I?'

And they'd make it together.

But she knows it's not going to happen. Of course she knows. But what you know and what you tell yourself don't always match up. But here's Irma, standing next to her in a house full of smiling people. She can't hide behind looking after everyone else for ever. It's time.

'Does anyone mind if me and Irma go for a half-an-hour walk?' she says, half-hoping one of the kids will say, 'Don't go, Mum!' but everyone nods or calls out, 'Of course!'

And Dylan says, 'Grandad and Isaac are going to help us set up Playmobil pirate ship.'

'Excuse me!' says Mrs Finch, smiling. 'I'm more than able to set up pirate ships as well, thank you very much.'

'And Mrs Finch!' says Patti, grinning.

'Ah-hem!' cough Tash and Jen loudly. 'Is there a rule that we're not allowed to play with pirate ships either?'

'Of course not!' says Dylan.

'And Sandy!' adds Patti as the tabby cat follows them all into the living room to set it up, while Joanie turns off the gas hobs, puts on her coat and leaves the flat holding hands with Irma.

As they walk, Joanie glances at Irma, who looks so beautiful. It's not just the make-up and the hair and her ridiculous attention to detail when it comes to making her outfits, although Joanie loves all those things. It's something else. The strength in her. The way she continues, when she doesn't have to.

'Are you going to move in?' Joanie says, softly. 'I'd like it if you did, but you don't have to.'

'I'm going to do more than that,' says Irma, squeezing her hand as they walk along in the cold and Joanie feels her heart beat faster.

11.45 a.m.

Christmas Day

Irma Woźniak

Earlham Cemetery

Irma feels the velvet box in her pocket as she walks. Some things have to be done the traditional way, and this is something she's been thinking about for months. Yesterday when she'd asked Frank for his blessing, she'd made it very clear she was going to ask Joanie anyway, whether he gave his blessing or not, that there would be none of that giving the bride away, or permission. But they'd both had their eyes fill up with hot tears, and embraced beside the bar. And she'd known it was the right thing to do.

When they get to the plaque with Allie's name, Joanie takes in a deep breath.

'Merry Christmas, Mum,' she says softly. 'I really miss you.' Irma thinks of Klara. All these people to miss.

The frost on the bushes and grass makes the whole cemetery look like it's a black and white drawing in an old story. It's misty too, almost, and the grass beneath their feet crunches. For a moment, Irma thinks she's got her timing wrong. It's not right to propose to someone who's visiting their mum's grave for the first time. But Joanie turns to look at her and smiles.

'Thank you so much for suggesting we come here. It's like . . .' Joanie looks up at the sky. 'It's like she's given me a kiss and said I'm doing OK. That might be wishful thinking, I know. But it does feel like that. I feel peaceful.'

'This might not be the time or place,' says Irma, thinking there is no harm in asking, and she's tired of being afraid of life just in case she gets hurt, or things she loves are taken away from her. 'And please don't do the saying yes because you feel you have to. It's just . . . I wanted to ask you,' she lifts the velvet box from her coat pocket and opens it up, the silver ring with the little emerald in the middle, just a small one, just a glint of green. '. . . If you'd do me the honour of agreeing to marry me.'

Joanie goes quiet. She looks from Allie's grave, to Irma, and back to Allie's grave again. She's smiling, Irma thinks, but she's not saying anything, just standing with her mouth open.

'It's no problem if we don't want to. I'm happy as we are.' Irma feels the need to let Joanie off the hook, but instead she throws her arms around Irma's neck and presses her cold face into her cheek. She turns back to the golden plaque and squeezes Irma's hand.

'Merry Christmas, Mum!' says Joanie, hot tears splashing down her face. 'Guess what? I'm getting married!'

It's the best way to be answered yes that Irma can think of.

12.00 p.m.

Christmas Day

DC Crane

DC Crane stands at the far end of Newbury Street and allows herself a few moments of quiet celebration. Not too much, because there had been too much suffering, for Tim Winters' victims, and for Cynthia Ellis too. She hates to think what might have happened if they hadn't turned up when they did. Cynthia had told them there and then about what John had done to the Finches. He'd blustered about it, of course, called her mad, hysterical, all the things he could to try and convince them she was making it up. She and DC Ado had watched her husband in The Mariner. Neither of them trusted him one bit, and had gone looking for evidence to prove their hunches right. It makes her angry to think of it, to think of Mr and Mrs Finch welcoming John in, making him cups of tea, letting him into their lives, just so he could rid them of all they'd saved for. A nasty bastard, and no mistake.

The voicemail left by Cynthia Ellis only confirmed what they already knew, but DC Crane was impressed with the woman's bravery when they'd arrived at her house last night.

Her testimony and that of Mrs Finch would make all the difference as they build the case. DC Crane is impressed with Mrs Finch too. Her husband never should have died. Not yet, at least. It will never cease to disgust and amaze DC Crane that people take advantage of those who are vulnerable. Human beings make no sense. They're a swirling mess of feelings and actions that only sometimes make sense.

Which is why kindness always moves her.

Are you feeling Christmassy yet? DC Crane sends a text to DC Ado and smiles as she gets into her grey Fiesta. She doesn't really want to spend Christmas with her dad, or with anyone really. She'd like to spend it with Walker and Freddie, eating seafood pasta with the radio on. How is it, that in her early forties, she still does the one Christmas at Mum's, one Christmas at Dad's thing that started when she was in her early teens? What would she do if she had a partner? And that partner had divorced parents? Would they spend the rest of their lives moving between each house, sharing their time out like pieces of cake at a children's birthday party?

And Dad doesn't even let the dogs come.

What sort of Christmas is that?

She picks up her phone and sends her dad a text too.

I'll pop in later Dad, I've got to work on a case. Love you. Merry Christmas. Xxx

That should do it.

Christmas this year would be her, Freddie and Walker, and exactly what she fancied.

The only way to survive in this job, DC Crane always said to new recruits, was to try not to think of all the people out there doing all the awful things at once. If you let it overwhelm you, then what you do would feel pointless, a drop in the ocean.

Just before she pulls away, Craig Mullany walks towards her car with his two sons on bright scooters and a Labrador on a lead. He taps on the window.

She smiles and hops out of the car. 'Do you mind if I . . .' she asks, although she's already bent over, rubbing under the ears and nose, making a fuss of the beautiful wet, white-gold fur. 'A dog is not just for Christmas, Mr Mullany.' She is smiling though. Craig Mullany looks different. His face is clear of whatever mood it was that made it even vaguely possible to imagine him a burglar.

'Agreed. I've been thinking, I can do the things I didn't do because of how I lived with Jen. Now there's no me and Jen. I've always wanted a dog. Grew up with them. Jen was always more of a cat person.'

'Some people are both,' she says, pushing her fingers into the lovely fur.

'Are you?' he asks.

'God no. I'm just dogs. Two of them. One big one small. What are you calling her?'

'Not sure yet. The boys think Spiderman, but I'm thinking something less . . . well.' He laughs.

'I have an aunt who says we should let dogs name themselves,' says DC Crane, smiling. 'I was supposed to spend most of today with my dad and her and the rest of the family, but realised I am old enough to do what I want on Christmas Day.'

'Maybe I'll let this one name herself. I was thinking something nice and hopeful.'

'I'm glad,' she says, standing up and looking up the street. 'A dog is the perfect way to start.'

'Yes. You know,' Craig Mullany looks about him, side to side, 'you could come for a drink and some Christmas food with me. If you fancy.'

DC Crane smiles at him, and is tempted, somehow. But she opens the door of her Fiesta, doesn't even try to hide all the food wrappers under one of the dog blankets like she would usually, and shakes her head. 'That's really kind of you, thanks,' she says. 'I've got two dogs and a load of linguine that needs me. Maybe another time though . . .' She lets that sentence hang for a moment. 'Have a lovely day. See you again, maybe. Merry Christmas, Mr Mullany.'

'Merry Christmas, DC Crane,' says Craig Mullany, as she pulls her door shut and turns the key in the ignition and he and his boys walk further up Newbury Street.

She's bought the dogs new blankets. They're sitting wrapped up nicely under the tree they've probably torn down again after Mrs Thomas, her neighbour, let herself in to feed and walk them this morning. Tomorrow she'll take a drive to the coast and she'll walk with her flask of tea and the bits of dried-out kidney.

Yes I'm feeling Christmassy yet. I hope you are too. Remember you're welcome tomorrow x

She smiles as she reads Michael Ado's reply. *Nobody has everything. And I've got enough.*

She pulls the Fiesta out onto the road and starts the drive towards home. She feels content in a way she that she never really expected when she was younger. A sort of calmness at knowing who she is. As she turns right onto Brighton Road, she sees the tabby cat that goes by all the different names wandering along the far end of Newbury Street with its tail high in the air and she gives him a little wave, which feels like such a silly thing to do, she laughs out loud. Then she turns on her window wipers. It has started to snow.

Acknowledgements

There are so many people who help make a book a book. There are some people who've always seemed to inspire my writing and I think they always will.

Still. There are people I definitely want to thank, because without them this book wouldn't exist. Thanks to Jo Unwin, agent extraordinaire and all-round excellent person. I'll never forget you checking in on me when I was low at the beginning of us. Thank you for reminding me I mattered. To Milly Reilly and Donna Greaves at JULA. You are both always so lovely to me, and I really appreciate it.

Thanks to Sam Eades who believed in this book, and whose notes about Allie being the heart of the story gave me the idea to have everyone dealing with her death, rather than her being in the book as a living character. I wanted to write about missing someone who's gone, and you helped me find how to do it. Thank you to Katie Brown for your thoughtful, generous edits (and some excellent cheering on of Tash that made me laugh out loud). Thanks too to Victoria Pepe, Jade Craddock and Rosie Pearce, who spotted things I could never have seen, and to everyone at Trapeze who helped bring this book to print and beyond, and for making the story shine.

There are friends who I couldn't have written this book without. Holly Seddon, you are a ridiculously talented writer and wonderful friend. The difference you make to my life is . . . well. I love you.

Lia Louis. You get it. You get the beauty in all the small, specific things. And you gave me sand.

Maureen Hardy. You are wonderful. Thank you for your unwavering belief in me and twenty years of kindness. Winter picnics and porridge and long chats at the kitchen table. More please.

Alice Broadway, Rachael Lucas and Keris Stainton. I love you three very much. Without caveat. Obviously, this time next year we'll be millionaires . . .

Others, in no particular order but who all had an impact on the writing of this book one way or another. Thank you. You're all brilliant and I don't know what I did to deserve you. Owen Booth, Antonia Honeywell, Erin Kelly, Will Dean, Shelley Harris, Fiona Cummings, Naomi Frisby, Nell Brown, Cornelia Prior, Bekka Staples, Chris Gribble, Kellee Rich, Sam Hacking, Louise Voss, Harley Jane Kozak, Gareth Hardy. Others too. Sorry if I missed you here. I hope I've told you in real life what a difference you make to me.

Thanks too to some early readers of various beginnings of this book a few years back when it was 70 per cent different and wasn't even set at Christmas. Some of you loved it like that. Some of you said it was too bleak. All of you helped that book become this book which deals with the same themes, but has love and hope at its core. Sometimes you just need someone to read your words, so thank you Wendy Vaizey, Anna Orridge, Ben Ingber, Alice Kuipers, Cath Martin and Nick Stone.

Thanks to Rebecca Bradley and Elizabeth Haynes for some policing details I had no clue about because my expertise only extends to Morse and Wexford and all those other fictional detectives I love (and thank) too. If I got anything wrong, it's totally my fault.

Cassie Crane. Thank you for letting me borrow your surname for a character who was going to be small but now has her own chapters and I'd love to write other books about. DC Crane is nothing like you, obviously, other than that she's great, and so are you.

Thanks to my sister Jodie, for playing ragamuffins in front of the Christmas tree at 6 a.m. and understanding Christmas Eve Eve Eve Eve Eve and putting up with me for years saying, 'Can we talk about Christmas?' as soon as bonfire night was over. I love you. In my childhood memories you *are* Christmas. (Thank you to Hollie, Jake, Noah and Dexter, for being yourselves, and coming to our Christmas puppet shows.)

To Nana and Gramps and Carol, who I miss. I'll never forget that Christmas I cooked for you all and we squeezed into that living room, nine of us, and we laughed and ate and Gramps and I waltzed in the kitchen while we did the washing up. I always thought I'd have lots of people to cook for at Christmas. Thank you for showing me what that would feel like. And for all the other Christmases. To Adam and Aiden too, for merry Christmas past.

Thank you to teaching and school colleagues, pupils and friends. Thank you for all your support, kindness, and for every time I've laughed or felt happy in a class or staff room.

To my dad, for teaching me I belong at any table and that everyone is equal but doesn't have equality of beginnings. And for the Christmas music. I never did go flat in 'Once in Royal David's City'. Honest.

To my mum. I didn't understand a lot of things when you were alive, but I do understand them now. I love you. For many reasons, this book is for you.

Thank you to Nell, who is the best person I know.

Everything I write is for you. Thanks too, for that time, at the start of last Christmas holidays when we watched every episode of *House of Anubis* in two days while we ate mince pies and had the foot heater on. You are brilliant.

Thank you to Nigella Lawson for filling in the gaps where my baking education ended after my mum died, and for being, without even knowing it, part of every Christmas I've had for the past twenty-one years.

Thank you to all the people on Twitter when I was @bookshaped who used to reply to my questions, and share my Twitter stories. And to Facebook friends who kept answering my questions about Christmas movies when I started this book. Thank you to Anne, who bought me *The Snowman* sheet music all those years ago and inspired the Twitter story that went viral, and thank you to J.K. Rowling, for sharing that thread, which made this book being published a possibility in the first place.

Merry Christmas everyone.

Credits

Trapeze would like to thank everyone at Orion who worked on the publication of *One Christmas Night*.

Agent
Jo Unwin

Editor
Katie Brown
Sam Eades

Copy-editor
Victoria Pepe
Jade Craddock

Proofreader
Patrick McConnell

Editorial Management
Rosie Pearce
Charlie Panayiotou
Jane Hughes
Alice Davis
Claire Boyle
Jeannelle Brew

Audio
Paul Stark
Amber Bates

Contracts
Anne Goddard
Paul Bulos
Jake Alderson

Design
Lucie Stericker
Joanna Ridley
Debbie Holmes
Nick May
Clare Sivell
Helen Ewing
Emily Courdelle

Finance
Jennifer Muchan
Jasdip Nandra
Afeera Ahmed

Elizabeth Beaumont
Sue Baker
Victor Falola

Marketing
Katie Moss

Production
Claire Keep
Fiona McIntosh

Publicity
Alex Layt

Sales
Jen Wilson
Victoria Laws
Esther Waters
Frances Doyle
Ben Goddard
Georgina Cutler
Jack Hallam
Ellie Kyrke-Smith
Inês Figuiera
Barbara Ronan
Andrew Hally
Dominic Smith
Deborah Deyong
Lauren Buck

Maggy Park
Linda McGregor
Sinead White
Jemimah James
Rachel Jones
Jack Dennison
Nigel Andrews
Ian Williamson
Julia Benson
Declan Kyle
Robert Mackenzie
Sinead White
Imogen Clarke
Megan Smith
Charlotte Clay
Rebecca Cobbold

Operations
Jo Jacobs
Sharon Willis
Lisa Pryde
Lucy Brem

Rights
Susan Howe
Richard King
Krystyna Kujawinska
Jessica Purdue
Louise Henderson